Drums of War

Drums of War

EDWARD MARSTON

First published in Great Britain in 2008 by
Allison & Busby Limited
13 Charlotte Mews
London W1T 4EJ
www.allisonandbusby.com

A CIP catalogue record for this book is available from
the British Library.

10 9 8 7 6 5 4 3 2 1

13-ISBN 978-0-7490-7976-5

Typeset in 12/16 pt Adobe Garamond Pro
by Lara Crisp

The paper used for this Allison & Busby publication
has been produced from trees that have been legally sourced
from well-managed and credibly certified forests.

PEFC
PEFC/01-01
CATG-PEFC-052
www.pefc.org

Printed and bound in Great Britain by
MPG Books Ltd, Bodmin, Cornwall

EDWARD MARSTON was born and brought up in South Wales. A full-time writer for over thirty years, he has worked in radio, film, television and the theatre, and is a former Chairman of the Crime Writers' Association. Prolific and highly successful, he is equally at home writing children's books or literary criticism, plays or biographies, and the settings for his crime novels range from the world of professional golf to the compilation of the Domesday Survey. *Drums of War* is the second in a new series of adventure novels featuring Captain Rawson.

Also available from
ALLISON & BUSBY

The Captain Rawson series
Soldier of Fortune

The Inspector Robert Colbeck series
The Railway Detective • *The Excursion Train*
The Railway Viaduct • *The Iron Horse*

The Christopher Redmayne series
The Frost Fair • *The Parliament House* • *The Painted Lady*

Also by Edward Marston

The Christopher Redmayne series
The King's Evil • *The Repentant Rake* • *The Amorous Nightingale*

The Nicholas Bracewell series
The Queen's Head • *The Merry Devils* • *The Trip to Jerusalem*
The Nine Giants • *The Mad Courtesan* • *The Silent Woman*
The Roaring Boy • *The Laughing Hangman* • *The Fair Maid of Bohemia*
The Wanton Angel • *The Devil's Apprentice* • *The Bawdy Basket*
The Vagabond Clown • *The Counterfeit Crank* • *The Malevolent Comedy*
The Princess of Denmark

The Domesday Books
The Wolves of Savernake • *The Ravens of Blackwater*
The Dragons of Archenfield • *The Lions of the North*
The Serpents of Harbledown • *The Stallions of Woodstock*
The Hawks of Delamere • *The Wildcats of Exeter* • *The Foxes of Warwick*
The Owls of Gloucester • *The Elephants of Norwich*

CHAPTER ONE

France, 1705

Daniel Rawson saw him coming. From his vantage point high up in the tree, he could command a view that stretched for almost a mile. With the aid of his telescope, he was even able to identify the man's regiment. The rider had a blue knee-length coat with red cuffs. He wore a cravat, a tricorne hat and black leather boots that glistened in the sun. The weapon holstered beside him was a rifled carbine. Daniel knew that he must therefore belong to the Royal-Carabinier corps. The horse was keeping up a steady canter, its hooves sending up clouds of dust from the dry track. At that pace, it would reach Daniel within a matter of minutes. It was time for him to climb down to a lower branch.

Though he was a captain in the 24th Foot, a seasoned British regiment engaged in fighting Louis XIV's mighty army, he was not in uniform now. Indeed, he would have been unrecognisable to most of his fellow-soldiers. Dressed in the nondescript garb of a French peasant, he'd grown a beard, dirtied his face and found a cap that hung low across his forehead. Since he was fluent in French and had the broad shoulders of someone accustomed to hard labour, he was confident that nobody would see through his disguise. What set him apart from other churls was that he had money in his purse and weapons under his smock. He also had a pretty accomplice.

When the rider got closer, Daniel gave the signal and Marie nodded in reply. Picking up her basket, she came out of her hiding place in the copse, walked across to the track and began to saunter along it. She was young, fresh-faced and buxom. Her long brown hair trailed down her back from beneath her bonnet. As her hips swayed rhythmically, her skirt swished to and fro. Hearing the clack of hooves behind her, Marie stopped and turned. The rider came round the angle of the trees and she had her first sight of him. He was tall in the saddle and, from what she could tell, passably handsome. The closer he got, the broader became her smile. He, in turn, was appraising her carefully and he liked what he saw. He took her for a farmer's daughter on her way to market in the next village. She stood obligingly aside as if to let him go past but – urgent as his business was – he felt that he could tarry for a short while. It was too good an opportunity to miss.

He slowed his horse to a trot and gave her a friendly greeting. Marie giggled in reply and flashed her eyes. It was all the invitation he needed. Tugging the animal to a halt, he dismounted, removed his hat and enjoyed a long, luscious kiss. Her lips were sweet and warm. He looked around to make sure that they were alone. The place seemed utterly deserted. Marie led him to the shelter of the trees. After tethering his mount, he discarded his hat, removed his sash then took off his coat. Tumbling a country wench on a bed of green grass was just the fillip he needed after several hours' ride on a hot day. She was clearly willing and far too wholesome to be a whore. He would not even have to pay for her favours. Setting her basket aside, she put her hands on her hips. When she giggled again, her breasts trembled irresistibly.

Daniel waited until the trooper lowered his breeches. It was the moment when his quarry was completely off guard and at his most vulnerable. Eyes fixed on the girl and loins already on fire, the man did not hear the branch creak or the leaves rustle above his head. Daniel timed his jump perfectly, hitting his target with such force that he knocked all the breath out of him, and using the butt of his pistol to club the man into unconsciousness. Letting out a gasp of fear, Marie turned away, horrified at the sudden violence. There had been no mention of murder when she agreed to help Daniel. He had told her that it was merely a jest played on an old friend yet he had just struck the so-called friend on the head. She could not bear to watch and was frightened that she might also be in danger.

Working swiftly, Daniel stripped the man of his remaining clothes then tied him securely to a tree with some rope he'd concealed nearby. When Marie dared to look again, she saw that the trooper she'd enticed from his horse was now bound and gagged, seated upright against a trunk with his head slumped forward on to his chest. What really caught her eye and banished her anxiety at once, however, was the fact that Daniel was naked from the waist up, clearly intending to put on the man's shirt and coat. She studied his slim, smooth, lightly tanned, muscular body with gathering interest. He was so different from the pot-bellied oafs she served at her father's inn. Though it bore the scars of war, his physique was truly impressive, hardened by combat and combining a sculptured beauty with latent power. Marie was roused and entranced. She forgot all about the victim of the assault. Her mind was on something else now. As Daniel reached for the shirt, she raised a hand.

'Wait!' she cried.

'Don't worry,' he said, taking some coins from his purse. 'I always honour a debt. You did well, Marie. Here's your reward.'

'I care nothing for the money, good sir.'

'But you earned it.'

'Begging your pardon, sir, I'd rather take my wages another way.'

'Then you shall have my horse – I need to ride his.'

'That's not what I meant, sir.'

'Oh?'

'I want neither payment nor the horse,' she said, stepping a little closer.

'Then what can I give you?' Even as he asked the question, he guessed the answer. Daniel grinned happily. 'Ah, I understand now.'

He had chosen the ideal accomplice. When he had spent the night at a nearby inn, Daniel sensed that Marie would be able to help him. She was comely and eager. He had told her a plausible tale about playing a trick on a friend in the army. Dressing up as a peasant, he'd explained, was all part of the jest. All that he'd hired her to do was to cause a distraction and she'd done that with surprising skill, unaware that she was actually assisting the enemy in the theft of royal dispatches. The giggle that had bewitched the trooper was now directed solely at Daniel and it was very tempting. As it grew louder, her whole body shook with sheer delight. Marie spread her arms wide to claim her reward, at once offering herself and pleading to be taken. Daniel needed only a second to reach his decision. Having got what he wanted, he could afford a little distraction.

'Let's find somewhere more private,' he said, glancing at his captive. 'We don't want to make him jealous, do we?'

* * *

'Confound it!' exclaimed the Duke of Marlborough, pacing up and down. 'Can there be anything worse than leading a coalition army? I'm fighting with one arm tied behind my back and both feet lashed together. Bickering and delay will be the ruination of me. I'm not allowed to move one solitary inch without a council of war beforehand.'

'The Dutch are awkward bedfellows, Your Grace,' agreed Cardonnel.

'They're the bane of my life, Adam. But for their caution, we could have won a decisive action on the Moselle and occupied French soil. We could have been giving nightmares to King Louis. Instead of that, we're back where we started.'

'The blame cannot be laid entirely on the Dutch.'

'No,' said Marlborough, heaving a sigh. 'We also have to contend with the problem of the Margrave of Baden. I ride all the way to see him in order to apprise him of my plans and what does he tell me? Not only is he unable to supply me with wagons, guns and horses but his wounded foot makes it impossible for him and his men to undertake the siege of Saarlouis. Yet another project has to be abandoned.'

'It's very frustrating, Your Grace.'

'It's positively infuriating!'

Marlborough and Adam Cardonnel were alone in the tent that acted as their headquarters. It was only because he could trust his secretary that Marlborough was able to vent his anger so openly. Most of the time, he had to conceal it behind soft words and a polite smile. As commander-in-chief of the Confederate army, he was hampered at every turn by his supposed allies. His triumph at the battle of Blenheim the previous year had sent tremors through France and been marked by wild celebrations in England, Austria, Germany and Savoy. Even the Dutch hailed

Marlborough as a hero, though praise was tempered with criticism of the high number of casualties among their regiments. On his return to England in December, he was greeted by cheering crowds and honours were heaped upon him.

When 1705 dawned and the campaigning season neared, there was justifiable optimism in the air. It was felt by many that Marlborough would build on the success of Blenheim, achieve other startling victories in the field and bring the War of the Spanish Succession to an end on terms dictated by the Allies. Optimism, however, was short-lived. The first setback occurred during the voyage to the Netherlands in April. Caught in a squall, Marlborough's yacht ran aground on the sandbanks of the Dutch coast. He had to endure a gruelling four-hour pull in an open boat against wind and tide. There were moments when it looked as if the elements would destroy a man who had survived fierce battles against the finest army in Europe. He was fortunate to reach dry land alive. The ordeal left him with a fever and a pounding headache.

There was worse to come. When he reached The Hague, he found the Dutch army unready to take the field and unwilling to fight far beyond its immediate borders. Always thinking ahead, Marlborough had arranged during the winter for his supply depots to be fully stocked so that his army never had to forage while on the march. To his dismay and fury, he discovered that the depots were half-empty owing to neglect, corruption and betrayal. Instead of being able to nourish his army's advance up the Moselle, his depleted stores were a huge problem. There were few opportunities to forage in the stark countryside and unseasonably cold weather was another distinct hazard. Marlborough complained bitterly that they were much more afraid of starving to death than of the enemy.

The loss of Huy, a citadel on the Meuse, had forced him to abandon his bold scheme to strike across the French border and he had to lead his entire army north. He did so with great reluctance but Marshal Overkirk – the one Dutch commander in whom he could confide – was desperate for reinforcements. It was almost two years since Marlborough had captured Huy from the French and it had both strategic and symbolic importance for him. It could not be left in enemy hands. Though the fortress was soon retaken, Marlborough remained depressed.

'We were out-manoeuvred, Adam,' he admitted.

'Circumstances conspired against us, Your Grace.'

'Fearing an attack up the Moselle valley, the French diverted us by attacking Huy. They knew that General Overkirk lacked the numbers to defend it. We simply *had* to retire in order to rescue them. Yet another plan of campaign was wrecked. With enough money, men, horses, artillery and commitment from our allies, I could bring this war to a satisfactory conclusion by the end of the summer.'

'It's not destined to be the summer of 1705,' noted Cardonnel, sadly.

'Nor any other, I fear. How can I attack the French where it will really hurt them when I'm trapped in the Low Countries?' He gave a weary smile. 'I'm sorry to rant on like this, Adam,' he went on. 'You know the difficulties we face only too well. Nothing can be gained by endless protestation. Forgive me.'

'There's nothing to forgive, Your Grace.'

Adam Cardonnel was extremely able and intensely loyal. He was the son of Huguenot refugees who had fled from the atrocities in France that followed the Revocation of the Edict of Nantes twenty years earlier. Sickened by the persecution, he had vowed to fight against the all-conquering army of Louis XIV; and Cardonnel's mastery of French was a potent weapon. Marlborough relied heavily on him and his secretary was never found wanting. The captain-general of the British forces was a striking figure even though he was now in his fifties. He was known for his grace, natural authority and infinite charm. Only close friends like Cardonnel were allowed to see him in blacker moods and to know his innermost feelings.

'We must be satisfied with more modest gains this year,' said Cardonnel. 'It's foolish to hope for another Blenheim every time we take up arms.'

'I know, I know,' said Marlborough, shaking his head. 'We must be patient. The trouble is that patience requires time and I'm fast running out of it. Most commanders have retired before they reach my venerable age.'

Cardonnel was about to point out that Marlborough looked far younger than he really was when he was interrupted by a noise outside the tent. A guard entered.

'There's a French prisoner who insists on seeing you in person, Your Grace. He says that he has something of great value.'

'Has he been relieved of his weapons?'

'He handed them over when he arrived in camp.'

'Then let's see the fellow.'

The guard withdrew for a few moments then entered again with a blue-coated trooper who wore a neat moustache and pointed beard. The prisoner bowed and released a stream of French, gesticulating with both hands as he did so. Marlborough was mystified but Cardonnel burst out laughing.

'I hope that *you* understand the rogue, Adam,' said Marlborough, 'because I could only translate one word in ten.'

'He was deliberately teasing you, Your Grace,' explained Cardonnel. 'Ask him to introduce himself and you'll understand why.'

'Captain Daniel Rawson, at your service,' said the prisoner, doffing his hat.

'Is that *you*, Daniel?' asked Marlborough, peering at him. He let out a cry of recognition. 'By Jove, I do believe it is! Since when did you join the Royal-Carabinier regiment?'

'It was a temporary enlistment, Your Grace. Luckily, the man who loaned me this uniform was close to my own height and build. I'll be happy to tell you the full story. First, however,' he added, reaching into his right boot to extract something, 'here are some dispatches sent to Marshal Villeroi. I had the good fortune to intercept them on the way.'

'Tell us how,' said Marlborough, dismissing the guard with a flick of his hand and taking the missives from Daniel. 'Are these from King Louis himself?'

'They're copies of his orders,' said Daniel. 'I had to deliver the originals. I broke the seals on them, noted their contents then sealed them up again with care. Only by handing them over in person to Marshal Villeroi could I be certain of being entrusted with his reply.'

Cardonnel was amazed. 'You went straight to the heart of the French camp?'

'It seemed a shame to waste this uniform.'

'And you have Villeroi's reply?'

'In his own fair hand,' said Daniel, fishing it out of his other boot and holding it up. 'He's expecting it to be opened in Versailles and not here.'

'You took a terrible risk, Daniel.'

'It was all in a good cause, sir.'

'This is wonderful,' said Marlborough, reading the two copies before passing them to his secretary. 'Villeroi has orders to retire to Tongres and adopt a defensive attitude. It was ever thus – defend, defend, defend. That's all they do. Bringing the French to battle is more difficult than passing through the eye of a needle with a herd of camels. What was the marshal's reply?' He took the sealed dispatch from Daniel and opened it, translating it as he ran his eyes over the looping calligraphy. 'He congratulates the King on the wisdom of his decision and promises to abide by it. Villeroi is far too circumspect to do anything as rash as to mount a major attack.' After giving the dispatch to Cardonnel, he turned his attention to Daniel. 'You promised us the full story,' he went on. 'When I sent you into enemy territory to gather intelligence, it never occurred to me that you'd bring back a haul like this. I congratulate you.'

'Did you undertake the enterprise alone?' asked Cardonnel.

'No, sir,' replied Daniel. 'I had the assistance of a young lady.'

Marlborough laughed. 'There's no surprise in that, Daniel,' he said. 'You're the scourge of the fairer sex. You have a tradition to maintain. Dressed like that, you could win over any woman.'

'Oh, I had a full beard when I persuaded this one to help me and I was disguised as a peasant at the time. It was only afterwards that I became a trooper in a French regiment. I shaved off most of the beard and kept what you see now.'

Daniel gave them a lengthy account of his adventures on the other side of the French border. Listening intently, Marlborough and his secretary were torn between amusement and admiration, smiling at the comical elements in his tale and struck yet again by his bravado. Daniel Rawson had patently enjoyed every moment of his escapades. He was now ready for more action.

'What must I do next, Your Grace?' he wondered.

'Await orders,' answered Marlborough. 'Since we've been prevented from piercing French defences along the Moselle, we'll attack them elsewhere.'

'And where will that be?'

'The Lines of Brabant.'

Daniel was surprised. 'But they're virtually impregnable.'

'Are they?' asked Marlborough, and there was a twinkle in his eye.

CHAPTER TWO

The friendship between Captain Daniel Rawson and Sergeant Henry Welbeck was an example of the attraction of opposites. Apart from the fact that they served in the same British regiment, the two men had nothing whatsoever in common. While Daniel was an eternal optimist who could pluck hope out of the direst circumstances, Welbeck was so deeply sunk into melancholy that he foresaw nothing but disaster. In appearance, too, the contrast between them was stark. While one was tall, strikingly handsome and debonair, the other was stocky, round-shouldered and decidedly ugly, the long scar down one cheek turning an already unprepossessing face into an almost hideous one. Daniel loved women yet Welbeck hated them. Son of a soldier, the captain was a devout Protestant, keen to fight a Roman Catholic enemy. The sergeant, on the other hand, was an unrepentant atheist, wondering what he was doing in the army and incessantly bemoaning his fate.

Notwithstanding their differences, the two men were very close. Daniel appreciated his friend's ability to turn raw recruits into efficient soldiers by cowing them into submission and making them fear their sergeant's wrath far more than the enemy.

For his part, Welbeck had a sneaking admiration for Daniel's daredevil streak, even though it sometimes threatened to bring a distinguished military career to a sudden end. He was also grateful to find one officer with whom he could talk on equal terms instead of having to adopt a deferential tone. When the two men were alone together, no rank existed between them. It was one of the few consolations in Welbeck's army career.

They were standing outside Daniel's tent on a warm July evening amid the routine clamour of camp life. When he heard the orders for the next day, Welbeck was contemptuous.

'We're attacking the Lines at Brabant?' he asked, eyes bulging.

'That's right, Henry.'

'Why doesn't the Duke simply issue us with razors so that we can all cut our throats? That's a much easier way to commit suicide than trying to storm well-defended French positions. They'll pick us off like so many rabbits.'

'The whole of the Lines are not fortified,' Daniel pointed out.

'That doesn't matter, Dan. As soon as we attack any part of it, Villeroi will rush troops to that particular spot and repel us.'

'They didn't repel us at Blenheim.'

'We had luck on our side that day.'

'I didn't think you believed in luck.'

'I don't believe in *anything*,' said Welbeck, gloomily. 'And I certainly don't believe in walking to certain death by leading my men against the Lines of Brabant.'

'You've led them into fierce skirmishes before now.'

'That was different. There was always a faint chance I'd come out alive, give or take a few nasty wounds.'

'You've certainly had your share of those, Henry.'

Whenever they'd bathed together in a river, Daniel had seen the injuries that Welbeck had collected over the years. Fearless in battle and driving his men on in the teeth of enemy fire, he had acquired many grotesque mementoes, including the marks on his thigh where a French musket ball had passed clean through and miraculously missed the bone. The slash of an enemy sword had been responsible for the gash on his cheek and the missing finger on one hand. His chest, back and shoulders were criss-crossed with other souvenirs of enemy blades. Only a strong man with a capacity to tolerate intense pain could have survived the battering taken by Henry Welbeck. He was a walking portrait of the perils of warfare.

'The Duke has finally taken leave of his senses,' he declared.

'He has a plan,' Daniel told him.

Welbeck sneered. 'Oh, yes, he always has a plan. He had a plan to strike into the heart of France through the Moselle valley but it came to nothing. All we did was to shiver in the cold and eat short rations because there wasn't enough food for us or the horses – so much for *that* brilliant fucking plan!'

'Have faith in him. As a soldier, he has no peer.'

'He's getting old, Dan. His judgement is starting to falter.'

'I disagree.'

'That's because you're so loyal to the Duke, you won't admit that he makes a wrong decision. I know he likes to give the impression that he's one of us and enjoys being called Corporal John, but we in the ranks pay for his mistakes. He gets off without a scratch.'

'His Grace is always ready to share our privations.'

'Yes – from the comfort of his coach.'

'You're being unfair, Henry.'

'I speak as I find,' said Welbeck, stoutly. 'You weren't there when we had to leave the Moselle in a hurry and charge all the way back up here to rescue the mutton-headed Dutch yet again. You went gallivanting off somewhere.'

'I was gathering intelligence on French soil.'

'Between the thighs of some trull, I daresay.'

Daniel chuckled. 'Well, yes,' he admitted. 'Except that she was no trull. Marie was a gorgeous young woman with a fondness for someone in a French uniform. Though, as it turned out, she was very reluctant to let me put it on.'

Welbeck raised a palm. 'Spare me the details, Dan. You know my view of females – they should be strangled at birth.'

'In that case, the human race would die out.'

'That's the best bloody thing that could possibly happen to it.'

He was about to launch into one of his tirades when he caught sight of a youth, walking briskly towards them with a regimental drum hanging at his side. Welbeck was irritated.

'Here's my latest affliction!' he said through clenched teeth.

'The drummer boy?'

'He's more than that, Dan. He's my nephew and he's got some lunatic idea that being a soldier is something to do with honour.'

'What's the lad's name?'

'Tom Hillier – he's my sister's boy.'

'You never told me that you had a sister.'

'It's something I try to forget.'

Daniel studied the approaching youth. Tom Hillier was tall, skinny and fair-haired with pleasant features yet to shake off all the signs of boyhood. His slender torso was emphasised by the fact that his uniform was too tight for him. From the look in his eyes, it was clear that he held his uncle in high regard.

Welbeck, however, stared at him with a mixture of distaste and resignation.

'What do you want?' he asked, gruffly.

'I just wanted to speak to you, Uncle Henry,' replied Hillier.

'This is an army engaged in a war, not a tavern where you can pass the day in idle chat.'

'I know that, Uncle.'

'Of course, you do,' said Daniel, looking him up and down. 'So you're Tom Hillier, are you?'

'Yes, Captain Rawson.'

Daniel was taken aback. 'You know who I am?'

'Everybody in the 24th knows who you are, sir,' said the drummer with a sense of awe in his voice. 'On my first day here, I was told about some of your escapades.'

'And when was that, Tom?'

'Two weeks ago.'

'You've only been with us two *weeks*?'

'Yes,' said Welbeck, sourly, 'and it's a fortnight too long. Tom ought to be at home, looking after his mother, instead of coming here to be butchered by the French.'

Hillier stiffened defensively. 'I'm not afraid of a fight, Uncle.'

'You can't kill anyone with a pair of drumsticks.'

'Strictly speaking, he can,' Daniel put in. 'Drums are vital instruments of war. Because they can be heard above the noise of battle, they're ideal for issuing commands. You know that as well as anyone, Henry. There was a time, many years ago, when *you* were merely a drummer boy.'

'That's why I joined this regiment,' Hillier explained. 'I wanted to follow my uncle's example. I've always looked up to him. I may begin with a drum but I hope to carry a musket in time.'

'More fool you, lad!' said Welbeck, scornfully.

'You couldn't have picked a better man on whom to pattern yourself,' Daniel observed. 'Henry Welbeck is the finest sergeant in the whole British army.' He winked at his friend. 'He's also the kindest and sweetest.'

Hillier smiled nervously. 'That's not what I've heard, sir.'

'Then you heard right,' said Welbeck. 'Look for no kindness from me, Tom, and expect no sweetness. Harsh words and a kick up that scrawny arse of yours are all you'll get from me or from any half-decent sergeant. We're here to mould recruits into good soldiers not to mollycoddle them. Your mother did you no favour, sending you here.'

'Mother tried to stop me joining the army.'

'Then you should have heeded her.'

'Why did you defy her?' asked Daniel.

'I've thought and dreamt of nothing else, Captain Rawson,' said Hillier, face igniting with pride. 'I love the sound of drums when a regiment is on parade. It stirs my blood. Back in England, I had a life of boredom on our farm. There's nothing heroic in doing all those chores. I want to see action on the battlefield. I want to fight against the French. I want to serve Queen and country.'

'Wait until the first musket ball whistles past your ear,' warned Welbeck. 'You'll change your mind then. Wait until you've filled your breeches with terror at the sight of an enemy attack. You'll forget all about Queen and bloody country.'

'I think the lad's got more backbone than you give him credit for, Henry,' said Daniel, tolerantly. 'A willing volunteer should be nurtured. Welcome to the regiment, Tom,' he added, giving him a friendly pat on the shoulder. 'I'll leave you and your uncle alone to become more closely acquainted.'

'I don't *want* a closer acquaintance!' insisted Welbeck. 'I joined the army to get away from my family. As far as I'm concerned, they don't exist.' He glowered at Hillier. 'Did you hear that?'

'Yes, Uncle,' said the drummer, backing away. 'I'm sorry. Forgive me for intruding.'

After bidding them farewell, he turned on his heel and walked disconsolately away. Daniel watched him go.

'You're being very cruel to the lad, Henry,' he said.

'Tom needed to be told the truth.'

'He's your *nephew*.'

'Yes,' said Welbeck, 'and that's what unnerves me. He reminds me of all the things I've struggled to put behind me.'

'Try to see it from his point of view.'

'He's a drummer, Dan. He doesn't *have* a point of view.'

'Tom is a callow youth, chasing his ambition. He's alone in a foreign country, cut off from his family and friends. He deserves a little guidance from his uncle. Is that too much to ask?'

'Yes, it is.'

'Even you are not that hard-hearted, Henry.'

'I don't want him here.'

'Why ever not?' said Daniel.

'Because he's a responsibility – Tom is someone I ought to care for, Dan. As soon as I do that, I know I'm going to be hurt. Let myself grow fond of the lad,' said Welbeck, ruefully, 'and what will happen? He'll be shot to pieces or trampled to death by a cavalry charge at the Lines of Brabant and *I'll* be the one who has to write to his mother.'

'You could at least be civil to the lad.'

'He has to respect my rank. Tom has to look at me as an army sergeant and not as a relative of his. If he were my own brother, I'd treat him the same way.'

'Blood is thicker than water, Henry.'

'It can be spilt just as easily.'

'Encouragement was all that Tom was after.'

'Well he won't get it from me,' said Welbeck, firmly. 'I'd never encourage anyone to join the army. It's a dog's life and my nephew will soon find that out – if he manages to stay alive long enough, that is. When he sees how many French regiments are defending the Lines of Brabant, he'll wish he stayed at home on the bloody farm.'

John Churchill, Duke of Marlborough, was nothing if not a supreme strategist. Having lost the initiative in the Moselle valley, he knew that he had to regain it swiftly in the Low Countries. First, however, he was obliged to have a council of war with his Dutch allies. Seated around a table in his tent, they did not show great confidence in his plan. They believed that the Lines of Brabant – a series of strongholds, ramparts, palisades, redoubts and trenches running all the way from Antwerp to Namur – were an insurmountable barrier. To cross anywhere along its seventy-mile extent would, in their opinion, be to court certain defeat and heavy losses.

As usual, the general who led the opposition to Marlborough's proposal was Frederik Johan van Baer, Lord of Slangenberg, a proud and resolute man of sixty. He stood out from his colleagues for a number of reasons, including the fact that he was a staunch Roman Catholic in an avowedly Protestant army. From the very start of the war, he had been a thorn in the side of the commander-in-chief, questioning his every move, delaying his campaigns and refusing to acknowledge the victory at Blenheim as Marlborough's crowning achievement. It made for frosty relations between the two men.

'I dislike the idea intensely,' said Slangenberg, stroking his beard with aristocratic disdain. 'It's fatally flawed and will not deceive the French for a moment.'

'I believe that it will,' countered Marlborough. 'You prevented me from forcing the Lines two years ago and it was a costly mistake. I mean to break through them near Leau. Marshal Villeroi will then be drawn to that sector, allowing your forces, General Slangenberg, to find an easy way through the weakened defences near the Meuse.'

'It will not work.'

'My feint will deceive the French.'

'It would not deceive a child,' said Slangenberg, snapping his fingers. 'Marshal Villeroi will stay where he is and we'll find ourselves up against his strongest battalions. It's a foolish plan.'

Marlborough stifled a sigh and exchanged a glance with Adam Cardonnel. Councils of war were invariably a contest between British boldness and Dutch caution. To Marlborough's consternation, those contests were often lost and some of his most daring projects never outlived discussion. Another strategy now seemed in danger of being overruled. Fortunately, Marshal Overkirk, commander-in-chief of Dutch forces, came to Marlborough's aid.

'It's a sensible plan,' he claimed, 'and well worth trying.'

'You've always argued *against* an assault on the Lines in the past,' said Slangenberg, pointedly, 'and rightly so. Geography favours the French. Where they've not built fortifications, they have natural defences of mountains, hills and rivers.'

'Those natural defences can be pierced.'

'Not when we're outnumbered, Marshal.'

'There's no possibility of that,' said Overkirk, meeting his gaze. 'Many of the regiments will have been withdrawn to stiffen resistance near Leau. We'll have a numerical advantage.'

'Nonsense!' cried Slangenberg.

'Try to moderate your language, General.'

'It's complete and utter nonsense!'

'We must agree to differ,' said Marlborough shooting Overkirk a look of gratitude for his support. 'I have the greatest respect for your military experience, General Slangenberg, but, if I'd listened to your advice in the past, I'd never have ventured outside Dutch territory and secured advances elsewhere in Europe.'

'To do that, Your Grace,' asserted Slangenberg, 'you gambled with the lives of Dutch soldiers.'

'The gamble paid off handsomely on the Danube last year.'

'It failed dismally this year on the Moselle.'

'We're bound to suffer reverses from time to time, General,' said Marlborough, stung by the comment but reining in his temper. 'We now have a chance to make amends for what happened on the Moselle. Behind the Lines of Brabant, the enemy feel that they are wholly invincible. Since they don't fear attack, we have the element of surprise on our side.'

'Then we must use it,' said Overkirk with an authority that silenced even Slangenberg. 'A clever strategy has been put to us by our commander-in-chief. We must adopt it bravely.'

There was a murmur of support from some of the Dutch generals but Slangenberg was unconvinced. He brooded sulkily. As the council broke up, British and Dutch commanders rose from their seats and dispersed. In the end, only Marlborough, Cardonnel and Overkirk remained. Marlborough shook hands with the Dutchman.

'Thank you,' he said. 'Your intervention was appreciated.'

Overkirk smiled. 'It's a brilliant strategy, Your Grace.'

'That's why you needed to understand the thinking behind it.'

'It was good of you to explain. Had you not done so, I would have been in the invidious position of having to agree with General Slangenberg. On the face of it, your plan is a poor one.'

'It will not deceive Villeroi for an instant,' said Marlborough. 'I'm counting on that fact.'

'I hope that he reacts in the way you anticipate.'

'We know the way that his mind works.'

'The marshal has one glaring fault, Your Grace,' remarked Cardonnel. 'He believes he knows the way that *your* mind works.'

Marlborough laughed. 'Then I'll take the utmost pleasure in disappointing him, Adam.'

CHAPTER THREE

On 17 July, 1705, Marshal Overkirk led the Dutch forces towards
the fortress of Namur at the southernmost tip of the Lines of
Brabant. Allied engineers worked hard to build twenty pontoon
bridges over the River Mehaigne so that the army could cross
with its equipment. As soon as French scouts became aware of the
operations, they sent urgent dispatches to Marshal Villeroi. He
responded by marching a substantial part of his army – 40,000
soldiers, in all – to a position between Merdorp and Namur.
The first part of Marlborough's plan had worked perfectly. He
had read the French commander's mind like a book. Instead of
being distracted by what he assumed was a deliberate feint in the
north, Villeroi hastened to repel an apparent attack in the south.
He had swallowed the bait dangled so temptingly before him.

Marlborough acted promptly. Gathering his army of British,
German and Danish troops, he hurried them north through
the night in the direction of Elixhem. The advance was led by
General Ingoldsby and Count Noyelles with 38 squadrons and
20 battalions supported by 600 pioneers. The cavalry carried large
trusses of hay to serve as makeshift fascines when they met ditches
or rivulets. Wider streams compelled them to make diversions.

Many complained about the rigours of a forced march through heavy mist and persistent drizzle but Captain Daniel Rawson was not one of them. Riding as part of Marlborough's staff, he was aware of the genius behind his commander's strategy. A double bluff had been used. Because there had been a feint near Leau in the north, Villeroi had been tricked into believing that the real danger lay in the south and the whole Dutch corps – with the exception of Marshal Overkirk – had also been misled. When they crossed the Mehaigne, they thought that they truly were the main strike force against the French. In fact, they merely acted as a decoy and would soon receive orders to withdraw.

By dawn on 18 July, Marlborough had reached his destination, a section of the Lines where the topography greatly favoured the French and where it had been reinforced with a series of fortifications. Had the defences been properly manned, it would have been virtually impossible to breach them. As it happened, they were more or less deserted. Scrambling over them, the advance guard sent the picquets scurrying away like startled animals. Pioneers laboured strenuously to level some of the ramparts to the ground and it was not long before Marlborough could take his cavalry and a detachment of foot soldiers over them. They dealt swiftly with any resistance and overwhelmed the defenders along a three-mile front, killing them, taking them prisoner or forcing a retreat. The dreaded Lines of Brabant, deemed impassable by the Dutch, had been broken apart with comparative ease. Progress had so far been rapid and largely unimpeded. It was a good omen.

Daniel Rawson was riding beside the commander-in-chief.

'We've put them to flight, Your Grace,' he said.

'They'll be back when they've had time to regroup and call up their reserves,' warned Marlborough. 'We'll be up against a strong French and Bavarian counter-attack. I daresay they'll have some Spanish horse as well.' He allowed himself a smile. 'But it was satisfying to draw first blood.'

'Where will Marshal Villeroi be now?'

'My hope is that he's still in the vicinity of Namur, wondering what happened to the Dutch army threatening his stronghold. By the time he realises that they stole away in the night to support us, it will be too late for him to get here in time.'

'It was a cunning strategy, Your Grace.'

'We've yet to bring it to a conclusion.'

'Do you have any accurate details of their numbers?'

'No, Daniel, but my guess is that we'll have an advantage.'

'Good.'

'If and when Marshal Overkirk gets here, of course, we'll have markedly superior numbers but the fighting may be over by then.'

'As long as I can play my part in it,' said Daniel, eagerly. 'I've seen no action in the field since Blenheim.'

'You've not exactly been idle,' noted Marlborough.

'I know, Your Grace, and I always enjoy the assignments you've given me. Gathering intelligence behind enemy lines is an adventure but it will never compete with the exhilaration of combat.'

'Sound intelligence helps to win battles.'

'Not on its own. It has to be backed up by heavy artillery and well-trained soldiers. And those troops have to be carefully deployed. I've watched you do that so many times. You're a master tactician.'

'My skills come from long experience.'

'It takes more than experience, Your Grace,' argued Daniel. 'Marshal Tallard had just as much experience as you and yet he was trounced at Blenheim. What he lacked was your instinct for victory.'

'Thank you, Daniel.'

'That's why he's now a prisoner in England while you're free to continue the fight. One day, under your command, we'll bring this war to an end and give Europe a taste of peace for once. Yes,' he added with a grin, 'and, while we're about it, we'll kick the Duc d'Anjou off the Spanish throne and give it to its rightful heir, Archduke Charles of Austria.' He raised a fist and recited the rallying cry of the Allies. 'No peace without Spain!'

Marlborough was practical. 'No peace without more battles.'

'Oh, yes – France is far from beaten yet.'

As they talked, their eyes were scanning the horizon ahead. It was Marlborough who first picked up the warning signal from one of his scouts. He turned to Daniel.

'When were you last involved in a cavalry charge?'

'Such opportunities don't exist in a foot regiment.'

'One may present itself very soon.'

'What makes you think that?' asked Daniel.

'Listen carefully.'

Marlborough knew that a counter-attack was at hand. It was only a matter of time before it took place. Minutes later, there was a distant rumble that built steadily until it became a roll of thunder. Bavarian cavalry then rode into sight, their black helmets and cuirasses glinting. Seeing themselves outnumbered, the enemy generals decided on an immediate attack. A charge was signalled. Marlborough took up the challenge at once. The order was given, the drums started to beat and the red-coated British cavalry kicked their horses into action. Battle was joined.

Daniel made sure that he was involved in it. Drawing his sword, he rode with the cavalry and felt the familiar surge of excitement. It never palled. He had first experienced the thrill when he was only a youth, fighting for King William III in the Dutch army. Now that he was in a British regiment, holding the rank of captain, the thrill was somehow intensified. Many soldiers were driven by a crude lust for blood. Others had enlisted out of blind patriotism. It was different for Daniel Rawson. He fought with a sense of mission and a kind of jubilation. War was his element.

The Allied force comprised 16 squadrons of British cavalry as well as the Hanoverian and Hessian horsemen of the advance guard. At their back were the infantry, drawn up in two lines near Elixhem, more troops arriving every minute. Facing them were 33 squadrons of French, Bavarian and Spanish horse with 11 battalions of foot. Though they had some triple-barrelled cannon at their disposal, there was little opportunity to use it. The battle was essentially a cavalry engagement with no quarter given. Both sides flung themselves at each other with determination, blood racing and sabres flashing.

In the first brush, Marlborough led the charge himself and Daniel rode alongside him. The first Bavarian line was routed, the Scots Greys going on to capture several cannon. When a second line of enemy cavalry approached, there was a renewed charge by the Allies with Marlborough once again leading by example. He and Daniel were everywhere, controlling their mounts with one hand while they hacked and thrust away with their swords. The earth was soon stained with gore and strewn with bodies. The frantic neighing of wounded horses added to the general cacophony. Because there was no large tract of open ground, most of the fighting took place along the narrow sunken lanes in the area. Daniel was embroiled in a series of individual duels. As one Bavarian fell from his saddle, another replaced him and Daniel had to hack him to death before taking on a third adversary. He was indefatigable. The weariness of the long march through the night was replaced by a frenetic energy.

Marlborough, too, was fighting with great vigour, scorning danger and inspiring his men. He almost paid the penalty for his audacity. Singling him out, a Bavarian trooper came at him and swung his sabre with murderous force. Had it made contact, the Allied army would have been mourning its commander-in-chief. As it was, the trooper put so much effort into his swing that, when his weapon missed its target, he lost his balance and fell to the ground. Cursing his misfortune, he quickly hauled himself up and tried to strike at Marlborough again but Daniel Rawson was now in his way. Parrying the sabre, Daniel kicked the man hard under the chin and sent him somersaulting backwards. Then he dismounted long enough to thrust his sword right through the man's heart, impaling him briefly on the ground. Back in the saddle, Daniel rejoined the ferocious melee with enthusiasm.

Though his men fought valiantly, Count Caraman, one of the enemy commanders, could see that there was no hope of victory. His second cavalry charge had failed and Allied infantry were arriving to swell the numbers against him. They were being demolished. A retreat was sounded. Daniel was able to knock one more Bavarian from his horse before the beaten cavalry turned tail. No signal was given for pursuit. The Allied army was left to savour its triumph. Marlborough was cheered to the echo by officers and troopers alike because they appreciated the significance of what he had done in crossing the Lines of Brabant at one of its strongest points. The defences were no longer an indestructible barrier. By skilful strategy, they had finally been smashed wide open.

The spoils of victory were heartening. French losses of almost 3000 dwarfed the number of Allied casualties. Many prisoners were taken, including the wounded French general, the Marquis d'Alegre, along with cannon, colours, standards and kettle-drums. Marlborough did not let his men rest. He ordered them to raze the barricades to the ground so that the French could never again hide behind them in complete safety and taunt him. The battle of Blenheim had shattered the myth of French invincibility. During the engagement at Elixhem, another telling blow had been inflicted on Louis XIV's army.

Daniel was always ready to give credit to an enemy. Their cavalry might have been chased from the field but the Bavarian infantry was not. Abandoned by their horse, the battalions withdrew by forming themselves into a hollow square. Even though they were surrounded by Allied horse and dragoons, they marched steadily on, maintaining their shape and sweeping the squadrons out of their way as they did so. Having fought exclusively in foot regiments throughout his career, Daniel was full of admiration for the discipline shown by the Bavarians. Not for the first time, he saw that well-drilled infantry could be a match for horse.

When he rode back to join Marlborough, he arrived in time to witness an argument. General Slangenberg had galloped ahead of the labouring Dutch columns to take part in the battle. He was aggrieved that it was all over and that Marlborough had not pressed home his advantage by harrying the enemy.

'We must pursue them,' he urged. 'This is nothing if we lie here.'

'I disagree, General,' said Marlborough, urbanely. 'In breaching the Lines, we've made a powerful statement this morning. It will make King Louis a very frightened man.'

'We achieve a greater victory if we deprive him of more soldiers.'

'My men are exhausted. They marched through the night.'

'So did we,' said Slangenberg, resentfully. 'Why was I not told that we were simply a decoy? We spent all that effort crossing the Mehaigne, only to be recalled by your orders. It was maddening.'

'The strategy *worked*, General,' said Marlborough. 'Surely that deserves congratulation even from you.'

'I congratulate nobody who gives up when the job is half-done.'

Slangenberg added some unflattering comments in Dutch and was amazed when Daniel answered him back in his native language.

'Pursuing the enemy is too dangerous,' he said, 'because we have no idea how close Marshal Villeroi is with his main army.'

The general blinked in annoyance. 'Who are you?'

'Captain Daniel Rawson, attached to His Grace's staff.'

'And working as his interpreter, I see.'

'Do you think you could speak in English?' said Marlborough, understanding nothing of the exchange.

'I'm sorry,' said Daniel. 'I was just explaining that Marshal Villeroi will have marched north as soon as he realised that he'd been duped. It would be folly to confront him when our men are so weary.'

'Captain Rawson is right. That's my view exactly and I suspect that it will accord with Marshal Overkirk's opinion. A long march over difficult terrain will not have whetted his appetite for pursuit of the enemy. We've achieved our objective, General, and must be satisfied with that.'

Slangenberg fumed for a few moments then swore in Dutch.

Daniel caught Marlborough's eye. 'I don't think I need to translate that, Your Grace,' he said. 'Do I?'

Having burst through the French defences, Marlborough steadily consolidated his position. Within a few days of the victory at Elixhem, the Allies had control of almost fifty miles of the Lines, including the towns of Aerschot, Diest and Leau. The success helped to atone for the disappointments in the Moselle valley. During a lull in activities, Daniel Rawson found time to return to his regiment and seek out Henry Welbeck in his tent. The sergeant had just finished dressing down two errant soldiers who crept away with their tails between their legs. Daniel saw the look of shame and anguish on their faces.

'What was their crime, Henry?' he asked.

'They upset me.'

'I'll wager they don't do that again in a hurry. I've heard men say that they'd rather be flogged than feel the lash of your tongue.'

'They have to be kept in line, Dan,' said Welbeck. 'If they can't control themselves in camp, how can they control their muskets in the heat of battle? We both know that obedience is everything in the army. I'll brook no waywardness in my ranks.' He looked his friend up and down. 'So you've deigned to visit us at last, have you? I thought you'd deserted us and joined the cavalry.'

'Only for one engagement,' Daniel told him. 'I happened to be in the right place at the crucial moment. And I can tell you now that your criticism of His Grace the other day was very unjust. Whatever you may think, he doesn't expect the lower ranks to do all the work. He led the charge against the enemy and fought like a demon.'

'So I heard and I take my hat off to him.'

'At his age, most commanders have long retired.'

'It's only poor buggers like us who keep going into our dotage.'

'That's because we love army life so much,' teased Daniel, giving him a slap on the shoulder. 'Without it, we'd probably die of boredom.'

Welbeck grimaced. 'War has its own kind of boredom, Dan. What can be more boring then trudging all night long then being denied a chance to fight? At least, you managed to see some action. All that we could do was to wait and watch.'

'That was probably a relief to young Tom.'

'Who?'

'Tom Hillier, that nephew you choose to ignore. He didn't get a baptism of fire in his first battle, after all. That will steady his nerves.'

'The lad will have to get by on his own.'

'You might show *some* sort of interest in him.'

'I will, Dan,' said Welbeck, coolly. 'I'll check every few weeks to see if the young fool is still alive.'

'I'm glad you're not *my* uncle.'

Before Welbeck could give a tart reply, they were interrupted by the arrival of Major Simon Cracknell. Slim, straight-backed and of medium height, he cut a fine figure in his impeccably tailored uniform. His boots had an almost pristine glow to them. When he stepped out from between some tents to confront them, neither man was pleased to see him. Welbeck thought the major supercilious and overbearing while Daniel found him difficult to like. Cracknell was a highly efficient officer but he and Daniel would never be soulmates. While one hailed from a wealthy family and had been able to buy his commission, the other had worked his way up slowly from the ranks. It annoyed Cracknell that Daniel was a favourite of Marlborough's and had now joined his staff. Though he treated the captain with surface politeness, he was seething with jealousy inside.

'What are you doing here, Captain Rawson?' he said, archly. 'I thought you'd moved on to higher things.'

'I do whatever I'm called upon to do, Major,' replied Daniel.

'Then why aren't you doing it at this moment?'

'I took the opportunity to call on a friend.'

'There's no such thing as friendship between a captain and a mere sergeant. Fraternise with the ranks and you lose their respect.'

'Captain Rawson will never lose *my* respect, sir,' said Welbeck.

Cracknell was curt. 'Your opinion is irrelevant here,' he said. 'I don't remember inviting it and I'll certainly pay no heed to it. In any case, Sergeant, you should reserve your respect for officers who remain with their regiment. Now that the captain has seen fit to leave us, he has no real function here.'

'His Grace gave me express permission to come, Major.'

'Really?' Cracknell lifted a patronising eyebrow. 'Given the way that you're indulged, I'm surprised that His Grace could spare you.'

Daniel bit back a reply. There had been unresolved tension between the two men since they had first met and he could do little to alleviate it. Though he admired Cracknell as a soldier, he loathed him as a man, finding his manner offensive and disapproving strongly of the way he treated those beneath him. All of the other officers in the regiment accepted that Daniel had unique qualities that gained him preferential treatment from their commander-in-chief. Major Cracknell was the sole exception. A mocking note came into his voice.

'What does it feel like to be the Chosen One?'

'I think you exaggerate my importance, Major,' said Daniel.

'Captain Rawson was promoted for one simple reason,' said Welbeck, bluntly. 'The Duke knows the difference between a good officer and a bad one.'

Cracknell bristled. 'Hold your tongue, Sergeant!'

'Yes, Major.'

'You're not part of this conversation.'

'No, Major.'

'You see what happens when you befriend someone from the ranks?' said Cracknell to Daniel. 'They get above themselves.'

'I've never found that in Sergeant Welbeck's case,' said Daniel. 'He's been in the army long enough to learn respect for the chain of command. How many years has it been now?'

'Twenty-five, sir,' answered Welbeck. 'My former regiment was disbanded and I joined this one when it was first raised in 1689.'

'There you are, Major – a quarter of a century of sterling service.'

'I'm not interested in *him*,' said Cracknell, dismissively. 'In fact, I'd prefer it if he went away so that we can talk in private.'

'I'll speak to you later, Henry,' said Daniel.

'Yes, Captain,' returned Welbeck.

After giving them a nod of farewell, he withdrew into his tent. Glad to have got rid of the sergeant, Cracknell was able to turn all his attention on Daniel. He gave a condescending smile.

'Well,' he said, 'what news from on high, Captain Rawson?'

'The chaplain is the best person to tell you that, Major,' replied

Daniel, mischievously. 'He can speak directly to God.'

'We can do without drollery. I was referring to His Grace, as you well know. What are his intentions?'

'You'll have to wait until he confides them in you.'

'But you have his ear. You must know what's in the wind.'

'I have no part in any decisions that may be made,' said Daniel. 'When orders are issued, you'll hear them as soon as I do.'

'You must have some notion of what's afoot.'

'We continue to secure our position, that's all I can tell you.'

'Surely we'll try to make further advances.'

'His Grace is never one to rest on his laurels.'

'What have you heard?' demanded Cracknell. 'What's the gossip among his coterie? Where will we move next?'

'Your guess is a good as mine, Major.'

'I think you're deliberately hiding the truth from me.'

'In all honesty,' said Daniel, 'I'm not. Being part of His Grace's staff does not entitle me to privileged information. As far as I know, immediate plans have not yet been agreed. Were we able to make a decisive move, I'm sure that we'd have done so by now but it seems as if the Dutch are delaying us once again.'

'The Dutch!' snarled Cracknell, curling a lip in disgust. 'What appalling allies they make! That beast, Slangenberg, is the worst of them. Had it not been for him and his ilk, we could have broken through the Lines two years ago. They've held us back at every turn. I hate their generals and I despise the whole rotten nation. The Dutch are nothing but a crew of flat-faced, addle-headed, pusillanimous old women. It pains me to fight alongside such cowards.'

'My mother was Dutch,' said Daniel, calmly.

'I was forgetting that. It explains everything.'

'About what, may I ask?'

'About *you*, Captain Rawson,' said Cracknell, nastily. 'It accounts for the flaws in your character. They're far too many to name. Your father, I know, was English but it's the Dutch influence that's uppermost in you. It's made you slow, shifty and unreliable. Worst of all, it's given you the stubbornness of a mule.'

Daniel smiled. 'I regard that as a compliment, Major.'

'Then it's the only one you'll ever get from me.'

Annoyed that he was unable to provoke Daniel, the major glared at him for a moment then stalked off. Henry Welbeck came out of his tent to rejoin his friend. He had heard every word through the canvas. He looked at the departing figure of Simon Cracknell then spat on the ground before speaking.

'Who's going to kill that bastard, Dan – you or me?'

CHAPTER FOUR

The euphoria engendered by the Allied success did not last long. Bad weather forced a delay of several days and the Dutch generals once again refused to approve a major engagement. With the enemy now drawn up behind the River Dyle, Slangenberg and the others could not even agree on the best point to attempt a crossing and they quarrelled for hours on end. Their hesitation caused even further delays. It was not until 30 July that the council of war authorised a move over the river south of Louvain with a diversion to the north. Marshal Villeroi moved smartly to block the first attempt but Allied troops managed to cross on pontoon bridges lower down the river. To Marlborough's delight, a battle at last seemed imminent. He carefully manoeuvred his men into position and was ready to strike. At the last moment, however, almost inevitably, General Slangenberg objected to an attack. The furious commander-in-chief had to call off the whole operation and march back to camp at Meldert.

'This is humiliating!' cried Marlborough in the privacy of his quarters. 'How can I conduct a war with such intolerable handicaps? The stupidity, pique and cowardice of the Dutch generals are beyond belief. It's almost as if they don't *want* to defeat the French.'

'Slangenberg is to blame, John,' said his brother, General Churchill. 'His behaviour has verged on insubordination. I think that you should bring it to the attention of the States-General.'

'It's not as simple as that, Charles.'

'Refuse to work with that bearded curmudgeon. He's been our nemesis from the start. I tell you, there are times when I believe that Slangenberg must be in the pay of the enemy.'

'I've tried everything to appease the old devil. I even told him it was an honour to have someone of his eminence under my command. But it was all to no avail. He continues to fester with jealousy and obstruct any plans we make.'

'Say as much to Grand Pensionary Heinsius,' advised Churchill. 'He's the one man with the power to dismiss Slangenberg.'

'I have to choose my words with care,' said Marlborough, biting his lip. 'Much as I'd love to show my rage, I must hold it in lest I upset people who are – when all is said and done – our major allies.'

'His Grace has shown a masterly control of his true feelings,' said Adam Cardonnel. 'Were he to commit them to paper, it would probably burst into flame.'

The three men shared a hollow laugh. They all knew that, in any correspondence, truth had to be mixed liberally with tact. In the wake of yet another missed opportunity to draw the French into battle, they were angry and jaded. The lustre of their victory at Blenheim was starting to wear off. They needed to prove that it had not been achieved by an isolated stroke of luck. Time was running out. Campaigning would be over in the autumn when food supplies dwindled. They did not wish to retire to winter quarters without having made at least some impression on the enemy.

Churchill was as distressed as his elder brother. General of Foot since 1702, he had seen his men performing heroically, only to have their efforts undermined by their allies. After the latest setback, he feared the worst.

'We'll end this year with very little to show for it,' he said.

'Not necessarily,' said Marlborough. 'We may yet do something of note before the summer is out.'

'Well, it will not be with the assistance of the Dutch.'

'It will have to be, Charles.'

'Then it's doomed from the start,' said Churchill. 'The truth of it is that the Dutch are sick of fighting. They have no stomachs for a long war. More and more voices in The Hague are suggesting that they sue for peace with France.'

'In that event,' Cardonnel pointed out, 'they'll have to accept a Frenchman as the King of Spain and that's anathema to us.'

'It's anathema to the Dutch as well,' said Marlborough.

'Is it, John?' questioned his brother. 'I begin to sniff betrayal here. I know I accused him earlier but I'd exonerate Slangenberg from being in league with the French even though he shares their Popish religion. However, I suspect one of our allies. When our first party tried to cross the river, Villeroi was waiting for them as if forewarned of their approach. I fancy there's a spy in the Dutch camp.'

'The warning could equally well have come from our camp.'

'That's even more worrying.'

'Only if there really was treachery,' said Marlborough, 'and I'm not persuaded of that. I think that Marshal Villeroi guessed right this time. It was too much to expect that we could fool him twice in a row. The only way to find out the truth,' he went on, 'is to capture him and ask if he had an informer in our ranks.'

'Capture him?' said Churchill in disbelief. 'How can we hope to do that when the Dutch will not let us get anywhere near the fellow?'

'Be patient, Charles,' said his brother, tapping his forehead with an index finger. 'Something is stirring in my brain.'

While his uncle was avoiding Tom Hillier, he hadn't been forgotten by Daniel Rawson. Wondering how the lad was faring, he sought the drummer boy out in a spare moment. Hillier was close to tears. He was staring up at a tall tree in dismay. Daniel realised why.

'How long has that been up there, Tom?' he asked.

Hillier gasped in surprise. 'Oh – Captain Rawson!'

'Somebody is enjoying a laugh at your expense, I see.'

'It's not the first time, sir.'

'New recruits always have to endure this kind of thing, I'm afraid. It's a rite of passage.'

'How can I get it *down*?'

Hillier had good reason to be upset. His drum had been stolen while he was in the latrines and wedged in the top branches of a tree. Some of the lower branches had been deliberately snapped off so that he could not use them to climb up. Shinning up the trunk would not be easy. It was too thick and smooth for him to get a good purchase on it.

'What else have they done, Tom?' said Daniel.

'They hid my uniform, they poured water over me while I was asleep and one of them put a dead mouse in my boot. Every day, it's something different,' said Hillier. 'They seem to like baiting me.'

'It's all in fun, lad. They may have stolen your drum but they've taken care not to damage it. As you can see, they've put it where it can't possibly fall.'

'But how do I get it down again, Captain?'

'Try using simple arithmetic.'

Hillier was puzzled. 'Arithmetic?'

'Yes, Tom,' said Daniel. 'Add six and six together for me.'

'The answer's twelve.'

'That means your six foot combined with mine will take you up to twelve feet, and you can add another two for reach. I'd say that lowest branch was no more than ten or eleven feet away. When you stand on my shoulders, you'll be able to grab it easily.'

'You're going to help me?' said Hillier in amazement.

'Well, there's nobody else here to offer you a hand.'

'Thank you, Captain Rawson. I'm so grateful.'

'Let's retrieve that drum first,' said Daniel. 'We can worry about gratitude afterwards. Come on, Tom.'

Facing the tree, Daniel knelt down so that Hillier could clamber on to his shoulders. As Daniel slowly lifted him up, the drummer boy used the trunk to steady himself. When he pulled himself up to his full height, his head was above the lowest branch. He took hold of it, got a firm grip then hauled himself up into the tree, sending some leaves fluttering down through the air like snowflakes. Daniel stood back to watch him. While he was not a natural climber, Hillier was determined. Inching his way up through the fretwork of branches, he finally reached his precious drum. After checking that it had not suffered any harm, he began the slow descent. By the time he reached the bottom branch, he was able to lower the instrument to Daniel.

Dropping to the grass, Hillier was now beaming.

'I got it,' he said, taking the drum and stroking it. 'I got it safely back. Thank you, Captain. I couldn't have done it without you.'

'Don't tell the others that, Tom. Let them think you did it all on your own. That will impress them.'

'Yes, sir.'

'And don't be the victim all the time.'

'What do you mean?'

'Do you know which of the others took your drum?'

'I'm fairly certain it was Hugh Dobbs.'

'Was he the one who put the dead mouse in your boot?'

'Yes – that was definitely his doing.'

'Then you wait until he's asleep tonight and put a dead rat in his boot. He won't be so keen to bait you if he knows you fight back.'

Hillier shrugged. 'Where will I get a dead rat from, sir?'

'Quite simple – you kill a live one. There are plenty of them about if you keep your eyes open.'

The drummer nodded then shifted his feet. 'Have you seen anything of my Uncle Henry?' he asked, tentatively.

'I've had brief glimpses of him,' said Daniel. 'Sergeants, as you've found out, are very busy men. Their duties are onerous and they rarely get much rest. *That's* why Sergeant Welbeck has been unable to get in touch with you.'

'No, it's not, Captain Rawson – he hates me.'

'That's not true.'

'Mother warned me that he would. According to her, even as a boy, he never liked being part of a family. He preferred to do things on his own. I remember Mother reading out some of his letters to us. They never showed any real interest in what *we* were doing.'

'I'm astonished to hear that he wrote at all, Tom.'

'It was only now and then, sir.'

'Did you get a letter after Blenheim?'

'Yes,' said Hillier, 'and for once it was quite long. Hearing his description of the battle made me want to join the army at once and do something worthwhile for a change. I had this strong urge to follow in Uncle Henry's footsteps.'

'Well, don't be too disheartened by the way he rebuffed you. Sergeant Welbeck will soften in time. I'll make a point of telling him how nimbly you climbed that tree.'

'Thank you.'

'As for these tricks they keep playing on you,' promised Daniel, 'they won't go on much longer. We'll be on the march again very soon. It's just as well you have that drum back, Tom,' he added, touching the instrument. 'You could well be beating it in battle.'

Given the unpromising circumstances, most commanders would have abandoned the idea of pursuing further success in Flanders but Marlborough was too tenacious to give up. Feeling that something positive could still be snatched out of a largely unsatisfactory year, he produced a new plan, reminding his reluctant allies that they did, after all, still hold the initiative. As a first step, he collected five days' ration of bread for the army and summoned a convoy from Liege with six days' biscuit. This made him independent from the supply depots and from the camp bakeries that normally worked every four days. At the same time, he ordered a siege train to Meldert, large enough to inflict damage but small enough to be moved easily. He now had operational flexibility.

Marlborough's intention was to march rapidly to the source of the River Dyle in an attempt to lure the French into battle before their reinforcements could arrive from the Upper Rhine. The advance began on 15 August with Overkirk's army to the left of

Marlborough's columns. Their combined force numbered 100 battalions and 160 squadrons. By dint of pressing on hard, they reached Corbaix and Sombreffe by nightfall. The development caused great unease in the enemy camp because they had no idea where the Allied armies would strike. Marlborough had positioned himself so that he could threaten Hal, Brussels, Louvain, Mons, Charleroi and even Dendermonde. As he had anticipated, his strategy sewed confusion in the French camp. In a panic, Villeroi dispersed his troops to strengthen every sector, thereby weakening his field force until it comprised only 70 battalions and 120 squadrons. They were outnumbered.

The Allies crossed the river at Genappes in blazing heat and swung north as if to attack Brussels. Villeroi immediately ordered General Grimaldi to block the high road running through Waterloo. The French commander-in-chief, meanwhile, concentrated his army behind the River Yssche. To his intense alarm, the Allies suddenly turned away from the high road and headed directly for the main French position, making it impossible for Villeroi to evade a major battle. All that he could do was to order his men to make frantic efforts to throw up earthworks along the line of the river. For the second time that summer, Marlborough had contrived to put the French army exactly where he wanted it.

There was another element to the plan. While enemy attention was concentrated on Marlborough and Overkirk, General Churchill took up a position in the Forest of Soignies. With 20 battalions and the same number of squadrons, he was poised to attack the French flank and rear from his hiding place among the trees. Everything pointed to an Allied victory. After consultation with General Overkirk, Marlborough secured full agreement to an immediate battle. All that they had to do was to wait for the artillery to arrive and hostilities could commence in earnest. Marlborough sent orders that the British train of artillery should come as quickly as possible. Then he waited.

Unfortunately, the delay was much longer than expected. When the artillery reached a narrow defile, they were stopped from entering it by General Slangenberg who wanted preference given to his baggage train. Frustrated artillery officers had to stand there for hours while the wagons rolled slowly past. Vital time had been wasted and the enemy had been able to bolster their numbers and strengthen their defences. It was noon when the British artillery was finally in place. Marlborough was at last ready to signal the start of what could prove to be a crucial battle.

Before he could do that, however, doubts were raised.

'Hell and damnation!' cried Marlborough, bringing both hands to his head in a gesture of despair. 'The Dutch are running scared yet again.'

'This is General Slangenberg's work,' said Daniel.

'He's the ringleader, I agree, but it's the subordinate generals who are pressing for further reconnaissance. They want to inspect the proposed crossing points on the river. All it will mean is more and more delay.'

'That will only favour the enemy, Your Grace.'

'It's unforgivable to dither like this.'

'I thought that General Overkirk recognised the wisdom of your plan,' said Daniel. 'You completely outwitted the French.'

'If only the other Dutch generals realised that!' Marlborough took a deep breath. 'I'm sorry, Daniel. I shouldn't rant on like this in front of you. I'll be much calmer when the council of war begins. I want you here as my interpreter. When they mutter away to each other in Dutch, I always feel at a disadvantage. I need you as an extra pair of ears.'

'I feel privileged to be able to help, Your Grace.'

Daniel Rawson had no time to say anything else because the tent was suddenly filled with officers. He sat beside Adam Cardonnel and in a good position to watch the Dutch generals. By studying their expressions, he feared that they had already made up their minds not to sanction an attack. Their spokesman, as usual, was Slangenberg.

'We need more time,' he insisted.

'We do not *have* time,' declared Marlborough. 'We've already delayed far too long.'

'We must be circumspect, Your Grace.'

'Circumspection does not decide the outcome of a battle.'

'Perhaps not,' said Slangenberg, sternly, 'but it can reduce the number of potential casualties. Taking an army into battle without careful reconnaissance beforehand is both rash and dangerous.'

'All the necessary steps have been taken, General.'

'I need to be absolutely certain of that.'

'Would you throw away the one chance we have of bringing Marshal Villeroi to battle? That's perverse.'

'We're pursuing a sensible course of action.'

'You're imperilling the whole strategy, General,' said Overkirk, irritably. 'His Grace devised a plan that bewildered the French and put them at our mercy. Had we attacked hours ago, we would surely have gained the upper hand by now.'

'That's idle speculation,' returned Slangenberg.

Daniel sat in silence while the argument continued and the minutes ticked by. Overkirk supported Marlborough but most of the Dutch generals and their field deputies were behind

Slangenberg. Marlborough was compelled for once to abandon his normally diplomatic tone. He appealed to them with real passion.

'Gentlemen,' he began, looking around the blank Dutch faces, 'everything needful has been done. I have reconnoitred the ground and made dispositions for an attack. I am convinced that conscientiously, and as men of honour, we cannot now retire without an action. Should we neglect this opportunity, we must be responsible before God and man.' He heard the snort from Slangenberg and raised his voice. 'You see the confusion which pervades the ranks of the enemy and their embarrassment at our manoeuvres. I leave you to judge whether we should attack today or wait until tomorrow. It is indeed late, but you must consider that, by throwing up entrenchments during the night, the enemy will render their position far more difficult to force.'

Daniel was impressed with his ardour and conviction but it had not won over his allies. Some of the comments he heard in Dutch were not ones he cared to translate for the commander-in-chief. General Slangenberg and his supporters felt hurt that they had not been taken fully into Marlborough's confidence before they had set out on the expedition. The argument waxed and waned then waxed afresh. By the time it was four o'clock in the afternoon, all possibility of action that day had completely vanished. The French had been let off the hook. Afternoon merged into evening yet still the dispute went on. It was a revelation to Daniel, the first time he had had some insight into the immense difficulty of making decisions in a coalition army. His admiration for Marlborough soared. In spite of the huge pressure on him, never once did he lose his temper. At the end of the meeting, when the disgruntled Dutch contingent had withdrawn, Daniel went across to the commander-in-chief.

'You argued your case superbly, Your Grace,' he said.

Marlborough was despondent. 'I failed, Daniel.'

'You persuaded some of them. I heard them say as much.'

'There was animosity in the eyes of the rest of them. General Slangenberg was more obstructive than ever. What kind of a commander believes that his personal baggage is more important than an artillery train? By causing that delay, he wrecked the whole enterprise.'

'Perhaps they'll agree to an attack tomorrow,' said Daniel.

'There's not the slightest hope of that,' conceded Marlborough. 'If they're afraid to attack the enemy when it's at its weakest and most disordered, they'll not even consider action tomorrow. The French will be too well-fortified. No, Daniel,' he continued, 'the only option for us is to withdraw and let Marshal Villeroi claim a victory. The moment he sees us pull back, he'll write to King Louis to boast that he scared us into an ignominious retreat.'

'But that's not what happened at all.'

'That's how it will be portrayed at Versailles and we can do nothing to stop it. I know that you have Dutch blood in you,' said Marlborough, bitterly, 'and I hope you'll not take offence at my opinion of your fellow-countrymen.'

'I'm as much English as Dutch, Your Grace.'

'Then I speak to you as an Englishman because I know that you fight like one. The conduct of this war has nearly driven me insane.' Pursing his lips, he shook his head dejectedly. 'There are times – and this is certainly one of them – when I'm forced to conclude that the Dutch, our allies, have caused us far more trouble than the French.'

Johannes Mytens was a big, fleshy man in his forties with heavy jowls that shook as he talked. As a member of the States-

General, the Dutch parliament, he had considerable influence and had garnered support both inside and outside the chamber. A wealthy man, he lived in a large house in the most fashionable quarter of The Hague. He was glad to welcome a visitor from Amsterdam that day. They sat either side of a walnut table in the sombre interior of the *voorhuis*.

'How is business, Willem?' asked Mytens.

'My business is thriving,' replied Willem Ketel, 'and it would thrive even more if we were not caught up in this damaging war. When roads are closed and enemy soldiers sit on our borders, merchants like me are hemmed in. When will it end? That's what I ask.'

'It's a question we often discuss in the chamber.'

'Are you any nearer to resolving the problem, Johannes?'

'No,' admitted the other.

'Then the war could drag on indefinitely.'

Mytens sighed. 'There's every indication that it might.'

'What a sickening prospect!'

Ketel was an old friend of the politician's. Short, angular and now in his fifties, he had small darting eyes set in a wizened face. His wig covered a head that was bald and mottled. While Mytens chose relatively flamboyant attire, Ketel preferred dark clothing that gave him a clerical air. He had a habit of sucking his teeth before he spoke.

'Nothing of consequence was gained this year,' he said. 'We were all misled by the happy outcome at the battle of Blenheim.'

'It was happier for the Duke of Marlborough than it was for us, Willem,' observed Mytens. 'He claimed all the glory while we lost a large number of men.'

'He's never given our army any credit.'

'All that we ever get from him are complaints. After the retreat from the River Yssche, he had the gall to write to Heinsius to demand that General Slangenberg be dismissed.'

'What did the Grand Pensionary do?'

'He foolishly acceded to the demand.'

Ketel was outraged. 'He dismissed a man of the general's ability?'

'Slangenberg was persuaded to retire. That kept his reputation intact and pacified the Duke. In my view, Slangenberg would have made a better commander-in-chief.'

'We need someone to *end* the war not to continue it.'

'What's the feeling in Amsterdam?'

'We've always been less hostile to France than you here in The Hague. We see the advantages of trade with her. I used to export almost a third of my goods to Paris. What we need is a peace treaty.'

'The Duke will not hear of it.'

'That's because he puts British interests before ours, Johannes. The French are ready to parley. They have no wish for this war to go on. It's very costly and they've suffered heavy casualties. I believe that King Louis wants peace as much as we do.'

'On what terms, Willem – there's the rub!'

'They must be honourable terms that satisfy both sides.'

'There's no such thing. Someone must lose and someone gain.'

'End the fighting and we're all beneficiaries,' said Ketel, eyes blazing with certainty. 'I know that the Duke will not give in until France renounces its claim to the Spanish throne but that will never happen. It's pointless to hold out for something that can never be attained.'

'I felt at the start that it *could* be attained,' said Mytens, his jowls wobbling. 'The thought that France could annexe Spain and take control of its empire was terrifying. It would have a monopoly on trade in all those colonies.'

'Nobody was more worried than me, Johannes. Yet now that it has happened – now that Spain has a French king – it doesn't seem quite so terrible. Besides,' he went on, adjusting his wig, 'we could gain concessions. Were we to sue for peace, we could insert terms in the treaty that would protect our merchants. We're a trading nation, for heaven's sake. That's our destiny. In fair competition, we're the equal of anyone.'

'You speak to the converted, Willem. For some time, I've been talking about the need to open negotiations with France.'

'What's been the response?'

'I hear that tired old slogan – No peace without Spain!'

'We strike too hard a bargain.'

The door opened and the maidservant brought in a flagon of wine and two glasses on a tray. When she had set the tray down on the table, Mytens dismissed her with a flick of the wrist. He poured wine into both glasses then handed one to Ketel.

'What shall we drink to, Willem?' he asked.

'To the only thing worth having,' said Ketel, 'and that's the prospect of peace.'

'It's a very long way off, I fear. Unless the Duke is dismissed from his command, there's no hope of an end to this war, even though it's killing our soldiers and bleeding our coffers dry.'

'Then the Duke must go. He's the barrier to peace.'

'Heinsius will not hear of it.'

'Why must the decision be left in *his* hands?'

'He'll always overrule critics like me, Willem.'

'Then let's find another way to remove the obstruction,' said Ketel, slyly. 'It's in everyone's interest to do so, after all. Let me ask you a straight question, Johannes.' He sucked his teeth. 'How far would you go to get rid of the Duke of Marlborough?'

Mytens met his gaze as he considered his reply. Instead of putting it into words, however, he simply raised his glass in a silent toast. Ketel gave a thin smile. They had sealed a bond.

CHAPTER FIVE

Tom Hillier had learnt his trade quickly. He had mastered the drum calls and could march in step with the others. Since he'd begun to stand up for himself, life in the army was much less of an ordeal. He no longer had cruel jokes played on him every day and had started to feel accepted. Even though hostilities against the French had now been suspended, the drummers did not rest. Like everyone else in camp, they continued to go through their drills so that they would be ready in the event of a sudden call to action. Longing to be tested in battle, Hillier brought a youthful zest to his playing. Henry Welbeck watched him from the shelter of some trees as his nephew marched up and down with the other drummers. The sergeant was startled when a firm hand fell on his shoulder.

'I've caught you, Henry,' said Daniel Rawson. 'In spite of what you pretended, I *knew* that you'd take an interest in the lad.'

'I just happened to be passing, Dan.'

'You never do anything by accident.'

'Very well,' confessed Welbeck. 'Perhaps I was curious to see how Tom was getting on. But that's all it was,' he added, wagging a finger. 'Curiosity.'

'And what have you discovered?'

'He seems to be faring quite well.'

'Things have settled down now,' explained Daniel. 'Ever since he had that fight with Hugh Dobbs, he's a different person.'

Welbeck was bemused. 'Who might Hugh Dobbs be?'

'He's one of the other drummers and he decided to make Tom's life a misery. You've seen the kind of japes that new recruits have to suffer. Dobbs even stole his drum and stuck it at the top of a tree.'

'How do you know all this?'

'I helped him to get the instrument down. I also advised him to give Dobbs a taste of his own medicine. What I suggested was putting a dead rat in his boot but Tom decided on something more drastic.'

'What did he do?' asked Welbeck with genuine interest.

'He challenged Dobbs to a fight and knocked him senseless. Tom may look spindly,' said Daniel, 'but, like me, he grew up on a farm. He's tough and wiry. Doing all those chores builds up your muscles. Also, of course, he comes from Welbeck stock. He's got your will to win, Henry.'

'How on earth did you get to hear about this fight, Dan?'

'He came and told me. It cost him a black eye but the other lad fared much worse. Dobbs won't bother him again.'

'I'm glad that Tom is finding his feet.'

'You might try talking to him yourself.'

'There's no need. I have no responsibility towards him.'

'But you do,' said Daniel. 'What really inspired him to join this regiment was that letter you wrote to your sister after the battle of Blenheim.' Welbeck flushed guiltily. 'I know your little secret, Henry. You *do* preserve family ties, after all.'

'I write a few lines once in a blue moon.'

'You're responsible for firing Tom's imagination and giving him the urge to be a soldier. The least you can do is to be a proper uncle to the lad. He's not asking for favours.'

'He'll get none,' said Welbeck.

'Stop treating him as a leper.'

'I've got far too much on my hands to bother about him.'

'Do you want him to go on thinking that his mother was right?' said Daniel. 'She told her son that you'd hate him simply because he was related to you. According to your sister, you never enjoyed being part of a family. It embarrassed you.'

'That's enough!' snapped Welbeck, interrupting him. 'I don't want to talk about my past. It doesn't exist anymore. As for Tom, I'll…watch him from a distance. It's all I'm prepared to do, Dan.' He took a last look at Hillier. 'In any case, I don't need to speak to him when I've got you to do that for me.'

'Oh, I won't be talking to him for a long time.'

'Why is that?'

'I'm leaving camp today. That's why I came looking for you. I wanted to bid farewell. His Grace has work for me.'

'What sort of work?'

'I've no idea,' said Daniel, shrugging. 'I'm on my way to find out.'

Seated at a table, the Duke of Marlborough finished the last of many letters he'd written that morning. He was alone in the tent with Adam Cardonnel. His secretary had been equally busy with correspondence. He sealed a letter then looked up.

'I wish that we had something of significance to report,' he said.

'Yes,' agreed Marlborough. 'It's been a fruitless campaign.'

'We did break through the Lines of Brabant.'

'Granted, but we were unable to build on that achievement. We had a chance to liberate the whole of the Spanish Netherlands and it disappeared into thin air. We both know why.'

'Our allies let us down, Your Grace. On the other hand, the retreat from the River Yssche did have one good result. You managed to get rid of General Slangenberg.'

'Not until he'd ruined the entire campaign,' said Marlborough, pulling a face. 'And while he may not be able to hinder us in the field again, he may well do so by other means – whispering in the ears of his friends in the States-General, for instance.'

'You still have their unreserved support,' said Cardonnel.

'But how long will it last, Adam? That's what worries me. War is hideously expensive. Like our own parliament, the States-General needs to feel that they're getting value for their money. That means we have to deliver a string of victories. We failed to do that this year.'

'The French failed equally, Your Grace.'

'King Louis will be well aware of that. We've reached a standstill. When the winter comes, I fancy he'll start to make peace overtures to the Dutch. He'll offer them all kinds of blandishments. He knows he can never tempt us.'

'The Dutch will surely hold firm and so will our other allies.'

'That's why we need to keep our relations with them in good repair, Adam. When we can no longer fight, we must turn diplomat.'

'It's a role in which you excel.'

The tent flap was pulled back and a guard stepped in.

'Captain Rawson is here, Your Grace,' he said.

'Show him in,' ordered Marlborough.

The guard retired and Daniel immediately entered the tent. After an exchange of greetings, he was offered a seat. He looked at the mound of correspondence on both tables.

'Have I been summoned to act as a messenger?' he asked.

'No, Daniel,' said Marlborough. 'We have a more important task for you. These letters are destined for our allies to warn them of my proposed visits. I have to go first to Dusseldorf to persuade the Elector Palatine to supply troops for service in Italy next year. Then we move on to Vienna so that I can meet the new, young Emperor Joseph. It seems that I'm to be invested with the Principality of Mindelheim.'

'It's a well-deserved honour, Your Grace,' said Cardonnel.

'It will entail pomp and ceremony and I never like that.'

'Will you be going to Berlin?' said Daniel.

'Of necessity,' replied Marlborough. 'We must keep Prussia on our side. I'll have to smooth King Frederick's ruffled feathers a little. I know how upset and angry he is at the behaviour of the Dutch and the Austrians. I share his feelings. When I've calmed him down, I hope to coax 8000 men out of him for the next Italian campaign. After that, we go to Hanover to meet Electress Sophia then on to The Hague.'

'It's a long journey, Your Grace.'

'Adam has calculated that we'll travel over 2000 miles.'

'Including the best part of a week sailing on the Danube,' said Cardonnel. 'We may find that tedious.'

'I'm sure that we will,' said Marlborough, picking up a sealed letter from the desk. 'You, Daniel, will have a much shorter journey to make but one that may be fraught with more danger.'

'Where am I to go?' asked Daniel.

'Paris.'

'You're sending me back again?'

'It's because you know the city so well that you are the ideal person for this assignment. I should warn you, however, that on this occasion, it will not be necessary for you to seduce the wife of a French general in order to gather intelligence. You did that last year and we profited greatly by the information you brought back.'

'Yes,' said Daniel, recalling his dalliance with Bérénice Salignac. 'Unfortunately, the lady's husband took exception to my methods. He was bent on revenge and hired two men to murder me. When they took me prisoner instead, General Salignac tried to kill me in a duel.'

'You have a gift for survival,' noted Cardonnel.

'He'll need it,' said Marlborough. 'I foresee many hazards. What I wish you to do, Daniel, is to find someone for me and bring him back to The Hague. Since he's a Dutchman, you'll be able to speak to him in his own language. I just pray that he's still alive.'

'Who is the fellow, Your Grace?'

'Emanuel Janssen.'

Daniel was thunderstruck. 'Do you mean the tapestry-maker?'

'The very same,' confirmed Marlborough. 'He's a master of his craft. King Louis was so dazzled by his artistry that he commissioned a tapestry to hang in Versailles alongside all the Gobelins tapestries. That shows how highly he prizes Janssen's work. He was prepared to pay a high price for it.'

'Emanuel Janssen is a traitor,' said Daniel, coldly. 'He was bought by the enemy and turned his back on his country. Instead of sending me to Paris to bring him home, you should be asking me to slit his throat.'

'Janssen is a braver man than you take him for, Daniel. The first thing he did when he was approached in secret by the French was to inform us. He's a fierce patriot. No amount of money would have made him defect to the enemy.'

'Then why did he do so?'

'Because that's what I asked him to do,' said Marlborough. 'It was too good an opportunity to miss. Janssen was going to be working at Versailles where all the major decisions are made. He would have direct contact with King Louis. Being a tapestry-maker was the perfect disguise behind which to hide.'

Daniel was sobered. 'Are you telling me that he is a spy?'

'He is indeed, Daniel, and quite an efficient one. He lacked the charm to extract information in the way that you do but he kept his ears open and heard much that was of value to us.'

'Why do you want me to bring him back, Your Grace?'

'We fear that he may have been found out. At all events, he's vanished and nobody has any idea where he is. It's very worrying. Having talked him into accepting such a risky business, I feel it's our duty to go to his rescue – if, that is, we can find him.'

'Where was he last seen?'

'Here are all the details,' said Marlborough, handing him the letter. 'When you've committed them to memory, destroy this.'

'Start your search at his house,' advised Cardonnel.

'What if he's already been executed?'

'That's a strong possibility, alas.'

'The French have no affection for our spies,' said Daniel, 'even if they can weave magical tapestries. My guess is that Janssen is dead.'

'Then why have we not heard of his death?' asked Marlborough. 'They would surely have made an example of him and boasted to us that they'd uncovered our ruse. No, Daniel, we must suppose that Emanuel Janssen is still alive.'

'And if he's not, Your Grace?'

'Then you're to bring the others safely out of France.'

Daniel frowned. 'You made no mention of any others.'

'He has an assistant and a servant with him,' said Marlborough. 'But the person who wrote to tell us that he was missing was his daughter. You should enjoy meeting the young lady, Daniel,' he went on with a smile. 'I'm told she's very beautiful.'

Amalia Janssen's face was clouded with misery. She was short and slight with elfin features framed by fair hair that peeped out from beneath her bonnet. Anxiety had etched deep lines into her forehead and lack of sleep had painted dark patches beneath her eyes. She was standing in the front bedroom of their house. Beatrix, the servant, was a plump, plain-faced, nervous woman in her thirties. She was peering out of the window in such a way that she could not be seen from the street. The two women spoke in Dutch.

'Well?' said Amalia.

'I think he's still there.'

'Did you actually *see* him?'

'I'm not sure,' replied Beatrix. 'But I sense that he's out there.'

'He has been every other day this week. Today should be no different.' Amalia bunched her fists. 'Why is he watching the house? I feel as if I'm a prisoner here.'

'I'm worried about Kees. He's been gone a long time.'

'The market is some distance away.'

'He should have been back by now.'

'He'll have a heavy basket to slow him down.'

'Oh, I hope we don't lose him as well, Miss Amalia,' said Beatrix, turning to face her. 'It's bad enough that your father has gone astray.'

'He's not gone astray, Beatrix. He's been deliberately taken from us and the worst of it is that I have no idea why. You couldn't meet anyone as mild or harmless as Father. He wouldn't hurt a soul.'

'It looks as if somebody might have hurt *him*.'

'Don't say that,' scolded Amalia. 'We must never give up hope. Even in Paris, the name of Emanuel Janssen compels respect. His reputation has reached every corner of Europe.'

'That may be the trouble, Miss Amalia.'

'What do you mean?'

'Some people might be very jealous of him.'

'Who could be jealous of my father? He's the kindest man in the world. Even his rivals like him. He has no enemies.'

'We're Dutch,' said Beatrix, morosely, 'and Holland is at war with France. We're bound to have enemies.'

'Yet we've lived here for months without any mishap. This is a beautiful, big house and the streets around here are safe to walk in. When people knew what we were doing here, they gave us a welcome. Father is weaving a tapestry by royal appointment.'

'Does the King know that he's disappeared?'

'He must do, Beatrix.'

Amalia wrung her hands. In the time they'd been in Paris, they'd settled into a comfortable routine. While her father and Dopff, his assistant, worked at the loom, she and Beatrix looked after the house. Janssen visited Versailles occasionally to report on progress and to meet some of the other tapestry-makers employed there. Amalia had been thrilled when she had been invited to join her father at a royal garden party. She had never been to such a glittering event and had stared in awe at the ostentation on display. It was an overwhelming spectacle. French nobles and their wives brought a colour and vivacity that made Amsterdam seem dull and lifeless by comparison. When she saw Louis XIV in his finery, moving like a god around the exquisite gardens and acting as a cynosure, she understood why he was called the Sun King. The heady experience had remained a happy memory until now. Suddenly, a dark shadow had been cast over their whole stay in France.

'I thought it was wrong at the start,' grumbled Beatrix. 'We should never have come here. We belong in Amsterdam.'

'Father couldn't refuse such an offer, Beatrix.'

'We betrayed our country.'

'You mustn't think that,' said Amalia, earnestly 'because it's not what happened. Try to remember what my father told you. Art has no boundaries. French painters, musicians and tapestry-makers have worked in our country many times. Why shouldn't someone from Amsterdam work here?'

Beatrix said nothing. It was not her place to argue with her mistress, especially at a time when she was in such distress. It was her job to offer succour. Amalia had grown to like Paris and learn enough French to hold a conversation but their servant had always felt uneasy there. In view of what had now happened, Beatrix was even more perturbed. They were foreigners and being treated as such. She yearned for the security of their home in Amsterdam.

'Let me take a turn at the window,' said Amalia, changing places with her. 'Perhaps I can catch a glimpse of him.'

'I think he stays there all night, Miss Amalia – or someone does. I can feel their eyes watching me.'

Standing back from the shutters, Amalia looked down the street to the nearby corner. People walked to and fro, a horseman trotted by then a cart rumbled past. There was no sign of anyone keeping the house under surveillance. After keeping her vigil for ten minutes, she felt confident that the man was no longer there and she stepped forward to put her head out through the window. It was a grave mistake. The moment she showed herself, a burly figure came around the corner and looked directly up at her as if issuing a challenge. When their eyes met, Amelia felt sick. She had never seen anyone look at her with such malevolence before. His smile was so menacing that it made her flesh creep. She jumped quickly back into the room.

'What is it, Miss Amelia?' asked Beatrix, worriedly.

'He's there.'

'Are you sure?'

'See for yourself,' said Amalia.

Taking care not to get too close to the window, Beatrix gazed down into the street. It was completely empty now. She looked in both directions but saw nobody.

'There's not a soul in sight,' she said.

'He's hiding around the corner.'

'Was it the same man as usual?'

'Yes, Beatrix. He gave me such a fright.'

'Well, he's not there now,' said the servant. 'Wait!' she added as someone came around the corner. She relaxed at once and let out a laugh of relief. 'It's only Kees, back from the market.'

'You'd better go down and let him in.'

Beatrix went out of the room and clattered noisily down the oak staircase. Left alone, Amalia brooded. The brief confrontation with the man outside had shaken her. His eyes had been dark pools of evil. Even though Dopff was back, she didn't feel safe. What troubled her was the thought that the disappearance of her father and the presence of the sinister man outside were in some way linked. She was overcome by a sense of hopelessness. Something else gnawed away at her mind. It was the realisation that her father, who had always been so honest with her, had deceived her.

In the event of anything untoward occurring, he had told her, she was to send word to an address in another part of Paris. At the time, she believed he was referring to an accident that might befall him or a disease he might contract. Her father's words now took on a different construction. It was almost as if he knew that he might be in danger. Amalia had obeyed his command. On the day that he failed to return from Versailles, she had dispatched Dopff with a letter to the address she'd been given. Explaining that her father was now missing, she begged for assistance. Over a week later, she was still waiting. Amalia was in such anguish that she opened her mouth to let out a silent cry of despair.

'Will nobody come to help us?'

Daniel Rawson had crossed the French border with ease. Pacing his horse carefully, he had reached Reims by nightfall and took a room at an inn. Having shed his uniform, he was now posing as a French wine merchant on his way to Paris, and he was dressed accordingly. Some travellers staying at the inn were also heading for the capital so he joined them for safety. His perfect command of the language allowed him to pass for a Frenchman and his knowledge of wines was good enough for him to discuss the subject at length. His companions, a dozen in number, were a mixed bunch. Three were merchants, two were musicians, one was a farmer, two were bankers, each with their wives, and the remaining two were former soldiers, returning to Paris in search of work.

Though Daniel would have liked it to go faster, the convoy kept up a reasonable speed. He spoke to as many of the others as he could and was interested to hear their views of the war.

They came in sharp contradiction to the opinions held in the Allied camp. He was irritated when one of the soldiers held forth about the way that Marshal Villeroi had forced the enemy into a hasty retreat from the River Yssche but Daniel said nothing. To all intents and purposes, he was one of them. When they broke their journey at another inn, he enjoyed sharing a meal with the bankers and their wives, the only people travelling by coach. Bowing to what they believed was his expertise, they let him choose the wine. The men had a prosperous air and the women were excited because they were being taken to Paris by indulgent husbands to look at the latest fashions. The war had not impinged on their life at all. It might have been happening on another continent.

His room was small but serviceable and overlooked the stables. Daniel removed his coat and shoes but kept most of his clothing on in case he had to make a sudden departure. When he got into bed, he kept his saddlebags within easy reach. Unlike the bankers, who had drunk themselves close to oblivion, Daniel had been abstemious at the table so that he could keep his mind clear. Even though he had been accepted into the group, it was important to keep his defences up. One slip could prove fatal.

It was after midnight when he finally dozed off but Daniel was a light sleeper. As soon as he heard the faint creak of floorboards in the passageway outside his room, he was wide awake. He lay there under the sheets as the door slowly opened. It was too dark for him to see anyone but he heard movement across the floor. The next sound that reached his ears was a slight clink. Someone was trying to undo the strap on his saddlebags. Thinking that it was a thief, Daniel reached for the dagger he kept under the pillow. Then he got up quickly and opened the shutters so that moonlight flooded into the room. He threatened the intruder with his dagger, only to find that he was staring at the barrel of a pistol. It was one of the discharged soldiers.

'I thought so,' said the man with a grin. 'You fooled the others but I knew there was something odd about you. How many wine merchants go to bed without undressing? And how many keep a dagger handy?' He gestured with the gun. 'Put it down on the bed.' Daniel tossed the weapon aside. 'That's better.'

'What do you want?' asked Daniel.

'I want to know who you really are.'

'I've told you – my name is Marcel Daron.'

'Then you'll have papers to prove it,' said the soldier. 'That's why I wanted to see inside your saddlebags.'

'Go ahead,' said Daniel, confidently. 'I've nothing to hide.'

'I think you do.' He opened one of the leather pouches and put his hand in. He brought out a purse. 'Do you always travel with so much money, Monsieur Daron?'

'I'll have a lot of expenses in Paris. The documents you want are in the other pouch,' said Daniel. 'If you give me leave to light the candle, you'll be able to read them properly.'

The man gestured with the gun again and Daniel lit the candle on the little table beside the bed. As he did so, he glanced at the door.

'I wouldn't advise you to make a run for it,' warned the man. 'My friend is at the other end of the passage and he'll run you through with his sword if you try to escape.' He looked at the saddlebag. 'Now then, what do we have here?'

Undoing the strap on the other pouch, he felt inside until his hand closed on a wad of papers bound with ribbon. He fished them out but was unable to untie the ribbon with one hand. When he put his pistol aside, he was momentarily unarmed. Daniel was on him in a flash, kicking the gun out of reach and punching the man's head with both fists until he was thoroughly dazed. Before the soldier could recover, Daniel had snatched the pillow and held it down over his face so that he could not cry out for help. Struggling frantically, the man tried to throw him off but Daniel was too strong and determined. With his life at stake, he had no sympathy for his victim. Grabbing his dagger from the bed, he inserted it between his adversary's ribs and thrust it home. The soldier gave a muffled gurgle and went limp.

Daniel had his shoes and coat on in an instant. He put the money and the documents back in the saddlebags then retrieved the pistol from the floor. The next thing he did was to haul the soldier on to the bed and cover him with a sheet. After blowing out the candle, he climbed nimbly through the window and dropped to the ground. Ten minutes later, Marcel Daron was riding hard along the road to Paris.

CHAPTER SIX

Kees Dopff was a small, thin, shy, sinewy man in his late twenties with a mobile face under a thatch of red hair. Mute since birth, he conversed by gesticulating with his hands or by rearranging his features into any one of a whole range of expressions. After serving Emanuel Janssen as an apprentice, Dopff had eventually become his trusted assistant but his talents were not confined to the loom. He was a gifted cook who prepared all the meals in the house, sparing them the trouble of hiring an outsider. When they had first moved to Paris, they had inherited a French servant but Janssen felt that she was there to watch him and dispensed with her services. The four of them had learnt to manage on their own.

Every time that Amalia Janssen left the house, she'd been followed and that unsettled her greatly. Beatrix was too frightened to venture out on her own so Dopff had taken over all the errands. He liked going to market because he could choose the ingredients for the various dishes in his repertoire. When he was not in the kitchen, he was following Janssen's orders and continuing to work on the tapestry that was now so close to completion. He was busy at the loom when Amalia came through the door. Dopff broke off immediately.

'I'm sorry to interrupt you, Kees,' she said, getting a quiet smile in return. 'I was upstairs when I heard you come back. Did you see the man again today?' Dopff nodded. 'Did he follow you?' There was a shake of the head. 'Was it the same man as yesterday?' Dopff nodded again, using his hands to describe the man's height and girth. 'Did he threaten you in any way?'

The weaver shook his head again but Amalia knew that he was lying. Dopff was capable, conscientious and extremely loyal but he lacked courage. The person watching the house intimidated him as much as the two women. Nevertheless, he wouldn't hesitate to protect them if they were in danger even though he could only put up a token defence. He was more than just an assistant to Emanuel Janssen. Dopff had become a member of the family, an adopted son whose disability was at once accepted and ignored. He was made to feel that he had no handicap at all.

When she looked at the tapestry yet again, Amalia had serious misgivings. It was as resplendent and detailed as all of her father's work. It would be much admired when it graced a wall at Versailles. She was, however, disturbed by its subject. It was a depiction of a battle fought almost forty years ago when the French invaded the Spanish Netherlands during the War of Devolution. Under the command of the brilliant Marshal Turenne, the invading army had captured Douai, Tournai, Lille and other cities, annexing Artois and Hainault in the process. It dismayed Amalia that her father was celebrating a French victory on the battlefield. Janssen had argued that it was an honour to have his work hanging in the most celebrated palace in Europe and that it did not matter what it portrayed. He claimed that he was serving his art rather than anything else.

As she viewed it once more, Amalia was struck anew by its subtle blend of colours and by the way the scene came dramatically to life. It was an extraordinary piece of work. She just wished that it did not glorify a nation still fighting against her own. Before she could make that point to Dopff, there was a loud knock at the front door. Tensing at once, she traded a nervous glance with him. A moment later, Beatrix bustled into the room in a state of apprehension.

'What shall I do, Miss Amalia?' she asked.

'Answer the door.'

'It may be that man who's been watching us.'

'Then we must show we're not afraid – go on, Beatrix.'

The servant ran a tongue over her dry lips and breathed in deeply. Dopff, meanwhile, opened a drawer and took out a dagger, hoping that he would never have to use it. Amalia's heart was beating rapidly. She sensed bad news on the other side of the front door.

Daniel had reached Paris without further trouble and entered one of the city gates after showing his forged passport. Because of its noise, filth, stench and crowded streets, he had always disliked the French capital, preferring Amsterdam in every way. It was a relief to find that the address he was after was in a quarter reserved for the rich and powerful. Emanuel Janssen had clearly been treated well since his arrival. When nobody responded to his knock, Daniel banged on the door again. He heard a bolt being drawn then the door opened wide enough for him to see the fretful countenance of Beatrix.

'Is this the home of Emanuel Janssen?' he asked in Dutch.

'The master is not here at the moment, sir.'

'You must be Beatrix.'

'That's right, sir,' she said, eyeing him uneasily.

'I'd like to speak to Miss Janssen, if I may.'

'What's your business with her?'

'I can't divulge that,' said Daniel. 'It's a private matter and I don't propose to discuss it on the doorstep. Tell the young lady that I bring news from home. I've ridden a long way to deliver it.'

Beatrix was unsure what to do. The visitor was very personable and had no resemblance to the man watching the house. At the same time, he was a complete stranger and she therefore distrusted him. She was spared the agony of making a decision.

'Invite the gentleman in,' Amalia called out.

'Yes, Miss Amalia,' replied Beatrix, opening the door wide.

'Thank you,' said Daniel.

Sweeping off his hat, he stepped into the house. Beatrix closed the door behind them and thrust home the bolt before she led him to the parlour. He went into the room to meet Amalia Janssen for the first time. Reports of her beauty had not been exaggerated. Even though she was under obvious stress, she was still arresting. He was taken aback at the sight of her.

'It's a pleasure to meet you, Miss Janssen,' he said, smiling.

'May I know your name, sir?'

'Of course,' said Daniel, 'when I'm certain that it's safe to tell it to you.' He glanced around. 'How many of you are there?'

'Apart from me, only Beatrix and my father's assistant are here.'

'That would be Kees Dopff.'

She was cautious. 'How do you know so much about us?'

'Because I've been sent to help you,' he explained. 'Your father is missing and you wrote to ask for assistance.' Smiling again, he spread his arms. 'Here I am.'

'Yet still you have no name, sir.'

'I travelled here as a French citizen by the name of Marcel Daron and I have papers to that effect. My real name is Daniel Rawson, Captain of the 24th Regiment of Foot, and I'm attached to the Duke of Marlborough's personal staff.'

Amalia was bewildered. 'What has the Duke got to do with this?'

'It was he who showed me your letter, Miss Janssen.'

'You *read* it?'

'I did indeed. You have a graceful hand.'

'However did it reach someone as eminent as a Duke?'

'The person to whom you gave it here passed it on to a courier. It was taken to Flanders at once. His Grace chose me to look into the problem.'

Daniel could see that she was both mystified and suspicious. In order to put her mind at rest, he invited her to interrogate him so that he could prove he was not deceiving her. Amalia offered him a seat then perched on a chair nearby. She fired a series of searching questions at him and he answered them with patent honesty. Very slowly, she began to trust him. However, she was still baffled by the involvement of the Duke of Marlborough. She'd heard her father speak in glowing terms of the British commander without realising that there might be a connection between the two men. Daniel sought to enlighten her.

'This may come as a shock to you, Miss Janssen,' he said, gently, 'but your father did not come to Paris solely to work for His Majesty, King Louis.'

She frowned innocently. 'Why else should he come?'

'He was helping to glean intelligence. Yes,' he went on, seeing her wonderment, 'I know that he was not trained in such work but he agreed to do it and he accepted the dangers that went with it.'

'Why didn't Father *tell* me?' she cried.

'The less you knew, the safer it was for you.'

'What about my father's safety, Captain Rawson? Did nobody consider that when he was asked to be a spy?'

'He was warned. To his credit, he was not frightened off.'

'Well, *I* certainly would have been.'

'That's one of the reasons you were kept in the dark.'

'If we'd stayed in Amsterdam where we belonged,' she said, hands clasped tight in her lap, 'none of this would have happened.'

'That's true,' he admitted. 'By the same token, if you hadn't come to Paris, we wouldn't have had such a stream of invaluable information, collected at Versailles by your father.'

'Is that what lies behind all this?' wondered Amalia, trying to work it out in her head. 'Father was welcomed when we first came here and everyone approved of his design for the tapestry. Like me, they didn't know that he had another purpose for being here.' Her eyes filled with tears. 'They must have found him out. My father is far too honest to dissemble for long. He must have given himself away.'

'That's one possibility we must consider.'

'What other is there, Captain Rawson?'

'He might have been attacked by robbers in the street or he might have been kidnapped by someone wanting a ransom.'

'We've received no demand.'

'It would not come here, Miss Jansson. It would go to Versailles and a large amount of money would be involved. Have you had any official word from the King?'

'None at all,' she said, using a delicate finger to wipe a tear from her cheek. 'We informed the authorities that Father was missing and they showed no interest. Since then, nobody has been in touch with us. It's unnerving.'

'Do you have any idea at all where your father might be?'

'No, Captain Rawson. At least, I didn't until you told me what he was really doing here. My fear is that Father's been arrested and put to death.' Amalia stemmed more tears with a handkerchief. 'Why ever did he take such a terrible risk?'

'It may yet prove to be worthwhile, Miss Janssen,' said Daniel, controlling the urge to put a consoling arm around her. 'There are ways of finding out the truth. Until we do that, there's no need to vex yourself unnecessarily.' He waited until she'd dried her eyes. 'The first thing I'll do is to speak to Pierre Lefeaux, the person who gave your letter to a courier. What manner of man is he?'

'I never met him. Kees delivered my letter.'

'What did he say about the fellow?'

'Nothing at all,' said Amalia with a wan smile. 'Kees is dumb, Captain Rawson. He talks with his hands.'

'I'll call on Monsieur Lefeaux this very afternoon.'

'Take great care. The house is being watched. A man has been standing near the corner all week. Whenever I leave the house, he follows me and it's very alarming.'

'Do you know who he is and what he's doing there?'

'No, Captain Rawson – I tried to speak to him once and he simply laughed. Since then, I haven't stirred from the house.'

'I can see why you and the others are so upset now,' he said, looking towards the window. 'Has this man made any attempt to get in here?'

'Not so far, but we thought it might be him when you knocked.'

Daniel was purposeful. 'This won't continue, Miss Janssen, I promise you. I'll soon find out what he's doing there. Before that, however, I must seek out Monsieur Lefeaux. He may have found out what happened to your father.'

'Then why hasn't he told us?' she demanded. 'It can only be that Father is dead and Monsieur Lefeaux doesn't have the heart to tell us.'

'There's a simpler explanation than that,' suggested Daniel. 'As far as Pierre Lefeaux is concerned, you know nothing at all about your father's other activities here in Paris. He'll certainly have been ordered to keep you ignorant of them.' He rose to his feet. 'I have his address. I'll go there at once.'

Amalia got up as well. 'What should we do, Captain Rawson?'

'Be ready to quit the house at short notice.'

'Leave *here*?' she said, becoming agitated. 'Is the situation that desperate?'

'It might be, Miss Janssen, which is why you need to be warned. With luck, you'll be able to stay here. In the event that you have to go, you'll have to travel light.'

'Would we leave Paris?'

'Not without your father,' he assured her. 'I know somewhere for us all to stay in the meanwhile and there'll be nobody at all watching that particular house.'

'How long will you be gone?' she asked, putting a hand on his arm as he tried to move to the door. 'Don't leave us too long.'

'I'll be back as soon as I can, Miss Janssen. Urgency is my watchword. When I've spoken to Pierre Lefeaux, I'll call on an old friend just in case we do require accommodation.' He chuckled. 'I fancy that he'll be surprised to see me again.'

'Why is that?'

'The last time we met we were on different sides in a battle.'

* * *

Henry Welbeck was not fond of officers. He had buried far too many men as a result of the incompetence of lieutenants or the misplaced bravado of captains. Having taken great pains to train those under his command, he liked to keep as many of them alive as possible. Taking stock of battlefield casualties was something that always darkened his melancholy. The social divide between officers and men was deep and wide. In his own idiosyncratic way, Welbeck was proud of the side on which he stood. The only person of his acquaintance who had bridged that gap was Daniel Rawson, allowing him to move from one world to the other without the slightest difficulty.

If his friend was an exception to the rule, Simon Cracknell embodied it. The major had, in Welbeck's opinion, all the defects of his breed. He was arrogant, disdainful and vindictive, treating those in the ranks as no more than cannon fodder. Among his colleagues, he was reckoned to be a good officer and had shown conspicuous gallantry on the field of battle. Welbeck was ready to acknowledge that. What he disliked most about Cracknell was his constant denigration of Daniel Rawson. It was spiteful and unjust.

Welbeck had just finished drilling his men when he saw that the major had been watching him. Cracknell beckoned him over with a lordly crook of his finger. The sergeant did not hurry.

'Good afternoon, Major,' he said.

'Your men were looking a bit ragged today, Sergeant. It's high time you taught them how to march in a straight line.'

'They were as straight as can be.'

'Not from where I'm standing,' said Cracknell. 'They were like the hind leg of a donkey.'

Welbeck knew that it was untrue and that Cracknell was trying to provoke him. It was pointless to argue with an officer, especially one as powerful as a major. Welbeck opted for gruff politeness.

'It won't happen again, Major.'

'I hope not,' said the other. 'I've got higher standards than Captain Rawson. Now that he's no longer here to protect you, there'll be more scrutiny of your work.'

'Yes, sir.'

'Rawson was far too lax.'

'I disagree, Major.'

'He let friendship interfere with duty and that's a fault in any officer. While he's away, you'll drill your men properly.'

'Yes, sir,' said Welbeck, hurt by the unfair criticism.

'Our regiment must be second to none. We have to set an example to the Dutch. If they were trained as they should be, they might even be prepared to fight a battle with us.'

'You're right, Major.'

'The Prussians know how to fight and so do the Austrians when they put their minds to it. Prince Eugene of Savoy is a true soldier, who leads his men from the front. Only the Dutch let us down and they will keep jabbering in that ridiculous language of theirs.' He gave a cold smile. 'When Captain Rawson talks in Dutch, he sounds like a goose having its neck wrung.'

'The captain is fluent in four languages, Major,' said Welbeck. 'How many do you speak?'

'The only one that matters,' retorted the other, stung by the question. 'Besides, I'm a soldier and everyone speaks the same language on the battlefield with swords and guns.' He tried to make his enquiry seem casual. 'When will we be seeing Rawson again?'

'You're more likely to know that, Major.'

'Didn't he tell you where he was going?'

'When we last spoke, Captain Rawson didn't know himself.'

'But he would surely have told you, if he had.'

'No, Major. He's very discreet.'

'Wouldn't he confide in a close friend?'

'The captain has never discussed any of his assignments beforehand,' said Welbeck. 'He's as close as the grave. I should imagine it's one of the reasons that the Duke entrusts him with such missions. A more boastful officer would be unable to keep secrets.'

Welbeck was delighted to see Cracknell wince slightly. The sergeant's thrust had gone home. Daniel had told him how conceited the major was and how quick to brag about his achievements. Any reminder of Daniel's closeness to their commander-in-chief annoyed Cracknell, who thought himself the better man and more deserving of Marlborough's attention. The major quickly retaliated.

'I understand you have a nephew in the regiment,' he said.

'Yes, Major.'

'I can't say that I approve. One Welbeck is more than enough.'

'The lad's name is Hillier, sir.'

'I know, sergeant. I made it my business to find out. Tom Hillier is a drummer. I shall be interested to see how he develops.'

Welbeck was worried. There was no reason why a major should take the slightest notice of the new recruit unless it was to use him as a means of wounding his uncle. It was the sort of thing that someone like Cracknell would do. In persecuting Hillier, the major would be hurting Welbeck and in doing that he would be assuaging his hatred of a fellow officer. Helpless to defend his nephew, the sergeant wished that Daniel Rawson was still there to come to his aid.

'Where the hell *are* you, Dan?' he said to himself.

Pierre Lefeaux was a cobbler in the city. While pursuing his trade, he also acted as a British spy, receiving and passing on intelligence to others. Because people came in and out of his shop all day, there was never any suspicion of him. Vital secrets had been concealed in shoes that needed to be repaired. Lefeaux had duly passed them on by all manner of devious means. His shop was in one of the more salubrious districts of Paris though Daniel had to ride through the teeming streets of the poorer quarters in order to find it. Even though it was afternoon, the place was closed. After tethering his horse, Daniel spoke to one of the neighbours and learnt that the cobbler's shop had not been open all week.

The news was disturbing. According to Daniel's information, Lefeaux was an important part of an intelligence system that had been developed in the French capital. He was unlikely to desert his post unless he had fled out of fear of discovery. The neighbour had told him that the cobbler lived above the shop with his wife but that nothing had been seen of either of them. Daniel studied the building. He could not leave without finding out what had happened to the couple. If one of his spies had gone astray, Marlborough would expect a full report. Daniel needed to get inside the premises to search for clues that indicated the fate of Pierre Lefeaux.

Making sure that he was not seen, Daniel went swiftly around to the rear of the house. The shutters were all locked and the little stable was empty, its door wide open. He moved to a ground floor window that was not overlooked by any of the neighbours and took out a dagger. Inserting it between the shutters, he tried to lift the catch but it was securely locked in place. He went back into the stable and looked for an implement that he could use as a lever. He found nothing suitable until his eye alighted on a pair of rusty horseshoes, lying in a corner as if tossed there. Seizing both of them, Daniel went back to the shutter. He used his dagger to saw away at the wood, making the slit wide enough to admit something thicker. Then he worked a horseshoe between the shutters and slowly applied pressure.

The catch held firm at first. As he put more effort into levering the timber apart, the shutters opened enough for him to push the other horseshoe into the gap further up. He now had two levers in play and the wood began to groan under the strain. All at once, with a loud bang, the lock snapped and the shutters flew open. Daniel had to leap back out of the way. He put the horseshoes aside and waited to see if the noise had been heard by anyone else. Nobody came. He flew into action. Removing his hat, he took hold of the window frame and pulled himself through it with speed and agility. He was in the kitchen and could see food left out on the table. The morsels of meat on the two platters were encircled by flies. Almost all of the butter had been eaten. When he felt the loaf of bread, it was dry and stale.

Daniel went through to the parlour but was unable to see much in the half-dark and did not want to open any other shutters in case he attracted attention. When he went through to the shop itself, he could smell the leather. A boot was affixed to a last and a hammer lay beside it. Shoes and boots in need of repair lined the shelves. Daniel had the feeling that many customers were going to be disappointed. As his eyes became more accustomed to the gloom, he went back into the parlour and up the staircase. A noisome smell soon hit his nostrils and it was all too familiar.

It was the unmistakable stink of death. Opening the door to the front bedroom, he blenched.

Pierre Lefeaux and his wife had been hanged from the main beam, their hands tied behind their backs. Their faces were badly bruised and dried blood stained their clothing. He surmised that they'd been tortured before execution. Flies buzzed noisily all around them. Maggots were dining on their rotting flesh. The reek of decomposition was overpowering. Daniel estimated that they'd been dead for several days. Hand over his mouth, he rushed down the stairs and climbed through the window so that he could breathe in fresh air again. His mind was racing and his stomach churning. It was a frightening development. The cobbler had obviously been punished for providing intelligence to the British army. As he rode away from the shop, Daniel was bound to wonder if Emanuel Janssen had met a similarly gruesome fate.

The news that they might have to flee from the house very soon had caused a commotion. Beatrix was close to hysteria and Kees Dopff flailed his arms like a windmill, pleading with Amalia Janssen not to abandon the tapestry on which her father had worked so sedulously and so long. It took some time to subdue them. Amalia sat them down in the parlour and tried to reason with them.

'It may be that we're able to stay right here,' she said.

'Then why this talk of running away?' asked Beatrix.

'That's only a last resort.'

'Who says so?'

'Captain Rawson.'

'And do you believe everything he tells you?'

'Yes, I do.'

'You hardly know him, Miss Amalia.'

'I know him well enough to trust him.'

'Well, I'm not sure that I do,' said Beatrix. 'After the things that have been going on here, I don't trust anyone.' She turned to Dopff. 'Do you?' He shook his head violently. 'There you are.'

Amalia was patient. 'Captain Rawson has been sent to help us,' she explained. 'There's no call for you to know why. Suffice it to say that his arrival has been the one thing to lift my spirits since my father went missing. I'm as reluctant as either of you to quit this house but, if it's essential, then we must do as we're told.'

'What about your father?'

'Captain Rawson is making enquiries about him.'

'Oh, I wish I knew what was going on,' Beatrix wailed. 'I never wanted to come here in the first place.' Dopff's expression showed that he agreed with her. 'But at least we had a fine house.'

'It may have served its purpose, Beatrix,' said Amalia. 'Now why don't you and Kees gather together the few belongings you'll be able to take if we're forced out of here.' She saw the anguish on Dopff's face. 'There's no call for alarm, Kees,' she went on, softly. 'I promise you that we won't leave the tapestry behind.' He brightened immediately. 'You'd better be ready to take it down from the loom.'

Dopff nodded and left the room. Amalia sent the servant off to pack her bags. About to go to her own bedroom, she saw a horse pull up outside the front window and recognised the rider. She ran to the door to admit Daniel then brought him into the parlour.

'Well?' she asked. 'Did you see Monsieur Lefeaux?'

'He was not able to help us,' replied Daniel, sadly.

'Didn't he know where Father was?'

'I'm afraid not, Miss Janssen.'

'What exactly did he say?'

'That doesn't matter,' said Daniel, keeping the awful truth from her. 'What has become clear is that you must leave here tonight. I called on my friend and he's willing to look after us for a while. He has a horse and cart.'

'How far must we go?'

'The house is on the other side of the city.'

'Who is this friend?'

'His name is Ronan Flynn and he has a warm Irish heart. He and his wife will look after us until we're ready to leave Paris.'

'And when will that be, Captain Rawson?'

'When we've discovered where your father is.'

'*Someone* must know,' she said with an edge of desperation.

'Yes, Miss Janssen, and I think he's standing outside in the street. That man who's been watching the house is still there. If anyone knows what's going on, he does.'

'What are you going to do?'

'I'm going to have a friendly word with him,' said Daniel.

CHAPTER SEVEN

They waited until evening shadows began to lengthen and the streets began to clear of people. Daniel then issued his instructions. Amalia Janssen was ready to obey them to the letter but Beatrix was fearful.

'I don't want to go out there, sir,' she said with a shudder.

'Why not?' asked Daniel.

'That dreadful man is waiting.'

'He won't trouble you for much longer.'

'What are you going to do?'

'I simply need to speak to him.'

'Well, why can't you go out there and do that, sir?'

'Listen to Captain Rawson,' said Amalia. 'He knows best. All that we have to do is to walk for ten minutes. No harm will come to us if we're together.'

Beatrix was not convinced and it was clear from Dopff's face that he, too, had qualms. On the other hand, the weaver had been impressed by their visitor's decisiveness and had no doubts about Daniel's good intentions. He just wished he understood why a British soldier had come to their assistance out of the blue. Daniel repeated his orders slowly.

'Give me five minutes and then leave the house together,' he said. 'Walk past the man at the corner and lead him around in a circle before coming back here. Is that understood?'

'Yes,' replied Amalia.

'Where will *you* be, Captain Rawson?' asked Beatrix.

'I'll be waiting for him,' said Daniel.

After giving them all a smile of encouragement, he let himself out into the street and mounted his horse. He trotted off in the opposite direction to the corner where the watcher was stationed. Turning into the adjacent street, he rode on until he reached another corner. When he turned right again, he kept his eyes peeled.

Amalia Janssen, Beatrix and Kees Dopff stood in the parlour and watched the pendulum of the clock as it swung to and fro. Dopff wanted to point out that it was a Dutch mathematician who first invented the pendulum clock over half a century earlier but he felt it inappropriate. It would also take far too long for him to convey the information by means of gesture and facial expression. When the five minutes had elapsed, Amalia gave a nod and led them to the front door. Beatrix was still reluctant but she could not refuse to go. She pulled a scarf around her shoulders and gritted her teeth. With mixed feelings, Dopff opened the front door and the women went out into the street. They heard the door being shut behind them.

'I don't like this,' confided Beatrix.

'Stay close to me,' said Amalia.

Crossing the street, they walked side by side, trying to appear as natural as they could. They turned left at the corner and expected the burly man to confront them but he was not there. For a second, they dared to relax. The man had apparently gone away. Their sense of relief was rudely shattered when he stepped out of a doorway opposite and tipped his hat in a mocking salute. They walked quickly on. His heavy footsteps soon fell in behind them. Neither of them dared to look over her shoulder. They were both quietly terrified.

Daniel had found a dark alleyway where both he and his horse could hide. It was only a question of waiting now. Certain that Emanuel Janssen had been identified as a spy, he prayed that the man was still alive and had been spared torture. He winced at the thought of having to tell Amalia that her father had been killed. She seemed so young and fragile that the news could destroy her. From the way Lefeaux and his wife had been summarily hanged, it was evident that no mercy would be shown to spies. He could only hope that Janssen's exceptional skill as a tapestry-maker had saved him. A monarch who took such delight in the work of artists of all kinds might think twice about condemning a supreme craftsman to death.

Daniel had no more time to reflect upon what was only a faint hope. A horse and cart went past then an old man staggered by on a walking stick. What he saw next as he peered around the corner of the alleyway were the two women, walking in step and staying close together. Yards behind them, he could just pick out a brawny figure in the gloom. Flattening his back against the wall, he was ready to pounce. Amalia Janssen and Beatrix got nearer and nearer until he could hear their matching footsteps. When they went past him, they didn't even think to look down the alleyway. Neither did their stalker and it was a bad mistake. Daniel leapt out, grabbed his collar to pull him into the alleyway then held a dagger at his throat.

'Who *are* you?' demanded Daniel.

'I've got no money if that's what you're after,' said the man.

'I want to know why you're following those two ladies and why you've been outside their house all week.' Daniel shoved him hard against the wall then pricked his neck with the point of his weapon. The man yelped. 'Next time, I'll cut your throat. Now – who are you?'

'My name is Jacques Serval,' admitted the other, 'and I wasn't following anybody. I live nearby and was on my way home.'

'Don't lie to me or I'll slice you to pieces.' Daniel reinforced the threat with a kick on the shin and a punch on the nose. Blood gushed down on to the man's beard. He glowered at Daniel. 'Where is Emanuel Janssen?'

'I've never heard of him,' said Serval, a hand to his nose.

'Why keep his house under surveillance?'

'I don't know what you're talking about.'

'Then you're no use to me,' said Daniel, pulling back his arm as if to thrust the dagger into him. 'Goodbye, my friend.'

'No – wait!' exclaimed Serval, cowering.

'Have I jogged your memory?'

'I didn't take him away. The others did that. I was just asked to watch the house to see what his daughter did. You've got no argument with me, sir. I'm not important.'

'You're important to me because you're the one person who can solve this mystery. I'll ask you once more and, if you still insist you don't know, I'll send you off to the Hell you deserve for tormenting those ladies.' With his free hand, he slammed the man against the wall, knocking off his hat. 'Consider your answer very carefully, my friend. Where is Emanuel Janssen?'

'Somewhere you'll never reach him,' said Serval, defiantly.

'He *is* alive, then?'

'Yes.'

'Is he still here in Paris?'

'Janssen won't ever be leaving here.'

'Why do you say that?'

'He's in the one place where nobody leaves.'

'And where's that?'

Serval smirked. 'The Bastille.'

Daniel was stunned. Relieved to hear that Janssen was still alive, he was dismayed to learn that he was being held in the city's most notorious prison. It was like a body blow to Daniel. As he tried to absorb the impact, he took a step backward. Serval saw his chance and took it. Lunging forward, he grabbed the wrist of the hand that held the dagger and tried to twist it away from him. Daniel fought back at once, grappling hard, looking into the Frenchman's crazed eyes and recoiling from his foul breath. With a sudden move and a swing of his leg, he managed to trip Serval up. Falling to the ground, Serval kept an iron grip on his wrist and pulled Daniel after him. They struggled violently. It was a trial of strength now.

Serval was a powerful man who had come off best in many tavern brawls. He spat into Daniel's face then turned his head sharply to bite his wrist, forcing him to drop the dagger. They were on even terms, needing to subdue or kill their opponent with bare hands. After trying to gouge Daniel's eyes, Serval rolled over so that he was on top for the first time, his substantial weight bearing down on Daniel. The Frenchman was sweating freely and panting hard but he now had the advantage. Rising up to sit astride Daniel, he got both hands to his throat and began to throttle him, blood from his nose dripping on to Daniel's face. Anticipating success, Serval let out a growl of triumph.

It was premature. Daniel was not finished yet. Gasping for breath, he put all his strength into a punch that caught Serval on the ear and knocked him sideways, weakening his hold on Daniel's neck. A second punch dislodged his hold altogether and Daniel was able to throw him off and scramble to his feet. Serval was quick to recover, getting to his knees and pulling out his own dagger. Daniel reacted by instinct. If he let the Frenchman get up, then the result would not be in doubt. Serval had to be disarmed. With a firm kick, Daniel caught him in the crotch and made him double up in agony. Then he dived in to grab Serval's wrist, twisting it so that the dagger turned towards the Frenchman's chest. With a howl of rage, Serval tried to pull himself upright and turn the weapon back on Daniel but he slipped on the cobbles and fell backwards. As Daniel tumbled to the ground on top of him, the dagger went straight through the Frenchman's heart. Serval's body convulsed for a moment then all resistance drained out of him.

When he was sure that the man was dead, Daniel searched him quickly and took some papers from his pocket. Then he lugged the body down the alleyway and hid it in a doorway. Retrieving his own dagger, he put it in its sheath and went to collect his horse. Now that the fight was over, he was able to address his mind to what he had found out. He did not relish the task of passing on the information to Amalia Janssen. Her father might be alive but he was incarcerated in the infamous Bastille. That was a death sentence in itself.

Amalia was increasingly worried. After their walk, she and Beatrix had returned safely to the house, expecting Daniel to join them almost at once. While they'd been on foot, he had a horse. She could not understand why he'd been delayed and was immediately prey to all kinds of fears. Daniel was the only person who had brought hope into her life and she needed him. Even on such a short acquaintance, Amalia had been drawn to Daniel, struck by his bravery, grateful for his honesty and touched by his charm. It was only when she heard the clip-clop of hooves in the street outside that she began to calm down. Instead of leaving the task to Beatrix, she ran to open the front door herself. Daniel had come back.

'What did you find out?' she asked, breathlessly.

'We must leave tonight,' he said, dismounting and holding the reins. 'I'll fetch the cart and be back within the hour.'

'What about my father?'

'He's alive, Miss Janssen.'

'Thank God!' she exclaimed. 'Where is he?'

'I'll explain that later,' he said. 'The important thing is for us to reach a place of safety as soon as we can. In due course, you'll understand why.'

Amalia gave a stifled cry. It was fairly dark in the street but she had just stepped close enough to Daniel to see the blood on his face and the tear in his coat. She also noticed the dirt on his clothing.

'What happened, Captain Rawson?' she said.

'This is no time to discuss that.'

'Were you involved in a fight with that man?'

'Forget him,' said Daniel. 'Impress upon Kees and Beatrix that this is an emergency. If they have to leave things behind, so be it. They must be ready to go the moment I get back. It won't be a coach and four,' he apologised, 'but it will get us there in one piece.'

'I'm worried about *you*, Captain. Are you badly injured?'

'I'm not injured at all, Miss Janssen.'

'Something has obviously happened.'

'Tell the others what I said,' he urged, mounting his horse.

'Where exactly are we going?'

'You'll find that out when we get there. Now please hurry up. There's no time to lose. If you stay in this house one more night, then all your lives will be in danger.'

Ronan Flynn was a lanky, raw-boned man in his early forties with long grey hair and curling eyebrows. Having served in an Irish regiment that fought in Louis XIV's army, he had picked up a certain amount of the French language. It was when he had met Charlotte Rousset that his fluency had perforce improved by leaps and bounds. Falling in love with the pretty young Parisian woman, he had courted and married her. Charlotte was almost eighteen years younger than her husband yet they were so contented that the age difference became irrelevant. Flynn lived happily in a small but comfortable house with his wife and baby daughter. It was, he reminded himself every day, far better than being a soldier.

'There are *four* of them?' said Charlotte with concern.

'It will only be for a short time, my darling.'

'But we don't have enough room for so many.'

'We'll fit them all in somehow,' said Flynn. 'There's room in the attic for the man and the two women will have to share.'

'What about your friend?'

'Oh, Dan Rawson will lay his head down anywhere. He's the one person you don't have to worry about. He's a soldier, used to sleeping on the ground in all weathers.'

'Why are they coming here, Ronan?'

He hunched his shoulders. 'They need a roof over their heads.'

Flynn had told his wife as little as possible. All that she knew was that Daniel and her husband had once fought alongside

each other in the army. Charlotte didn't realise that Flynn had
been in the British army at the time. She assumed that both men
had served under the French flag. The salient point about their
friendship was that Daniel had rescued the Irishman when he'd
been captured by the enemy. There was an unpaid debt that had
to be honoured. Flynn would not, in any case, have been able
to give his wife full details of why four strangers were about
to descend on her because he didn't know them himself and
didn't wish to know. A friend was in trouble. That was enough
for Ronan Flynn.

'Who *are* these people?' asked Charlotte.

'They're friends of Daniel and they've had to leave their
house.'

'Why?'

'I've no idea, my darling,' he said, kissing the chevron of
concern on her brow. 'Let's wait until they tell us, shall we?'

'It seems so odd, coming here at this time of night.'

He beamed at her. 'Paris is an odd place. Where else could an
ugly old Irishman like me marry the most beautiful woman in
the world?' Charlotte softened and hugged him in gratitude for
the compliment. 'If looking after these people for a few days is all
we have to put up with, I'd say that we were very lucky. Doesn't
the priest tell us every Sunday that it's good to help others? Or
has my French let me down? It sounds to me as if that's what he's
saying.'

She was still worried. 'Are they in trouble, Ronan?'

'Yes – they have nowhere to sleep.'

'Where is their house?'

'I don't know,' he told her. 'Somewhere on the other side of
the city, I think. There are all kinds of reasons why people have
to look for accommodation. Perhaps they had a quarrel with

the landlord or discovered the place was infested with vermin. Maybe there was a fire. Whatever the cause, we mustn't pester them with questions. Be nice to them, Charlotte, please. Will you do that for me?'

'I'll do anything for you,' she said.

Flynn embraced her and kissed her on the lips. Before they could savour the moment, however, there was a cry from upstairs as the baby came awake again. Charlotte smiled tolerantly and went off up the steps. Flynn followed her.

For the three Dutch passengers, the ride through Paris at night was nothing short of an ordeal. Having lived in such a pleasant quarter of the city, they hadn't realised that most of it was given over to narrow, fetid, swarming streets lined with tenements and decaying old buildings. The pervading stink was matched by a continuous din. Boisterous taverns and pleading beggars supplied most of the noise. Yapping dogs and screeching cats added a descant. Daniel drove the rattling cart with Amalia beside him. Amid a pile of belongings, the others sat uncomfortably behind them. Beatrix clung to her bag so that none of the grasping hands could steal it while Kees Dopff held the tapestry in his arms as if clinging to a piece of timber in a swollen river. Both of them were highly distressed at the number of drunks who lunged wildly at the cart or threw missiles out of random malice. They were all relieved when they entered the wide thoroughfare of a more respectable district. As the hubbub subsided, they were able to hold a conversation at last.

'Who is this friend of yours?' asked Amalia.

'He's a mad Irishman,' said Daniel, 'and his name is Ronan Flynn. We met when he served in the British army but he later joined a French regiment. That's when we were on opposite sides.'

'Is he ready to help an enemy?'

'We're good friends, Miss Janssen, and we're no longer on the battlefield. Ronan owes me a favour, that's all I'll say.'

'How much does he know about us?'

'Precious little,' said Daniel, 'and I wish to keep it that way. Kees is not going to tell them anything and I doubt if your servant speaks much French but you're obviously an intelligent young lady. I daresay you have some knowledge of the language.'

'I like to think that I do, Captain Rawson.'

'Don't admit that or you're likely to be interrogated.'

'Am I?'

'Ronan won't ask you any questions but his wife is a different matter. Charlotte is French and can't be expected to show the same sympathy to foreigners.'

'I understand.'

'Do you like children?'

The question surprised her. 'Yes, of course I do.'

'They have a baby daughter,' said Daniel. 'I only caught a glimpse of her but she's a gorgeous child. Ronan loves showing her off. Luckily, I'd had time to wash the blood off my face before he handed her over to me or I'd have frightened her.'

'You still haven't told me what happened with that man.'

'We exchanged blows, Miss Janssen.'

'Won't he run off and summon help?' she asked. When Daniel remained silent, she gulped. 'You didn't *kill* him, did you?'

'I stopped him from bothering you ever again.'

Amalia reeled from the shock. 'No wonder you were covered in blood,' she said. 'This is terrible, Captain Rawson. I had no idea you'd have to go to that extreme.'

'My hand was forced.'

'I can see now why we had to leave in a hurry.'

'It's only a matter of time before the body is found,' said Daniel. 'When that happens, the first place they'll go to is your house. We need to be as far away as possible.'

'What about my father?'

'We'll talk about that later.'

'I want to know now,' she insisted. 'Where is he?'

'Your father is being held, Miss Janssen. He's in prison.'

Her face fell. '*Prison*? What have they done to him? Is he being fed? Has he been tortured? Father's not a strong man. Being locked up will break him, Captain Rawson.' She tried to hold back tears. 'How can we possibly reach him if he's held in prison?'

'There has to be a way,' said Daniel, thoughtfully. 'All that I have to do is to find out what it is.'

When they finally reached their destination, they were given a cordial welcome by Ronan Flynn and his wife. Charlotte had prepared a meal for them so they all sat around the table together. Even Beatrix, who, as a servant, always ate apart as a rule, was allowed to join them. Dopff was very impressed with the cooking and went into an elaborate mime to congratulate Charlotte. There were some awkward moments but the supper passed off without incident. Having always had her own bedchamber, Amalia was unhappy that she had to share her bed with Beatrix but accepted the situation without complaint. Dopff was content to sleep in the bare attic as long as he could have the tapestry beside him. Daniel agreed to spend the night downstairs.

The visitors adapted slowly to a house that was very much smaller than the one they'd just left and possessed none of its luxuries. They all seemed to be on top of each other. When the women had finally retired, and when Dopff was snoring in the attic, Flynn produced another flagon of wine so that he and Daniel could talk over a cup of it in private. The first thing the Irishman did was to clap his friend heartily on the shoulder.

'You always *did* have an eye for the ladies, Dan,' he said. 'She's a real beauty is that Amalia. If it wasn't for the fact that I have a lovely wife waiting for me upstairs, I'd be very jealous.'

'I'm simply here to look after her,' said Daniel.

'It always starts that way.'

'I'm serious, Ronan. The girl is young and innocent.'

Flynn laughed. 'They're the best kind.'

'There's nothing like that going on.'

'Well, there damn well ought to be, man,' said Flynn, nudging him with an elbow. 'Look at those eyes of hers. Think of that divine face. Saints in heaven, Amalia could seduce the Pope!'

'She's a frightened woman who needs protection.'

'Then why aren't you in her bed, protecting her?'

Daniel sipped his wine until Flynn had finished his jocular teasing. When they'd first met, they'd been two of a kind, lusty young soldiers who fought bravely on the battlefield and took their pleasures where they could find them. Flynn had now settled down into family life but he had some warm memories. Daniel tried to steer him away from them so that they could talk about something more serious.

'What made you give up army life?' he asked.

'Old age and the sight of Charlotte Rousset,' replied Flynn.

'Was that her maiden name?'

'Yes, Dan, but she didn't hold on to it much longer once I'd met her. I worship that woman. She's changed my life and given me that little angel of a daughter. And that's not all,' he went on. 'When her father heard that I had a little money to invest, he took me into the family business. I'm a baker now, *un boulanger de Paris*. You tasted some of my bread earlier on.'

'It was delicious, Ronan.'

'The only problem is that I have to be up so early to make sure the servant has lit the ovens. Then we toil away while the city sleeps. When the bread is baked, I help to deliver it with the horse and cart. We've a lot of customers and they expect fresh bread every morning.'

'Which do you prefer – being a soldier or being a baker?'

'If you'd asked me twenty years ago, I'd have said that nothing could compare with army life. It was tough, I grant you,' said Flynn, 'and it could wear you down at times, but it was just the thing for a young fellow like me with fire in his belly. I craved the excitement of it all. I loved the danger.'

'You loved other things as well, as I recall,' said Daniel.

'That was my downfall, Dan. It wasn't the women. I think every man has the right to spread his love far and wide. No, it was the drink and the fighting. When I'd had too much of the one, I couldn't get enough of the other.' He gave a rueful laugh. 'I probably did more damage to my fellow-soldiers with my fists than I ever did to the enemy with a musket. It's the reason I never rose higher than a corporal. I had warning after warning but there was no heeding them when the drink had a hold on me.'

'You knocked out a captain, didn't you?'

'He was a lieutenant, actually,' said Flynn, 'and he deserved every blow. But striking an officer is a crime. When they'd finished flogging me, they threw me out of the regiment altogether.'

'Is that when you went over to the French?'

'No, Dan, I had a spell of drifting all over the place, taking whatever job I could lay my hands on. But I couldn't stay out of the war too long. I had friends in an Irish regiment serving the French so I threw in my lot with them.' He looked quizzically at Daniel. 'What about you? When we first met, we were both black-hearted corporals. Then you got yourself promoted.'

'I was lucky,' said Daniel, modestly.

'That's nonsense, man! Luck doesn't come into it. I know what it takes to work your way up and why so few people manage to do it. Captain Daniel Rawson, is it?' he added with a twinkle. 'I like it, Dan. It has a ring to it.'

'Thank you, Ronan.'

'It also gives the game away. If someone like you tricks his way into Paris, then it's to do with something more important than wishing three Dutch guests on the Flynn household.'

'It is,' confessed Daniel, 'but I'd rather not go into details.'

'It's probably better if I don't hear them, Dan. I count myself a loyal Frenchman now. On the other hand, I have to think of my wife and child. You and your friends are welcome to stay here as long as you don't endanger us.'

'If it reaches that point, Ronan, we'll move out immediately.'

'Then I won't pry any further.'

He poured them both a second cup of wine and they shared army reminiscences for a while. When his friend was in a mellow mood, Daniel turned to another subject.

'What do you know about the Bastille?' he asked.

'I know that I'd much rather be outside its walls than inside.'

'It's in the Rue Saint-Antoine, isn't it?'

'Yes,' said Flynn, 'and I get quite close to it when I deliver my bread. It gives me the shivers. My father-in-law would love to have the contract to provide bread for the Bastille itself but one of his rivals has got that. Mind you,' he went on, 'the bread probably only goes to the turnkeys. They starve any prisoners locked away in there. What are you interested in the Bastille for?'

'I've heard so many tales about it. If your delivery round takes you in that direction, you must have a wide circle of customers.'

'They've heard how tasty Flynn bread is. Strictly speaking, it's Rousset bread because my father-in-law taught me everything I know. There's a real art to baking, Dan. It took me a year to master it.'

'I'd like to see you at work, Ronan.'

'You won't get much sleep if you do that.'

'Who cares?' said Daniel, intrigued by the fact that Flynn would be going close to the Bastille. 'I'm used to broken nights. Would I be in the way if I came with you to the bakery tomorrow?'

'No,' said Flynn, 'you can help to load the cart.'

'In that case, I'll snatch a few hours' sleep while I can.' He drank the last of his wine. 'I can't thank you enough, Ronan. You helped us in our hour of need. We simply couldn't have stayed where we were.'

When the body of Jacques Serval was discovered that night, the police were informed at once. While some of them removed the corpse, others rushed to the house occupied by the Dutch visitors. Two constables were sent around to the rear of the building to block off any attempt at escape then someone banged loudly on the door. When there was no response, he pounded even harder with his fist. Still nobody stirred within the house. Forced entry was required. Two of the heftiest men threw their combined strength at the door until the lock gave way and it swung open on its hinges. Policemen poured into the dark house with lanterns and searched every room. When they met again in the hall, it was the sergeant who summed up the situation.

'They've gone,' he declared, purple with fury. 'We must catch them before they can leave Paris.'

Chapter Eight

Tom Hillier was disappointed. Army life was neither as thrilling nor as rewarding as he thought it would be. He had left the safety of his farm and family back in England in the hope of adventure abroad and it had not been forthcoming. Expecting to take an active part in famous victories, he'd twice been denied the chance to march into battle and had spent most of his time being drilled or moving from place to place. The novelty of being in a foreign country had soon worn off. He began to feel homesick. Of all the things that had disillusioned him, the most painful was the way in which his uncle had effectively disowned him. Though he'd only known Welbeck from the sergeant's letters, and from what his mother had told him about her brother, Hillier had an image of him as a hero and wanted to emulate his achievements. Yet he'd been rebuffed in the most hurtful way.

Set against the disappointments was one consolation. Having fought the drummer who'd been teasing him remorselessly, he not only won the contest but made himself a real friend in the process. In beating Hugh Dobbs, he'd earned his respect. Dobbs was a sturdy, potato-faced youth of eighteen summers with a roguish grin and a dislike of authority. He gave Hillier a lot of useful advice about the technique of drumming and told him lively tales about the regiment's involvement in the victory at Blenheim. Dobbs also acted as a kind of unofficial biographer to Daniel Rawson and the new recruit never tired of hearing tales of the captain's exploits. As they lay side by side that night in the tent they shared with the other drummers, Dobbs resumed his narrative.

'Do you know what else Captain Rawson did?'

'No,' said Hillier, attentively.

'I overheard Lieutenant Ainley talking about it,' said Dobbs, 'so it must be true. When the captain was sent across the border to act as a spy, he captured some dispatches from a French courier then dressed up in the man's uniform and delivered them in person to Marshal Villeroi.'

Hillier gaped. 'He rode into the French camp?'

'He rode out again as well with Villeroi's dispatches to King Louis. Who else would have the nerve to do that?'

'Who else would take part in a Forlorn Hope?'

'Yes,' said Dobbs, 'Captain Rawson has done that twice now. When we reached the Danube last year, he joined in the Forlorn Hope at the Schellenberg. Most of the others were killed on the slope but he survived to fight on.'

'Tell me about Blenheim again.'

'Be quiet, you two!' someone called out. 'We're trying to get some sleep over here.'

'I'm sorry,' said Hillier before whispering to Dobbs, 'Tell me about Blenheim.'

'Ask me tomorrow,' suggested Dobbs, yawning.

'I want to hear it now.'

'Your uncle is the person to ask. Sergeant Welbeck was right in the thick of it. All that we did was to beat the drums.'

'I'd rather listen to you,' said Hillier. 'I want to know what it's like to be in a battle.'

'Tomorrow, Tom – I'm tired.'

'All right, but answer me this before you doze off. Is it true that Captain Rawson is no longer in camp? I heard a rumour that he was seen riding off days ago in civilian clothes.'

'I heard the same thing.'

'Where was he going?'

'He wants to take on the French fucking army all on his own.'

Hillier laughed aloud until someone threw a boot at him. The conversation was over. He lay on his back and gingerly rubbed the side of his head where the boot had hit him. Hillier then closed his eyes. It was time to dream again of the military glory that had so far eluded him.

After sleeping on the floor downstairs, Daniel came awake when he heard the sound of footsteps in the room above. Ronan Flynn was on the move. By the time that the Irishman crept downstairs, Daniel was dressed and wide awake. After a mouthful of bread and a drink, they harnessed the horse between the shafts and set off on the cart. The bakery was half a mile away so the journey gave them time to talk. They raised their voices over the clack of hooves and rattle of the cart.

'So this is how bakers live, is it?' said Daniel.

'We start early and finish early.'

'Then it's better than working on a farm. When I was a lad, we started early and finished late. In summer we never seemed to stop.'

'What happened to the farm?'

'It was commandeered when my father fought against the

King's army at the battle of Sedgemoor. He was taken prisoner. Father was sentenced to hang at the Bloody Assizes. Mother and I had to flee to Amsterdam.'

'What rank did your father hold?'

'He was a captain.'

'So you followed in his footsteps.'

'Not exactly, Ronan. My father fought *against* His Grace – or Lord Churchill as he was then – while I serve under his command.'

'I'd much rather be on the Duke's side.'

'Then you should've drunk less and kept out of brawls.'

'Ah,' said Flynn, expansively, 'a man can't deny his own nature. I was born to fight and given the strength for it. And if I hadn't ended up in the French ranks, I'd never have met Charlotte.'

'You have a lovely wife,' said Daniel, enviously. 'I'm grateful that she made us feel so welcome last night. But we don't wish to be a burden on her while we're here. Beatrix will help around the house and Kees will take his turn in the kitchen. I'm told he's a wonderful cook. Amalia says that he makes all the meals at home.'

'What about her? How will Amalia pass the time?'

'When she sees that daughter of yours, I'm sure she'll want to hold her. Anyone would dote on Louise. She's a delight, Ronan.'

'That's because she takes after her mother. She's got Charlotte's beauty and my brains. That should stand her in good stead.' He gave a sigh. 'To be sure, I'd rather bring my child up in Ireland but she'll have a much better life here. I have to accept that. If I went home, I'd have no earthly notion of what to do. Here in Paris, I have a trade.'

'You had one when you were in the army, Ronan.'

Flynn guffawed. 'Yes,' he said, 'I was paid to kill people then. Nowadays, my bread tries to keep them alive.'

Daniel was fascinated to see the bakery in operation. He had watched army bakers preparing bread in vast quantities and dispensing with any subtleties as they did so. At the Rousset bakery, a large, low building with a number of ovens, far more attention was given to each individual loaf. They arrived to find the place already warmed up. A servant was bringing the ingredients in while Flynn's two assistants were making a start.

'Does your father-in-law still work here?' asked Daniel.

'Emile has more or less retired, Dan. He pretends that he's still in charge by looking in each day but I run the bakery. We'll probably be gone before he even gets here.'

'He obviously trusts you, Ronan.'

'With good reason,' said Flynn. 'I look after his daughter, his grandchild and his bakery. What more can a man ask?'

While he was talking, Flynn was already putting on a white apron and moving to one of the tables. Daniel stood back out of the way. Watching from a corner, he admired the speed and precision with which the Irishman shaped a loaf, albeit in a snowstorm of flour. Though the assistants were industrious, they had nothing like the skill of their employer. Nor did they take such an obvious delight in their work. Having got him into trouble as a soldier, Flynn's enormous hands were now put to more delicate use than knocking people unconscious. Two of the large ovens were set aside for him and they'd been the first to be lit. As a result, it was Flynn's bread that was first to be baked. Bringing it proudly out of an oven, the Irishman set it out on a tray. The aroma was enticing.

'There you are, Dan,' he said, inserting a new batch into the oven. 'When it's cooled down a little, you can have a taste.'

'Thank you. It smells wonderful.'

'Tempt the nose and fill the belly – that's my motto.'

As the hours rolled by, Paris came slowly awake and the noise from the street steadily increased in volume. Traders went past on their way to market, followed by housewives in search of the best bargains and the freshest meat. Some of the bread was destined for a stall there. It would still be warm when it was handed over. There was a shop at the front of the bakery and many of the loaves were stacked on the shelves in there. The old woman who ran the shop was a distant relative of Emile Rousset. She lumbered in well before the place was due to open. Candles burnt in the bakery but much of the light came from the ovens. Every time one of them was opened, a bright glow illumined the whole room and filled it with a gust of warm air. The assistants chatted amiably to each other. Flynn liked to sing Irish songs out of tune as he worked.

When the sky began to lighten outside, Daniel turned to glance through the window. The first thing he saw was his own reflection and he was jolted. Having dressed in the dark earlier on, he'd not been able to inspect the coat that had been torn and scuffed during the death grapple with Jacques Serval. Now that he did so, he saw to his amazement that the tear had been expertly mended and the dirt had been brushed off. The repair could only have happened while he was asleep with the coat over the chair beside him. Daniel couldn't believe that someone could remove the garment without disturbing him.

Though he'd washed his hands before they left, Flynn's face and hair were still flecked with white flour. The cart was now loaded with bread and loaves were delivered to various customers.

Dozens were dropped off at the market. Flynn didn't only deal in large deliveries. Daniel was touched to see him hand over two loaves to an elderly couple, too infirm to walk all the way to the shop. It was towards the end of the round that Daniel finally caught sight of the Bastille. While Flynn was delivering bread to a tavern in an adjacent boulevard, Daniel slipped around the corner into the Rue Saint-Antoine.

He stared up at the forbidding exterior of the Bastille. It was an enormous structure. Built as a gate during the Hundred Years' War, it had been considerably extended to create a looming fortress. The irregular rectangle had eight towers that seemed to climb up into the sky. What made it particularly daunting was that the walls and the towers were the same height and connected by a broad terrace. It meant that soldiers inside the stronghold could move quickly to the point of attack without having to go up and down the circular staircases in the towers. A wide moat completed its defences.

Somewhere inside the prison was Emanuel Janssen. Finding a means of rescuing him seemed an impossible task. Yet it had to be attempted. On the ride back to the bakery, Daniel heard very little of Flynn's hearty monologue because his mind was fettered to the Bastille.

Charlotte Flynn had been uneasy at the threat of having her home invaded by strangers. Now that they were actually there, however, she found them less intrusive than she feared. Dopff helped to make and serve breakfast while Beatrix seized a broom and started to clean the house. All of Amalia's maternal instincts were aroused when she set eyes on Louise and she couldn't stop smiling as she cuddled the baby. When she was alone with Charlotte in the parlour, she was reluctant to yield up the child to its mother.

As Daniel had advised, Amalia did not reveal how much of the French language she'd mastered. Instead, she spoke haltingly and deliberately groped for words so that conversation with Charlotte was laboured. There was one thing that she wished to make clear.

'While we here,' she said, 'we help, yes?'

'Thank you,' replied Charlotte, gratefully. 'Until last week, we had a servant but Ronan caught her stealing and got rid of her. We are looking for someone else.'

'With baby, the help you need.'

'We know that.'

Sensing that Amalia was in some kind of trouble, Charlotte warmed to her. The two of them went off to market together. While Charlotte chose the food, Amalia insisted on paying for it. As a reward for her generosity, she was allowed to carry the baby on the journey home. When they got back to the house, it was visibly tidier. Beatrix felt much happier in her role as a servant and knew how to keep out of the way. Seeing the food bought at the market, Dopff's face became more expressive than ever. It was clear that he was volunteering to prepare the next meal.

Daniel and Flynn eventually returned and walked in on a quiet domestic scene. Amalia was rocking the baby in its wooden crib while Charlotte was mending a dress. At the sight of needle and thread, Daniel recalled the repair made to his coat and wondered if Charlotte had been responsible. Since he'd been away from his wife and child for so long, it was evident that Flynn would appreciate some time alone with them. Daniel therefore invited Amalia to join him in a walk. They stepped out into the sunshine.

'What have you been doing?' she asked.

'I watched Ronan make bread then helped to deliver it.'

'Why did you do that, Captain Rawson?'

'His delivery round took him close to the prison where your father is being held,' explained Daniel. 'I wanted to take a look at it.'

Amalia came to a halt. 'Where is it?'

He'd deliberately not told her before because he knew that she'd be distressed. Amalia had been in Paris for several months. In that time, she'd surely have heard of the Bastille and been aware of its reputation. It was a place where political prisoners were kept in chains and where those who'd offended the King in some way were routinely dispatched. Many who entered the grim portals never came out alive again. Emanuel Janssen could not be in a worse place.

'Well,' she pressed, 'which prison is it?'

She had to be told. 'The Bastille,' he said.

'Oh!'

Amalia almost swooned and he had to support her with both hands for a moment. Thanking him for his help, she eased him away and made an effort to compose herself. They continued their walk.

'I can see why you didn't tell me earlier,' she said.

'You've had enough distress in the last twenty-four hours, Miss Janssen. I had no wish to add to it.'

'That was considerate of you.' She turned to him in despair. 'I've heard the most terrible stories about the Bastille. We drove past it in a coach once and the very sight of it frightened me. I'm horrified to think that Father is locked up in there.'

'It shows that he's still alive,' said Daniel, trying to strike an optimistic note. 'That's a sign of clemency.'

'Should I make an appeal for mercy to the King?'

'Oh, no, Miss Janssen. It would certainly be rejected and you would give your whereabouts away. After what happened to the man who watched your house, the police will be looking for you and the others. That's why I brought you to a part of the city where they'd be unlikely to search. I want them to think that you've left Paris.'

'I could never do that while Father is still here.'

'You may not have to,' he said.

'Is there *any* chance at all that he can be rescued?'

'I think so, Miss Janssen.'

'How will you go about it?'

'I'm not sure yet but, thanks to Ronan, an idea is forming in my brain. It may require me to leave you alone at the house for a while.'

'Where will you be, Captain Rawson?'

'Perhaps you ought to stop calling me that,' he suggested. 'It's not wise to keep reminding me that I'm a British soldier. If that name slips out in front of Charlotte, she'll become too curious. It might be safer if you called me "Daniel" from now on.'

'In that case, I will – Daniel. And in view of what you've already done for us in the short time you've been here, I think you're entitled to call me by my Christian name.'

'Thank you, Amalia. I regard that as a privilege.'

Their eyes locked for a moment. Daniel's smile was broad and Amalia's more cautious but both acknowledged that they had just crossed a little boundary. Their friendship had deepened and they were drawn insensibly closer. It was a very pleasant feeling and Daniel luxuriated in it until he remembered the repair to his coat.

'There's something else I must thank you for, Amalia.'

'Is there?'

'During the night, you brushed and mended my coat.'

'But I didn't. Had you asked, I'd have been happy to do so. I may not aspire to the heights of making a tapestry but my father taught me a long time ago how to use a needle.'

Daniel was puzzled. 'If it wasn't you,' he said, 'who was it?'

'Well, it was certainly not Beatrix,' she replied. 'She lay snoring beside me all night. That leaves only one person.'

'It has to be someone capable of moving silently in the dark.'

'Kees can do that. *He's* the one you have to thank, Daniel.'

Seeing his uncle walking towards him, Tom Hillier quailed. It was one thing to be ignored by Henry Welbeck but he sensed that it would be even worse to be berated by him. The sergeant was known for his ability to harangue recruits. Judging by his dour expression, he was about to turn his venom on his nephew. Hillier swallowed hard.

'Good morning, Sergeant,' he said, meekly.

'I need a word with you, lad.'

'Have I done anything wrong?'

'Yes,' said Welbeck, darkly. 'When you joined the army, you made the mistake of signing your life away to a lost cause. However, that's behind you. What you have to do now is to make the best of a bad situation.'

'That's what I've tried to do, sir.'

'So I hear. You've been fighting with one of the other lads.'

Hillier flushed. 'Who told you that?'

'I have my spies.'

'It was only in fun, Sergeant. Hugh Dobbs and I are friends really. He's helped me a lot with my drumming and he seems to know everything that happens in this regiment. Hugh's been telling me about Captain Rawson.'

'Don't believe all of it.'

'He described how the captain took part in a Forlorn Hope.'

'We're *all* involved in a Forlorn Hope,' moaned Welbeck. 'Army life is one long, pointless charge up a hillside with the enemy firing at will. It's not bravery, it's sheer bloody lunacy.'

'Then why have you stayed in uniform so long?'

'That's my business.'

'Mother says that you…' His voice trailed off as he saw the menace in Welbeck's eye. 'I'm sorry, Sergeant. I won't mention the family again.'

'*This* is your bleeding family now,' said Welbeck with a gesture that took in the whole camp. 'You're in a madhouse under canvas.'

'I think that's being unfair.'

'I've been here long enough to find out.'

His nephew avoided argument. 'Then I'll accept your word, sir.'

Welbeck stood back to weigh him up. His nephew's uniform was too tight but he looked smart and alert. Much of the early wonder had been sponged off his face by cold reality. Hillier was no longer in thrall to the idea of bearing arms. It was now a commitment he'd made rather than a patriotic duty that set his heart alight. There was something about him that Welbeck had never noticed before. He had a definite resemblance to his mother. The sergeant was looking at his sister's nose, chin and pale complexion. Hillier even had some of his mother's mannerisms. Welbeck had never been close to his sister but he felt an impulse of affection towards her now.

'What was the name of that friend of yours?' he asked.

'Hugh – Hugh Dobbs.'

'Was he the one who hid your drum in a tree?'

'You've been talking to Captain Rawson, haven't you?'

'That's neither here nor there, lad. All I want to know is this. If Hugh Dobbs knows everything that happens in the 24th Foot, has he ever mentioned the name of Major Cracknell to you?'

Hillier pondered. 'No, I don't think so,' he said at length.

'Be on guard against him,' warned Welbeck.

'Why is that?'

'It doesn't matter – just do as I tell you.'

'I've never even heard of Major Cracknell.'

'You will.'

'What business could he have with me, Sergeant?'

'You're my nephew.'

'I thought you didn't have a nephew any more, sir.'

Welbeck gave him a hard stare that slowly evanesced into a grudging smile. He stepped forward to pat Hillier on the shoulder.

'I like what I've heard about you, Tom,' he said, briskly, 'but not everyone in this regiment will want to be your friend. I've told you a name to remember. It's Major Simon Cracknell. Watch out for him and don't tell anyone I gave you this warning.'

In taking Daniel close to the Bastille, Ronan Flynn had unwittingly given him an idea relating to Emanuel Janssen. Flynn had delivered bread to a tavern nearby. It might well be the place where some of the turnkeys from the prison came to drink. If not, there was bound to be another tavern within walking distance of the edifice. After telling his friend that he was going away for a while, Daniel left the others in the care of the Flynn family and rode to the Marais, a quarter inhabited largely by people with money and position. In the boulevard close to the Rue Saint-Antoine, he located the tavern that Flynn had visited that morning. The one thing he did know about the Fleur de Lys was that it would serve excellent bread.

Daniel took a room at the tavern and immediately changed out of his guise as a wine merchant. Putting on more workaday apparel and a large cap, he went out to study the Bastille in more detail and to walk along the bank of the Seine. To rescue the tapestry-maker from the prison was the major problem but a second one then had to be solved. Daniel would have to spirit four people out of the city. Since the police would certainly be searching for the Dutch contingent, it would be another test of his initiative. As he watched the boats and barges gliding serenely past on the glistening water, he wondered if the river might be the best route out of Paris.

Returning to the tavern, he lay on his bed and spent hours considering the possibilities. Each one involved putting himself into jeopardy but Daniel was accustomed to doing that. His personal safety was never a concern. What he had to ensure was the security of other people. His orders had been to find and rescue Emanuel Janssen but it was Amalia who occupied his mind. He was aware of the intense stress under which she'd been and the indignities she'd suffered. The only way that Daniel could bring relief was to reunite her with her beloved father. His fondness for Amalia was an additional spur. He longed to take the nagging anxiety out of her life and help her to return home.

When evening gently squeezed the last daylight out of the sky, Daniel returned to the Rue Saint Antoine and watched the Bastille from a distance. At a rough guess, he decided, the walls had to be around eighty feet high, ruling out any hope of climbing into the prison or of climbing out again. Emanuel Janssen was a middle-aged man who worked at a loom all day. He could hardly be expected to descend a very long rope in the darkness, especially as he might not be in the best of health as a result of his incarceration. The one conceivable exit was through the front doors. In order to bring him out of the Bastille, Daniel first had to get inside it himself.

Assuming that the turnkeys worked in shifts, he was pleased to see that he was right. Various men trudged up to the entrance in twos and threes. Those whom they replaced on duty eventually started to come out. Many dispersed to go to their homes but, as Daniel had predicted, some preferred a drink after a long day in the macabre surroundings of the prison. Instead of going to the tavern where he was staying, however, they walked along the river until they reached a smaller and noisier establishment. Daniel followed a group of them into the tavern. When they sat around a table and drank heavily, he stayed within earshot. After a while, when the wine had helped them to relax somewhat, Daniel hobbled across to them as if he had an injured foot.

'Did I hear someone mention the Bastille?' he said.

'Yes,' answered a thickset man with warts all over his face. 'We're all prisoners there.' The others laughed. 'Who are you?'

'I was a soldier until I got shot in the foot. I've had to look for something else to do. A friend suggested they always need turnkeys at the Bastille.'

'That's right, my friend. The stench kills off three of us a week.' The others shook with mirth. 'What's your name?'

'Marcel Daron.'

'Where are you from?'

'I was born here in Paris but joined the army when I was a lad.'

'Oh?' said the man with the warts, indicating the one-eyed turnkey who sat beside him. 'Georges was a soldier until he lost his eye at Blenheim. What regiment were you in?'

'I was a trooper in the Royal-Carabinier,' replied Daniel, thinking of his brief time in the courier's stolen uniform. 'I fought at Blenheim as well.'

'Tell us about it,' goaded the one-eyed man.

It was clear that they didn't trust him and that he would have to win their confidence. As they aimed questions at him, he was able to answer them all convincingly because he'd been at the heart of the battle. He reeled off the names of the French generals and talked about their disposition on the battlefield. At the start, Georges, the former soldier, was the most suspicious but Daniel's detailed knowledge persuaded him that he had no cause to be wary.

'He's telling the truth,' announced Georges.

'Then he can pull up a seat and join us,' said the wart-faced man. When Daniel ordered a flagon of wine, he got a slap on the back. 'You can come here any time you wish, Marcel.'

As the wine flowed, Daniel spent the first few minutes getting to know their names and finding out how long they'd worked at the prison. All of them grumbled about their work but none actually talked about giving it up.

'Long hours and poor pay,' said Georges. 'That's all we get at the Bastille. Then there's the stink, of course. The straw's never changed in some cells. I'd hate to be locked up in those shit-holes.'

'What sort of prisoners are they?' asked Daniel.

'There's only one kind, Marcel. Whatever they're like when they go in there, they soon end up the same. It doesn't matter what they did to get locked away. All we see is a lot of miserable, godforsaken wretches, crawling slowly towards death.'

'Our work is boring,' said Philippe, the man with the warts. 'We lock them up, we feed them and, if they're very lucky, we take them out for exercise. Most of them never leave their cells. And if they try to complain, we have some fun knocking them about.'

Georges smirked. 'That's what I enjoy,' he said. 'When one of them dared to throw food at me today, I beat him black and blue. That'll teach him.'

They were an uncouth bunch and, in the normal course of events, nothing would have induced Daniel to befriend them. Since he wanted to penetrate the Bastille, however, he would have to do so as part of its large staff. The men laughed, sang, joked and boasted about the way they mistreated the prisoners. At the end of the evening, Philippe wrapped an arm around Daniel's shoulders and grinned at him.

'Do you still want to be a turnkey, Marcel?' he asked.

'Yes,' said Daniel. 'I guarded prisoners in the army. I liked it.'

'Meet me outside the main gate at noon tomorrow. I'll take you along to meet someone. I can't promise anything, mind you,' he added, drunkenly, 'but I'll put in a good word for you.'

'Thanks.'

When Daniel eventually limped away, he was equally satisfied and dismayed. He was pleased to have the possibility of work at the Bastille but alarmed to hear how some of the inmates were treated. There was no point in trying to liberate Emanuel Janssen if the Dutchman was in no condition to walk out. In the brutal regime of the prison, he might by now be barely alive. On the other hand, if the intention had been to kill him, Janssen would already have been executed as a spy. For some reason, he'd been spared. Daniel therefore consoled himself with the thought that he might – if he was fortunate enough to secure employment at the Bastille – find out exactly what that reason was.

CHAPTER NINE

When business took him back to The Hague again, Willem Ketel made a point of calling on his close friend. Johannes Mytens shook him warmly by the hand then conducted him to the parlour. It was a large room with a polished oak floor and solid oak furniture. Paintings by Rembrandt, Vermeer and Hobbema adorned three walls. The fourth was covered by a magnificent tapestry depicting The Hague. They went through the social niceties before turning to the subject that exercised their minds most.

'What's the feeling in the States-General?' asked Ketel.

Mytens sounded weary. 'Most of us are as tired of this war as you are, Willem,' he said. 'We've spent far too long fighting the French with no prospect of ultimate victory. I freely admit that I was carried away by the rhetoric when the Grand Alliance was first formed. With England, Prussia, Austria and others to help us, I felt that we could defeat the French army at last. They've held sway over Europe for far too long.'

'It's easy to see why, Johannes. They've always had the finest soldiers and the most astute commanders.'

'I'd hoped that the Duke of Marlborough could match their commanders and, in all fairness, from time to time he did.'

'It was only because he was supported by able Dutch generals.'

'Marlborough says that our generals held him back.'

'They merely saved him from making rash decisions.'

'Our soldiers are brave,' said Mytens, 'but the fact remains that we fight best at sea. While our army is competent, our navy is our real strength. Unfortunately, there's little chance of using them in this war. We're restricted largely to land battles.'

'That's one of my complaints.The English steal all the glory at sea.'

'I don't see much glory,' said Ketel, removing his wig to scratch his head. 'I know that they captured Gibraltar and withstood a French siege but what else has the navy done? Those leaky, old, disease-ridden ships of theirs have spent most of their time carrying soldiers to Portugal and Spain.'

'I approved of the treaty with Portugal,' admitted Mytens, his jowls wobbling more than ever. 'I accepted Marlborough's argument that he needed naval bases there. He was eager for his men to cross the border into Spain supported by the Portuguese army.'

'Never trust the Portuguese, I say.'

'They've been dubious allies, I grant you.'

'It's a question of resources,' argued Ketel, replacing his wig. 'We need all the men we have to defend our boundaries and to advance into French territory. Yet Marlborough, our commander-in-chief, the self-proclaimed hero of Blenheim, the man who boasts that he has a grand strategy, has diverted almost as many soldiers to Spain.'

'His mistake was in thinking that he could control operations in the peninsula from here.'

'We're all paying a high price for that mistake.'

'I agree, Willem.'

'On a single voyage from Lisbon to Valencia, we lost over four thousand men who could have been put to better use in Flanders.'

Mytens smiled. 'You're remarkably well-informed.'

'I'm a merchant, Johannes. My success depends on knowing what happens where. When a ship of mine puts into port, I always go out of my way to talk to the captain to hear what news he has for me.' He sucked his teeth. 'And I have other sources of information as well.'

'It's no wonder that you've prospered.'

'There are ways of making money out of war and I've used every one of them. I don't deny it. That's what anyone in my position would do. But my prosperity – *our* prosperity as a nation – relies on a long period of peace that allows us to invest our money prudently instead of wasting it on a war we can never win.'

Mytens clasped his hands across his paunch and gave a nod. 'We've had this conversation before, Willem.'

'And are you still of the same mind?'

'I am. Marlborough must go.'

'But whatever means necessary?'

'By *whatever* means,' repeated Mytens, firmly.

'Where is he at the moment?'

'I thought you'd know that. You seem to know everything else.'

'Is he still in Flanders?'

'No, Willem, he's on his way to Dusseldorf to wheedle more troops out of the Elector Palatine. After that, he's visiting our other allies to get promises of men and money out of them. Give the man his due,' he continued, 'Marlborough is a sublime diplomat. That English charm of his works time and again.'

'And it sends men off to pointless deaths on the battlefield.'

'Why did you ask about his whereabouts?'

'I wanted to make sure that he'd be out of the way.'

'Marlborough won't be back here until December.'

'That will give us ample time,' said Ketel. 'I hope to be bringing a friend to meet you in due course, Johannes.'

'Is it someone from Amsterdam?'

'No – he comes from Paris.'

Mytens was guarded. 'Who is the fellow?'

'You don't need to know his name yet and you certainly don't need to feel perturbed. My friend wants exactly what we want and that's a promise of peace and a rest from this perpetual warfare.' He slipped a hand under his wig for another scratch. 'If we can reach agreement with France, we all stand to benefit.'

'Marlborough will oppose any peace manoeuvres.'

'He won't be here to do so, will he?' said Ketel with a smile before turning to look at the tapestry. 'I'd know the work of Emanuel Janssen anywhere. Whenever I'm in this room, I always admire it.'

'I'm not sure that I should keep it, Willem.'

'Nothing would make me part with such a masterpiece.'

'Emanuel Janssen is a traitor. He's working at Versailles.'

'King Louis always had exquisite taste.'

'That doesn't entitle him to lure away our best tapestry-maker. It's true,' said Mytens, studying the tapestry, 'that it's a masterpiece but should I have it hanging there when the man who created it is now in the pay of the enemy?'

'Leave it where it is, Johannes,' urged Ketel. 'It deserves a place in any house. Besides, Janssen may be in the pay of our enemy at the moment but that enemy could soon become our friend.'

* * *

Daniel rose early next morning and, after breakfast at the tavern, rode off to explore the city carefully and to find the best way out of it for them. Because it covered a relatively small area, it was densely populated. Straddling the river, it was bounded on the north by the boulevards from Porte Saint-Antoine to Porte Saint-Honore. Its southern border was the Boulevard Saint-Germain. Paris was divided into 20 *quartiers* and had something close to 500,000 inhabitants. Early in his reign – and he had been on the throne for over four decades now – Louis XIV had instructed Jean-Baptiste Colbert, his Superintendent of Finance, to create a capital city worthy of the name. The enterprising Colbert did so by embarking on an ambitious programme of building and he transformed Paris.

Working people, along with the poor and sickly, were forced out to the suburbs so that the centre of the city could be occupied by wide new thoroughfares, impressive monuments, grandiose palaces, vast mansions and splendid gardens. New bridges spanned the Seine and factories manufacturing glass and carpets were set up. It was a compact, bustling city where beauty and ugliness lived cheek by jowl and where fabulous riches contrasted with the most degrading poverty. Though Daniel was bound to marvel at the superb architecture of buildings like the Invalides hospital and the Hotel Colbert, he preferred Amsterdam in every way. The Dutch city, the greatest port in the world, was altogether cleaner, healthier, safer, more modest in its aspirations and, because of its plethora of lamps, the best lit city in Europe.

Daniel yearned to be there again, ideally in the company of Amalia Janssen. His orders had been to take her father to The Hague but the Janssen family would in time return to their home. He hoped that his friendship with Amalia would continue and blossom. When it was known that the tapestry-maker had not after all betrayed his country, he'd be acclaimed once more in Amsterdam. All that Daniel had to do was to convey him there. The task seemed more difficult every time he contemplated it but he responded to the challenge. Riding from gate to gate, he saw how well-guarded all the exits were and was sure that those on duty had descriptions of Amalia and her companions. It was Daniel who'd killed Jacques Serval but the others would be regarded as confederates and punished accordingly.

After his tour of the city's portals, he returned to the tavern well before noon and stabled his horse there. As midday was approaching, Daniel was lurking outside the Bastille. Among the many faces coming towards him, he recognised those of Philippe and Georges, the turnkeys with whom he'd been drinking the previous night. They greeted him with a wave then escorted him to the main gate. Daniel had put a stone in one shoe so that he was forced to limp as he walked. Having passed himself off as a wounded French soldier, he had to keep up the pretence. When the gate was opened, the gaolers went through it for another day's work. Before they were allowed to go to their posts, their names were checked off in turn. The man in charge of the list was tall, cadaverous and beady-eyed. He wore a dark uniform. Philippe spoke to him and indicated Daniel. After subjecting the newcomer to a long stare, the man flicked a hand to make him stand aside. Philippe and Georges bade him a cheery farewell before going off to one of the towers.

Daniel waited until the incoming turnkeys had all been accounted for and those they'd relieved had all departed. Only when his ledger had all the requisite ticks on it did the emaciated man look up. Daniel felt the intensity of his scrutiny. The man's eyes were so keen that they seemed to see right through the newcomer.

'What's your name?' he demanded.

'Marcel Daron, sir.'

'Do you have papers?'

'Yes, sir,' replied Daniel, taking them out and handing them over. He stood there for several minutes while his papers were inspected. They were eventually handed back to him. 'I was a soldier until I was wounded in battle,' he explained. 'They have no room in the army for invalids.'

'We have no call for them here either. Our turnkeys must be fit and strong enough to control unruly prisoners.'

'Apart from my foot, I'm in good health, sir. Being a soldier has kept me strong. Put me to the test, if you doubt it.'

The man did so at once, shooting out a hand to grasp him by the neck and pulling him close. Daniel's response was equally swift. He grabbed the man's wrist and squeezed it tighter and tighter until he saw the pain clouding his eyes. Strong though he was, the man was soon compelled to release his grip. Tucking the ledger under one arm, he massaged his wrist with the other hand.

'You're a powerful man, Marcel Daron.'

'You'll not find me wanting, sir.'

'Have you guarded prisoners before?'

'I did so many times in the army.'

'Why do you want to work here?'

'The work appeals to me, sir.'

'But why choose the Bastille?' asked the other. 'Why not go to the Châtelet or the Evêque? They are always looking for new men.'

'I heard that there might be a job for me here, sir.'

The man sniffed then walked around him, as if examining livestock at a fair. He opened his ledger and glanced down the list of names. The beady eyes shifted to Daniel once more.

'Are you afraid of the dark?' he asked.

'No, sir.'

'Are you frightened by rats and mice?'

'Nothing frightens me,' said Daniel, levelly.

'Very well,' decided the man after another prolonged survey of him. 'You can go on duty tonight. There'll be a uniform waiting for you when you arrive. If you're late, you'll be turned away.'

'Yes, sir.'

'My name is Bermutier – *Sergeant* Bermutier.'

'I'll be here on time, Sergeant.'

Bermutier gave him full details of how long he'd be expected to work, where he'd be assigned and what wage he could expect if he proved himself capable. Daniel thanked him before being let out through the door. As it closed behind him with a loud thud, he was profoundly grateful. Even during his brief visit to the place, he'd felt extremely oppressed by the high, thick walls of the Bastille. He could imagine how much worse it was to be imprisoned there.

Ronan Flynn was a genial host. Unfailingly pleasant to Amalia and Dopff, he was so impressed by the way that Beatrix had cleaned the house that he jokingly offered her a permanent job there. Amalia didn't even bother to translate the words into Dutch for her servant. She knew that Beatrix was as eager as she to leave Paris altogether and would hope never to set foot in France again. While they were there, however, it was important for the visitors to express their gratitude by giving the Flynn family ample time on their own. That was what prompted Amalia to take Beatrix for a walk that afternoon. Dopff, meanwhile, retreated to the attic.

Alone with his wife and child, Flynn sat in a chair and dandled Louise on his knee, chuckling as she gave him her toothless grin and happy burble. Charlotte watched them fondly. Her thoughts then turned to their guests.

'They're very good,' she conceded. 'They've been no trouble while you were at the bakery. Amalia looked after Louise for me.'

'They all adore her.'

'Yes, she's getting a lot of attention from them.'

'She deserves it,' he said, lifting the child high to shake her before bringing her down and planting a kiss on her forehead.'

'Where is your friend, Daniel?'

'He'll be back in a few days, my darling.'

'A few *days*,' echoed Charlotte. 'They've already been here two nights. I thought they'd have been on their way by now.'

'Dan has some business to see to first.'

'What kind of business?'

'He didn't say.'

'There are lots of things he hasn't told you, Ronan. He hasn't said why they're all here, for a start. And he hasn't explained why they're all so nervous.'

'They're nervous because they're in a strange house in a foreign country and unable to speak the language.'

'Then what are they doing here? Why come to Paris when they can't speak French and when they have nowhere to stay?'

'Who knows?' said Flynn, tolerantly. 'I don't want to poke my nose into their business. I told you how Dan Rawson came to my aid when I was captured by the enemy. He risked his life to do that, Charlotte, and it's not something you forget in a hurry, believe me. I owe him a great deal. These people are

Dan's friends and I was willing to help. I'd hoped that you'd be just as willing, my darling.'

'I am,' she said, 'in some ways.'

Seeing her concern, he put the baby gently into the crib then took his wife by the shoulders. He kissed her tenderly.

'Something is upsetting you, isn't it?'

She shook her head. 'It puzzles me, Ronan, that's all.'

'What does?'

'Why they seem so ill at ease and whisper in corners.'

'You can't accuse Kees of whispering anywhere,' he said with a laugh. 'The poor fellow can't utter a word.'

'He's the one who puzzles me most. I never know what he's thinking. Have you seen what he has up there in the attic?'

'A lot of dust and spiders' webs, I daresay.'

'I slipped up there when he was in the garden.'

'You shouldn't pry, Charlotte.'

'This is our house,' she said with spirit. 'I've the right to go anywhere I like in it. That's why I went up to the attic.'

'And what did you find there?' asked Flynn.

'I found a tapestry. It was the most beautiful thing I've ever seen and must be worth a small fortune. Do you understand why I'm so puzzled now?' she asked. 'Why does a man like that have such a valuable tapestry with him?'

'Follow me and do as I do,' ordered the Frenchman.

'I will,' said Daniel.

'And don't breathe in too deeply.'

'Why?'

'You'll soon find out.'

Daniel arrived for work late that evening to be met by another duty sergeant. He was issued with a nondescript uniform, the most significant feature of which was the thick leather belt to which a large metal ring of keys was attached. His partner for the night was Jules Rivot, a fat, slovenly man in his forties with a dark complexion. Rivot's manner was less than friendly and his face was a study in solemnity. Daniel could smell the beer on his breath. He trailed round obediently after the Frenchman. Rivot was slow and methodical. Patently hating the work, he unloaded as much of it as he could on Daniel.

'Give this one more water,' he said.

'Yes,' replied Daniel, filling a cup with a brackish liquid out of a wooden bucket before passing it through the bars to a prisoner. 'What about food?'

'He gets none till breakfast and only if I'm in a good mood.'

That seemed highly unlikely to Daniel but he said nothing. Rivot's warning had been timely. The reek was so powerful at first that it made him retch. He'd been assigned to the *cachots*, cold, dark, slimy, vermin-infested cells below ground where people were locked away and often forgotten. Some had clearly been there for a very long time because their clothes had worn away to shreds. One man, a human skeleton with hair down to his shoulders and a beard down to his chest, was almost naked. Rivot showed them no compassion. He simply held up his lantern so that he could see the occupants of each cell. The prisoners knew better than to try to talk to him but the sight of a new face roused a few of them. They came to the doors and gave Daniel ingratiating smiles.

'Ignore the bastards,' advised Rivot. 'They all want favours.'

'They don't seem to get any of those.'

'Not when I'm on duty.'

'Are all the prisoners kept in these foul conditions?'

'These are the ones nobody cares about,' said Rivot. 'We bury them underground like so many corpses. It's just as bad in the *calottes*, the cells under the roof. They're open to the weather up there. They get soaked by the rain and burnt by the sun. In winter, some of them freeze to death.'

'What crimes have they committed?' asked Daniel.

'It doesn't matter.'

'Are they thieves or kidnappers?'

'They upset important people.'

Daniel knew that the King had sent many of the inmates there by means of *lettres de cachet*, a pernicious document that had victims thrown into a rank cell without any judicial process. There was no appeal against such an indeterminate sentence. Louis XIV's favourites were also indulged. If one of them suffered a slight or was openly insulted, the offender could find himself deprived of his liberty on a royal whim. During their dismal tour of the *cachots*, Daniel checked every name and looked through every set of bars. Relieved that Emanuel Janssen was not among the miserable wretches kept there, he feared that the Dutchman might be housed instead under the roof and exposed to the elements. In some weathers, that amounted to continuous torture.

Some time during the night, they had a break from their duties and shared a tankard of beer and a piece of bread with the other turnkeys. Rivot preferred to eat in silence but one of the men was more talkative. He told Daniel that not everyone in the Bastille was treated like those in the *cachots*. Those imprisoned on the middle level of the towers had a more comfortable time. Being locked up was their only punishment. To relieve the boredom, they were allowed books, writing materials, visitors, pets and, if they could afford to pay for it, excellent food and wine.

'We had a Duke in there last year,' confided the man, 'and he lived in luxury. He was even allowed to have his mistress in the cell twice a week.' Nudging Daniel, he cackled. 'It must have been interesting to watch them in bed together. They say she was a beauty.'

'Who looks after prisoners like that?' asked Daniel.

'Not the likes of you and me. We only deal with the dross down here, my friend. Only the lucky ones get to work up there. They can earn a lot of money sometimes.'

'By taking bribes, you mean?'

'By doing a few favours,' said the man.

Daniel was heartened for the first time. It might be that Janssen had been given privileges as well. If he was imprisoned somewhere on the middle level of a tower, his health might not have deteriorated. His tapestries had earned him substantial rewards. Janssen would be rich enough to buy concessions from his gaolers. That vague hope helped to sustain Daniel through the long, malodorous, depressing hours below ground with inmates who might never see the light of day again. He put up with Rivot's bleak companionship and learnt not to be startled when a rat darted across his path. When his stint finally came to an end, he climbed back up into the courtyard and had to shield his eyes from the sun for several minutes.

He looked up at the imposing towers, wondering in which one of them Janssen was being kept. Daniel would never have the time or opportunity to search them all in rotation. He had to find another way to locate the tapestry-maker. He remembered the ledger that the duty sergeant used to check people in and out. That would surely contain the names and whereabouts of prisoners as well. Daniel had to gain access to it somehow. For the time being, however, he had to content himself with what he'd so far achieved. He was inside the Bastille and he'd acquired a convincing disguise. Further progress would have to wait. What he needed most now was fresh air, the chance to wash and a reviving sleep.

Major Simon Cracknell came into Tom Hillier's life when he least expected it. The drummer had been on the edge of the camp with Hugh Dobbs, throwing missiles playfully at him and trying to dodge the ones that were aimed at him. Twigs, clumps of grass and handfuls of earth flew through the air until Cracknell suddenly appeared. Both of the youths immediately dropped their next missile and stood self-consciously to attention.

'Is *this* how you spend your time?' said the major, looking at the dirty marks on their uniforms. 'You should be ashamed of yourselves.'

'We're sorry, Major,' said Dobbs.

'How long have you been in the army?'

'Four years, sir.'

'Then you should have grown out of these childish games.'

'We were doing no harm, sir.'

'Yes, you were,' said Cracknell. 'Apart from anything else, you were soiling your uniforms. This regiment prides itself on its appearance and your coats are covered in filth. What the devil did the pair of you think you were doing?'

'It won't happen again, Major,' said Dobbs. 'Tom and I didn't mean to get dirty. It was just horseplay.'

'Disappear and clean up that uniform. No, not you, Hillier,' said Cracknell as he tried to leave with Dobbs. 'I want to speak to you.'

'Yes, Major,' said Hillier, stopping in his tracks.

'What do you have to say for yourself?'

'I apologise, sir.'

'How often does this kind of thing happen?'

'It's the first time, sir.'

'Don't tell lies, boy!'

'Hugh Dobbs and I have never done this before.'

'Then what's this I hear about your getting into a fight?'

Hillier was startled. 'That was nothing, sir,' he said, guiltily.

'It's evidence of gross indiscipline and I deplore it.' He stood very close to the young drummer. 'Do you know who I am?'

'I think that you must be Major Cracknell, sir.'

'And how did you decide *that*, I wonder?' said the officer, leaning over to whisper in his ear. 'Could it be that your uncle told you about me, perhaps?'

'I have no uncle in this regiment, sir.'

'What else is Sergeant Welbeck?'

'The sergeant made it clear to me that family ties have no place in the army, sir. I've accepted that I'm no longer his nephew.'

'And yet he goes out of his way to warn you about me.'

'Sergeant Welbeck has no reason to speak to me, sir.'

'I don't believe that,' said Cracknell. 'The fact is that you know who I am so it's time you discovered *what* I am as well. I loathe horseplay of any kind, Hillier. I hate indiscipline. In my view – and it's been informed by years in this regiment – transgressors need to be taught a lesson they won't forget.'

'Yes, Major.'

'Do you like being a drummer?'

'I like it well enough, sir.'

'Do you enjoy marching with the others?'

'I do, sir.'

'Well, you're going to do some marching on your own now. Do you see that wagon?' asked Cracknell, pointing a finger.

'I want you to find your drum and meet me there as quickly as you can.'

'Yes, Major,' said Hillier before running off.

It was the best part of a hundred yards to the wagon indicated. By the time that Cracknell had reached it, Hillier came panting up with his drum. He awaited instructions.

'You won't need the drumsticks,' said Cracknell.

'Then how shall I play it, sir?'

'You're not going to play it. You're going to hold it high above your head with both hands then you march from here all the way to where we were standing a while ago. When you reach that point,' said Cracknell, 'you simply turn round and march straight back here.'

'Yes, Major.'

'You'll keep going to and fro until I stop you. Is that understood, Tom Hillier?'

'Yes, Major.'

'Then let me see that drum held at arm's length.'

Hillier obeyed. Tucking the drumsticks into his belt, he held the drum above his head and set off, certain that the punishment would continue for a long time. As he marched across the grass, he knew that Major Cracknell would be watching him with grim satisfaction.

Refreshed by a morning's sleep, Daniel changed into the attire he'd worn on his arrival in Paris and rode off to the Flynn household. They were all pleased to see him again. Amalia's face brightened instantly, Beatrix burst into tears and Dopff grinned from ear to ear. It was Ronan Flynn who led the questioning.

'The Prodigal Son has returned,' he said, jocularly. 'Kill

the fatted calf, Charlotte. We must celebrate.' He embraced Daniel warmly. 'Where have you been, man?'

'I've been attending to business,' replied Daniel.

'Here in Paris?'

'Yes, Ronan.'

'Then why didn't you stay with us?'

'You already had plenty of guests.'

'Isn't our floor good enough for you to sleep on?' teased Flynn.

'It's a wonderful floor,' said Daniel, 'and I have fond memories of it. With me out of the way, however, there was more room for the rest of you. Is all well here?'

There was a long pause filled by an exchange of glances between the others. Something was evidently amiss. Flynn broke the tension by offering Daniel a drink and the atmosphere became more convivial. Beatrix and Dopff soon drifted out of the room but it was a long time before Daniel was able to talk to Amalia alone. Flynn and his wife took the baby upstairs for her afternoon sleep, leaving the couple to speak in private. Amalia was desperate for good news.

'What have you found out, Daniel?' she asked.

'The situation is not as hopeless as it seemed.'

'But you told me Father was imprisoned in the Bastille.'

'Yes,' said Daniel, 'he is. Don't ask me how – it would take too long to explain – but I'm trying to get in touch with him.'

'Has he been badly treated?'

'I won't know until I can reach him, Amalia, and that may take days. I don't think you can stay here for that long. I have the feeling that you're not as welcome here as you were.'

'They've been very kind to us and I can't thank them enough. It must have been a shock for them to have us arrive on their doorstep the way that we did. But,' Amalia went on, 'we've been here for three nights now and I can see that Charlotte feels that we're in the way. We're starting to become a real burden.'

'I'll find somewhere else for you all to stay.'

'We have plenty of money, Daniel. That's one thing we don't have to worry about. There must be a tavern where we could hire some rooms.'

'There are dozens of them,' he told her. 'On the night that we fled across the city, however, I wanted you to be somewhere I knew was completely safe. That's why I thought of Ronan Flynn.'

Amalia smiled softly. 'He told me what you did for him when he was in the army,' she said. 'You rescued him from the enemy.'

'It was a long time ago.'

'It's still fresh in his mind. Now you're doing the same for us. If we do ever manage to get back home, then I'll never forget it, Daniel. You've been our guardian angel.'

She reached out a hand and he squeezed it gently, resisting the desire to bring it to his lips so that he could kiss it. Instead, he held on to her hand and Amalia made no effort to withdraw it. Searching each other's eyes, they realised the depth of their mutual affection. It was not the time to put feelings into words. In any case, Flynn chose that moment to come downstairs. The Irishman saw the way that their hands suddenly parted.

'Forgive me,' he said, winking slyly at Daniel. 'I didn't mean to interrupt a tête-à-tête.'

'We were just talking about moving out, Ronan,' said Daniel. 'Amalia feels that she's imposed on you too long.'

'*Imposed* on us? What gave you that idea? Instead of three guests, we had a cook, a servant and someone to nurse the baby.

And we didn't even have to *pay* them for their services.'

'You and Charlotte have been wonderful.'

'Then why desert us?'

'We have to go,' said Amalia. 'Thank you very, very much.'

She excused herself so that she could warn Beatrix and Dopff about their imminent departure. Flynn spread his arms.

'Have I frightened them away?'

'Yes,' said Daniel. 'They enjoyed your bread so much that they're afraid they'll double their weight if they stay here. Seriously,' he said over Flynn's chortle, 'the business that brought us here is nearing completion. We need to be in another part of Paris.'

'I can't deny that it will be a relief to Charlotte.'

'Have they been that much of a nuisance?'

'No, no, they've been very well-behaved.'

'Then what's upset your wife?'

'Charlotte is a very law-abiding woman,' said Flynn, 'so I haven't told her about some of the trouble I used to get into in the old days. What's worrying her now is that we've been harbouring stolen goods.'

Daniel blinked in amazement. 'Stolen goods?'

'Well, one item, anyway. Charlotte went up into the attic when Kees wasn't there and she saw that tapestry. She couldn't believe that a man like that could afford something so ruinously expensive. She thinks that he must have stolen it.'

'Would you steal a loaf of bread from your own bakery?'

'It would never even cross my mind.'

'Well, that's the position Kees is in,' said Daniel. 'He didn't rob anyone of that tapestry, Ronan, because he helped to make it. You can't steal what you already own.'

'It's magnificent, Dan. I sneaked up there to take a peep at it myself. Are you telling me that Kees helped to create it?'

'He was working to someone else's design.'

'I don't care. He's a fine artist. Wait until I tell Charlotte.'

'That's all you must tell her,' advised Daniel. 'Neither of you must know why the tapestry ended up here. I'd be grateful if you didn't talk about it to anyone else.'

'We can keep our mouths shut.' He looked his friend in the eye. 'There's danger ahead, isn't there?'

'There may be.'

'You're carrying all three of them on your shoulders, Dan. I can see that. All I asked of you was that you didn't do anything that would put my family in any kind of peril.'

'It's the main reason I'm taking them away.'

'Let me help,' offered Flynn. 'As long as it's well away from this house, I've always got time for an old friend. Kees might be a wizard at a loom but I reckon he's not the man you need in a crisis, and the two ladies would be even less useful. You know my mettle, Dan,' he added, tapping his own chest. 'If there's adventure at hand and you need someone you can rely on, Ronan Flynn is your man.'

'Thank you,' said Daniel, gratefully. 'I may well call on you, Ronan, though you might live to regret your offer.'

Flynn grinned. 'Ah, who's worried about regrets?' he said, airily. 'A man who has no regrets has led a pretty dull life in my opinion. Turn to me when you need me, Dan. I'll be there.'

Chapter Ten

'He kept you out there for well over an hour,' said Hugh Dobbs
with a blend of sympathy and anger. 'Major Cracknell is a
bastard.'

'He was waiting for me to drop my drum,' explained Tom
Hillier, rubbing an arm, 'but I didn't give him that pleasure.'

'*I* could never have kept it up there that long.'

'It was hard work.'

'By rights, I should have been there with you. We were both
caught by the major yet he let me go. Why was that?'

'Go and ask him.'

'Oh no, I'll keep well clear of that cruel bugger.'

'I'll try to do the same, Hugh.'

They were in their tent. After suffering the pain and
humiliation of marching up and down for so long, Hillier felt
that his arms were about to drop off. His drum had got heavier
and heavier until he felt that he was holding a ton of lead above
his head. What came to his rescue was his determination not
to buckle under the strain and the fact that his muscles had
been toughened on the farm. He'd also recited some verses he'd
memorised as a child and it helped to take his mind off the

growing agony. Seeing that he couldn't bring the drummer to his knees, Major Cracknell had eventually stalked off.

'He came looking for you,' said Dobbs. 'Officers have got much more important things to do than watch a couple of lads having some fun. If he was that worried about us, he could have sent a corporal to break up the fight and bellow at us.'

'You could be right, Hugh.'

'I usually am.'

'Major Cracknell went out of his way to find us.'

'To find *you*, Tom,' corrected the other. 'He doesn't care a fiddler's fart about me even though I'm a lot prettier than you.'

'I hadn't noticed that,' said Hillier with a laugh, starting to rub the other arm. 'You should look in a mirror, Hugh.'

'I'm the handsomest drummer in the regiment.'

'Then the rest of us must be as ugly as sin.'

'You all are.' He saw the fatigue in his friend's face. 'Here, let me do the rubbing for you, Tom. You look as if you're going to fall over.'

Dobbs used both hands to massage one of Hillier's weary arms, managing to impart discomfort and relief at the same time. He then moved on to the other arm before turning his attention to the searing ache in his friend's shoulders. Hillier could scarcely bear the pain at first but it slowly eased.

'You should tell your uncle about this,' counselled Dobbs.

'Why?'

'He ought to know.'

'There's nothing he can do about it,' said Hillier. 'Anyway, he told me to stay away from him. He wants me to get by on my own.'

'I still think you should speak to Sergeant Welbeck.'

'There's no point, Hugh.'

'I believe there is.'

'What can a sergeant do against an officer?'

'He can fight fire with fire,' said Dobbs, knowledgeably.

'I don't understand.'

'He can set an officer on an officer, Tom.'

'Can he?'

'Yes, he can, and he couldn't pick a better man. According to you, your Uncle Henry is a friend of Captain Rawson. You saw them together that day. Tell the sergeant what happened to you and you can be sure it will get back to the captain.'

'But I don't want it to,' protested Hillier. 'I don't need any help. I can fight my own battles.'

'Not if you're up against a vicious tyrant like Major Cracknell. If he has his knife in you, Tom, he'll twist it until you beg for mercy. You need an officer on your side.'

'Captain Rawson wouldn't bother about someone like me.'

'He'd bother about anyone being unfairly treated,' said Dobbs. 'He's that sort of man. Speak to your uncle, that's all you have to do. Don't you want to have Captain Rawson defending you?'

'He's not even here in camp, Hugh.'

'He soon will be, I daresay. Captain Rawson never stays away for too long. He's probably on his way back this very minute.'

Daniel arrived for his second night at the Bastille in a more sanguine frame of mind. He knew what would be expected of him and, though his duties were deeply unpleasant, they were not taxing. The burden on him had eased slightly. In moving Amalia and the others out of the house, he'd rid himself of some anxieties. He no longer had to worry about getting Flynn into serious trouble or of arousing Charlotte's suspicions to the point where she would feel endangered. Nor did he have to worry about his charges. Daniel had settled all three of them in a respectable tavern that ensured them a degree of comfort and privacy without leaving them feeling obligated to anyone. Amalia's safety was paramount to Daniel. He could now forget her for a while and concentrate on her father.

Night duty began with another trudge through the *cachots* in the uninspiring company of Jules Rivot. If anything, the stench was stronger, the rats more abundant, the cries of the prisoners more pitiable and the mood of his fellow-turnkey even more morose. Rivot belonged underground. He was a human mole going endlessly back and forth along his runs with blind resignation. He was not a creature of daylight. The subterranean darkness suited him. It was Daniel who carried the lantern. Rivot could find his way around by instinct. He only spoke to give Daniel a curt command. As a source of information about the other parts of the prison, he was useless.

When the gaolers broke off for refreshment, some of them slipped away to relieve themselves, either urinating in a corner or climbing up to one of the *garderobes* in the nearest tower. Daniel took the opportunity to visit the gatehouse. Crossing the courtyard in the eerie light from flaming torches, he knocked on the heavy oak door. After a few moments, it was opened by a portly man of middle years. From the way that the duty sergeant rubbed his piggy eyes, Daniel guessed that he'd been taking a nap. Rudely awakened, the man was brusque and unwelcoming.

'Who are you?' he demanded.

'Marcel Daron, sir,' replied Daniel.

'What are you doing here?'

'I have a favour to ask.'

'You should be on duty.'

'We're having a rest, sir. I'll go back down to the *cachots* in a matter of minutes. I simply wanted to find out if what Sergeant Bermutier said is true.'

'Bermutier?' There was a note of respect in the man's voice.

'He was kind enough to offer me work here, sir.'

'So?'

'I overheard him say that the Comte de Lerebour was being held in one of the towers.'

'What's that to you, Daron?'

'I served under him in the army, sir. He was a fine commander. If he's here, I'd like to visit him to pay my respects.'

'Lerebour, Lerebour,' said the other. 'I don't recall the name but then we have so many prisoners here. In which tower is he held?'

'Sergeant Bermutier didn't say, sir.'

'Let me have a look.'

Daniel was in luck. He'd invented the name of the Comte de Lerebour but coupled it with that of Bermutier. It was enough to get him through the door of the gatehouse. The sergeant opened his desk, took out the ledger and flipped through the pages by the light of a candle. Over his shoulder, Daniel saw all the names that had been crossed out with a date beside them. He was not sure if they'd been released, executed or simply allowed to rot away in their cells. At all events, the numbers had mounted up over the years. The sergeant eventually came to the lists of those currently held in the middle levels of the towers. Daniel peered intently as the sergeant's stubby finger went up and down the various names. In the end, he snapped the ledger shut and spun round.

'He's not here,' he said.

'Are you sure, Sergeant?'

'You must be mistaken.'

'I could've sworn that I heard the Comte de Lerebour's name,' said Daniel, scratching his head. 'Mind you, there were a lot of us milling around when Sergeant Bermutier spoke. With all that noise going on, I might have misheard him.'

The sergeant was terse. 'Go back to your duties.'

'Yes, sir.'

'And don't bother me again.'

'I'm sorry to disturb you, sir.'

'Get out!'

Pushing Daniel through the door, he shut it firmly in his face. As a result, the duty sergeant did not see Daniel's broad smile. The Comte de Lerebour was not detained in the Bastille but Emanuel Janssen certainly was. His name was on the list and Daniel now knew exactly where to find him. Though work in the *cachots* was dispiriting he was now able to rejoin Rivot with something akin to enthusiasm.

The War of the Spanish Succession was not merely a conflict played out on a series of battlefields around Europe. During the months when bad weather and a lack of provisions curtailed any fighting, it continued by other means. Allies had to be courted, money had to be raised, soldiers had to be found and plans for campaigns in the following year had to be discussed and agreed upon. No commander on either side combined military prowess with diplomatic skills as effectively as the Duke of Marlborough. When he was not leading his men into battle, he was keeping in constant touch with his allies and soothing them with honeyed words. Adam Cardonnel never stopped admiring his political shrewdness.

'You are Restraint personified,' he observed.

'There are times when one must learn to subordinate one's

personal feelings, Adam,' said Marlborough. 'In my dealings with the Dutch, alas, those occasions are all too frequent.'

'I fear they are, Your Grace. After our untimely withdrawal from the River Yssche, you behaved impeccably. Any other commander-in-chief would have stormed off to The Hague to confront the whole States-General.'

'What would that have achieved?'

'You'd have had the satisfaction of speaking your mind.'

'True,' said Marlborough, 'but I'd also have stirred up all those who oppose this war. They'd be glad of an excuse to turn on a tetchy commander-in-chief from England. There are too many of them who wish to open peace negotiations with France. That's why we can't afford to antagonise the Dutch. Policy must come before petulance.'

'It's not petulance, Your Grace, but justifiable fury.'

Marlborough smiled. 'Some of that fury was assuaged by the dismissal of General Slangenberg. I regard that as a small triumph.'

The two men were travelling in a coach over a bumpy road. With their entourage, they were on their way to Dusseldorf, the city on the Rhine in which the Elector Palatine had chosen to reside in preference to the badly damaged Heidelberg. Marlborough was confident that he could persuade Johann Wilhelm II to provide an appreciable number of troops for the Italian campaign when it resumed in the following spring. He was also assured of a welcome that befitted the victor at the battle of Blenheim. Marlborough had another reason for looking forward to renewing his acquaintance with the Elector.

'He's such a cultured man,' he recalled. 'His court has given work to many artists and musicians over the years.'

'The same could be said of Louis XIV's court,' said Cardonnel drily. 'Versailles has an art collection second to none.'

'I doubt if even King Louis has as many paintings by Rubens. The Elector seems to own a vast number of them. I envy him the time to look at them. Having an art gallery presupposes leisure.'

'We shall enjoy it one day, Your Grace.'

'Not if we continue to be baulked by the Dutch and hampered by some of our other allies. Then there is the small matter of our own Parliament,' said Marlborough. 'Every letter I receive from Sidney Godolphin tells of growing disillusion with this war. The Tories seem never to have heard of what we did at Blenheim or, if they have, they choose to disregard it. Thank heaven we still have so many staunch friends back in England.'

'None stauncher than Her Majesty, the Queen,' said Cardonnel.

'My dear wife must take some credit there, Adam. Queen Anne and the Duchess are as close as sisters.'

'I've known sisters who do nothing but squabble.'

'Happily, that's not the case here.' Marlborough was jolted as the coach came to a sudden halt. 'What's going on?'

'A courier,' said his secretary, looking through the window. 'He's riding hard. He must be bringing a billet-doux from Slangenberg.'

Marlborough laughed and waited for the horseman to arrive. Even though he was in transit, he received a regular supply of dispatches and private correspondence. It kept him in touch with events elsewhere and alleviated the monotony of travel. When the courier pulled up outside the coach, Marlborough descended to take a pile of letters from him. After enquiring about the man's journey, he thanked him for the latest delivery then climbed back into the coach. He immediately began to sift through the missives. Spotting one that had been sent from Paris, he opened it first. His jaw tightened as he read the message.

'Is is bad news, Your Grace?' asked Cardonnel.

'Yes, Adam,' said Marlborough, passing the letter to him. 'One of our most reliable agents in Paris has been discovered and hanged. As for Emanuel Janssen, it appears that he's entombed in the Bastille.'

'The Bastille!'

'Daniel Rawson has been sent on an impossible mission.'

'Quite so,' agreed the other. 'The captain is doomed to fail. How could he even *think* of getting Janssen out of there?'

Daniel moved quickly. Snatching only a couple of hours' sleep, he left the tavern and rode to Ronan Flynn's bakery. The Irishman was about to set off on his cart to deliver bread. He greeted his friend with a flour-covered grin.

'You're just in time to help me deliver these, Dan,' he said.

'Very well but you must do something for me in return.'

'I always return a favour.'

'You've proved that, Ronan.'

Tethering his horse to the back of the cart, Daniel sat beside Flynn so that they could talk as they rolled through the streets. Their conversation was interrupted by stoppages. Daniel helped to unload bread and hand it over to the various customers. Towards the end of the round, he had enough time to broach the subject that had taken him to the bakery in the first place.

'Do you know anyone with a boat?' he asked.

'To be sure I do,' replied Flynn, jovially. 'The French navy has hundreds of them. They've got boats, ships, yachts and anything that sails on water.'

'That's not what I had in mind, Ronan.'

'I know. I was only pulling your leg.'

'It was a serious question.'

'Then I'll give you a serious answer. As it happens, I do know someone who plies his trade on the Seine. When I first got married to Charlotte, I paid him to row a couple of miles downstream.'

'How big is the boat?'

'It's big enough to take three or four passengers.'

'Then it might be what we need.'

'Are you thinking of leaving us then?'

'I have to, Ronan.'

'Well, don't tell me where you're going for I've a terrible loose tongue, so I have. I'd probably shout the news all over Paris.' He tugged on the reins to bring the horse to a halt then jumped off the cart to deliver an armful of bread. He soon leapt up beside Daniel again. 'When might you want this boat?'

'I'm not certain – as early as tomorrow, perhaps.'

'Then you'd better meet the fellow this morning. He's getting old but he knows the river and he'll do whatever you pay him to do.'

'He'll be well rewarded.'

'If there's a lot of money involved,' said Flynn, eagerly, 'then I'll row you myself.'

'You have a wife and child to consider.'

'Ah, I see. There could be hazards.'

'How do I find this man?'

'I'll take you to him when I've finished delivering bread.'

'Thank you,' said Daniel. 'I'm very grateful. You've been a true friend, Ronan.'

'Oh, I'm not doing it for your sake, Dan. It's for my own benefit. I want my wife to stop asking what you're all doing here and whether or not you'll bring the police down on us. I'll be glad to wave you off,' he teased. 'As long as you leave Amalia behind,' he added, wickedly. 'She can work beside me at the bakery. I'll teach the little darling how to make bread – among other things, that is.'

While she was pleased to leave the Flynn house, Amalia was not entirely happy in the tavern that Daniel had found for them. It guaranteed their anonymity but they were no longer enjoying the hospitality of friends. Kees Dopff was patient and undemanding, quite content to spend the day guarding the tapestry or taking a walk near the river. Beatrix, however, was less able to cope with the waiting.

'The police are still looking for us, aren't they?' she asked.

'I expect that they are,' said Amalia.

'They're bound to find us one day and then what will happen?'

'Try not to think about that.'

'I can't help thinking about it, Miss Amalia.'

'Captain Rawson has a plan.'

'How can he get all of us out of Paris?'

'I don't know, Beatrix, but I believe that he can.'

'Why does he keep leaving us alone like this?'

'I'm sure there's a good reason,' said Amalia. 'All that we can do is to watch and pray.'

'Oh, I've been praying every hour of the day,' confessed the servant. 'I've been praying that we all get safely back to Amsterdam but that's like asking for a miracle.'

They were still at the tavern. Though Amalia tried valiantly to still Beatrix's doubts, she still had several of her own but she didn't voice them in case she turned the servant's fears into complete panic. When Daniel finally called on them that afternoon,

Amalia wanted to fling herself into his arms in gratitude but Beatrix's presence deterred her. Sensing the taut atmosphere, Daniel managed to reassure the older woman a little before asking her to leave them alone so that they could have a private conversation. As soon as the door closed behind the servant, Amalia gave vent to her feelings, taking Daniel by both hands and imploring him to tell her where he'd been.

'I've been searching for a boat,' he explained.

She was perplexed. 'A boat?'

'I want you to leave the city by river.'

'What about Father?'

'God willing, he may be able to quit Paris at the same time.'

'How will you get him out of the Bastille?'

'I think I may have found a way,' said Daniel. 'First, however, I need you to describe him to me.'

'Why do you want me to do that, Daniel?'

'I need to know how old he is, how tall, how fat or how thin. Tell me everything, Amalia. I have to be able to recognise him at a glance.'

'There's a chance that you'll *see* him, then?' she said, excitedly.

'I hope so. Your father's being held in one of the towers at the Bastille. Prisoners get far better treatment there. It's likely that he's still in good health.'

'Thank goodness!' she exclaimed.

'Tell me what he looks like.'

Amalia gave a detailed description of her father and there was a mingled respect and affection in her voice. Since her mother's early death, she'd been brought up almost exclusively by Emanuel Janssen and the bond between them was very strong. Daniel was interested to hear that the tapestry-maker was stout, bearded, in his fifties and of medium height. The plan forming in his mind took on more definition.

'Do you have any idea when we might leave?' she asked.

'It could be as soon as tomorrow or as late as next week.'

Her face crumpled. 'Next *week*?'

'I have to seize the moment when it comes, Amalia,' he said. 'It will depend on a number of things over which I have no control.'

'The longer we stay, the more worried everyone becomes.'

'I could see that Beatrix is suffering badly.'

'Unless we leave soon, Daniel, she'll vex herself to death.'

'I said this to you when we first met and I must say it again. You must all be ready to leave at a moment's notice. In your case, Amalia,' he said, feasting his eyes on her face, 'you must disguise yourself in some way.'

'Why must I do that?'

'Everyone guarding the exits to the city will have been furnished with a description of a beautiful young lady with fair hair and blue eyes. If you're seen looking like that,' he went on, 'you'll be recognised at once. There'll be guards on the river as well as at the gates.'

'What about my passport, Daniel? It bears my name.'

'His Grace thought about that in advance. The Duke of Marlborough always looks ahead for possible difficulties. It's the secret behind all our victories in the field. I not only travelled with a forged passport for myself – as Marcel Daron – but I've brought papers for you and the others.'

'Does that include Father?'

Daniel grinned. 'We can hardly leave him behind.'

'Oh, you've done so much for us, Daniel,' she said, taking him by the arms. 'I can't believe that anyone else would have gone to such lengths to help us.'

'I'm simply obeying orders.'

'But they could arrest you at any minute.'

'They could, Amalia,' he agreed, cheerfully, 'but they'll have to catch me first and I'm determined not to be caught. That's why I chose the perfect hiding place.'

'And where's that?'

'It's inside the Bastille.'

Henry Welbeck's voice had developed over the years into something akin to the boom of a cannon gun. It had a volume and intensity that compelled his soldiers to listen even as it threatened to burst their eardrums. Drilling his men that afternoon, he yelled out his orders and excoriated anyone who failed to obey them correctly. After the criticism received from Major Cracknell, he paid especial attention to the alignment of his men, keeping them in serried ranks that were perfectly symmetrical. The sergeant didn't notice anyone watching him until the drill was over. Out of the corner of his eye, he then caught sight of a figure standing beneath a tree. It was not the fault-finding major this time. It was a potato-faced drummer boy. The youth took time to pluck up enough courage to approach Welbeck. All that he got by way of a greeting was a bellicose question.

'What do you want, lad?'

'I'd like to speak to you, Sergeant.'

'Who are you?'

'Private Dobbs, sir. I'm a drummer.'

'Then why aren't you practising with your drumsticks? You've no need to be in this part of the camp at all.'

'I needed to tell you something,' said Dobbs.

'Well, speak your mind then bugger off.'

'First of all, you ought to know that he didn't send me. In fact, if he knew I was here, he'd probably punch me on the nose.'

'It might improve your appearance,' said Welbeck.

'I came of my own accord. Tom would never come himself.'

'Tom?'

'Your nephew, Sergeant.'

'I don't *have* a nephew in this regiment.'

'He said you'd deny it.'

Welbeck checked himself from making a sharp retort. He could see that Dobbs was already in a state of trepidation. It was unfair to rebuke someone who was acting out of simple friendship. He'd already worked out that the youth must be the same Hugh Dobbs who'd tormented Tom Hillier on his arrival and had taken a beating as a consequence. Clearly, they had now settled their differences.

'I don't like people who run to me with tales,' warned Welbeck.

'I know, Sergeant, and I've never done this before – not even on my own account. When I joined this regiment,' said Dobbs, 'the other drummers had great sport with me. It's what any new recruit must expect. One day, they stripped me naked and threw me into a patch of nettles. It stung for weeks but I never thought to report it.'

'I'm not interested in your memoirs, Dobbs.'

'No, sir, and nor should you be. Tom is different, though.'

'Private Hillier's affairs are nothing to do with me.'

'That's what he told me.'

'Then why didn't you have the sense to listen to him?'

'I worry about him,' said Dobbs, earnestly. 'I know what it's like to fall foul of a sergeant. I did it myself once. When it's an officer, it's far worse. He can grind you into the dust.'

'What are you talking about?'

'His name is Major Cracknell.'

'Be very careful what you say, lad,' Welbeck cautioned. 'You're not in the army to question any decision made by an officer. Your duty is to obey. If you have grudges, you keep them to yourself.'

'This is more than a grudge, Sergeant.'

Welbeck held back the expletive that jumped to his lips. If anyone from the ranks came to him with a complaint, they usually received short shrift. He told soldiers that they had to address their own problems and not turn to him like a child running to its father. When disagreements between the men spilt over into violence, the sergeant invariably banged heads together, telling the disputants that they had to learn to get along. Facing this new situation, however, he was torn between involvement and indifference, wanting to know the details yet needing to remain detached from it all. After minutes of pondering, he reached a decision.

'What happened?' he asked.

Dobbs told him about the way that they'd been caught by Major Cracknell and about the punishment meted out to Hillier. There had been a second incident on the same day when the major found a spurious excuse to subject the drummer to further punishment. On that occasion, Hillier had been made to run in a wide circle with a heavy pack on his back. Dobbs talked about the ugly red weals left on his friend's shoulders by the straps.

'It started all over again this morning,' Dobbs continued. 'The major singled out Tom again and made him—'

'That's enough!' snapped Welbeck, interrupting him. 'I want no more of this whining. This regiment is full of people with grudges against certain officers and they're almost always without any foundation. I suggest that you do as Private Hillier seems to be doing and that's to keep your mouth firmly shut.'

'I thought you'd like to know.'

'Then you were badly mistaken, lad.'

Dobbs was crushed. 'Yes, Sergeant,' he mumbled.

'Don't bring any more of these silly stories to me.'

'No, Sergeant.'

'Be off with you!'

Wounded by the rebuff, Dobbs scampered off. Welbeck looked after him and was grateful that his nephew had such a good friend. He was impressed that Tom Hillier had taken his punishment without feeling the need to complain and was struck by something else as well. It was evident that Dobbs knew nothing of the warning that the sergeant had issued to Hillier about Major Cracknell. The drummer had kept it to himself. That pleased Welbeck. Where an officer was concerned, however, the sergeant was powerless to intervene. If he so wished, a major could beat someone from the ranks black and blue without even needing an excuse to do so. Hillier was in grave danger.

His third night as a turnkey at the Bastille followed the same dreary pattern as the others except that, on this occasion, Rivot unloaded more of the drudgery on to Daniel. Now that the new man was familiar with the routine, Rivot kept sneaking off for short, unscheduled rests. This allowed Daniel to be more generous with the distribution of water and to converse with some of the prisoners. Those who stirred from their straw to come to the door were extremely grateful for what they saw as a concession. When Rivot was on duty, they had virtually no human contact. Suddenly, they had a friend who showed interest in them. Daniel was astonished to learn that one of the ragged inmates had once been a member of the *Parlement*.

'How did you end up here?' asked Daniel.

'I spoke my mind,' replied the man.

'How long have you been imprisoned?'

'Over two years.'

'When will you be released?'

The prisoner gave a hollow laugh. 'There's no talk of release down here. I'm locked up for having the courage of my convictions. And I'd do the same again,' he went on with a battered dignity. 'If I see corruption in government, I have to speak out.'

'Do you have a wife and family?'

'I did have. They're dead to me now.'

'You must have been a person of consequence at one time.'

'That's why I was dragged from my bed one night and arrested. They were afraid I'd persuade others to join in my crusade. I had to be silenced.'

It was a salutary tale and there were others just like it. Talking to some of them, Daniel could see how paltry their so-called crimes were and that they were really victims of rank injustice. All that he could do was to offer them a sympathetic ear and as much water as they wanted. His main interest was in someone confined in less sordid conditions. It was not until the turnkeys reached their break in the middle of the night that he was able to go in search of Emanuel Janssen. Daniel came up from the *cachots*, gulped in fresh air then crossed the courtyard to a tower on the eastern side of the building. He went swiftly up the stairs, looking into rooms at every level for the Dutchman. Turnkeys who saw him assumed that he had business higher up the tower. Halfway up the circular stone staircase, he reached an open area with a large wooden bench against the wall. Lying full length on it, snoring contentedly, was one of the gaolers.

Daniel tiptoed past him then looked into the next cell. It

was cold, bare and featureless. At the same time, it was more spacious than the cells below ground and was occupied by only one person. The candle burning in the corner shed enough light for him to see a body on the mattress, concealed by a sheet. When the man turned over in his sleep, Daniel's heart began to pound. Amalia had described her father's silver hair and beard. It had to be Emanuel Janssen. Daniel took a small stone from his pocket. Wrapped carefully around it was a message written in Dutch. Putting an arm through the bars, he tossed it at the man's head so that it grazed his temple.

Janssen came awake immediately, rubbing his head and trying to sit up. It took him time to open his eyes properly. When he did so, he saw Daniel outside the bars, holding a finger to his lips to enforce silence then using it to call him over. Janssen was bewildered. He was a sorry figure, stooping, round-shouldered and looking much older than Daniel had expected. He shuffled across to the door.

'Read the message I threw at you,' whispered Daniel.

Janssen rallied at the sound of his own language. 'Who are you?' he murmured.

'I'm a friend. Your daughter and the others are safe.'

'You've seen Amalia?'

'She sends her love.' Daniel glanced over his shoulder. 'I must go. I'll be back.'

Janssen reached through the bars to grab Daniel's shoulder and to ask the question that had troubled him throughout the whole of his incarceration.

'Where's the tapestry?'

CHAPTER ELEVEN

Alphonse Cornudet had worked on the river for many years, rowing passengers from one bank of the Seine to the other when they were too lazy to walk to the nearest bridge or when they preferred a more leisurely way of crossing the wide stretch of water that slid through the nation's capital like a capricious serpent. In spring and summer, he took families for a day out on the river or delivered small cargo to certain destinations or carried lovers to sheltered spots along the banks where romance could burgeon. Cornudet served all needs and tastes. He was a short, balding, barrel-chested man with a weather-beaten face that always wore the same sad, world-weary expression. Toughened by a lifetime of pulling on oars, his compact frame had deceptive power and stamina. Nothing short of a blizzard deterred him. For a tempting fare, he was ready to battle against the strongest wind or the heaviest rain.

After his third night as a turnkey, Daniel permitted himself a longer time in bed the following morning. He then had a late breakfast and went down to the river to make arrangements. Cornudet was sitting on the wharf with his legs dangling over the side. Moored below him was his skiff. Daniel could see the smoke coming from the old man's pipe. When he got closer, he could smell the tobacco.

'Good morning, Monsieur,' he said.

'Good morning,' returned Cornudet, looking up. 'Oh, it's you again, Monsieur Daron.'

'How are you today?'

'I'm still alive, as you see.'

'We may need your boat tomorrow.'

The old man grunted. 'Will you need it or won't you?'

'I can't be sure.'

'I have other customers, Monsieur.'

'Yes, I appreciate that.'

'I can't be at your beck and call.'

'I'll pay you to keep your boat free tomorrow morning,' said Daniel, taking out a purse. 'We may or may not make use of it then. I'm sorry that I can't be more definite, Monsieur Cornudet, but there are other people involved.'

'How many of them are there?'

'That, too, has yet to be decided.'

'Is there anything you *do* know?' asked Cornudet without removing the pipe from his mouth. 'Have you any idea in which direction you wish to go, for instance?'

'We'll go downstream and leave the city that way.'

'Am I to take you there and back?'

'No, you'll drop off your passengers at a given place.'

'And what place is that, Monsieur?'

'It's yet to be determined.'

'I like to know where I'm going,' said Cornudet, irritably. 'That's little enough to ask of a customer. Where exactly are you heading?'

'We're going to Mantes.'

The old man snatched the pipe from his mouth. 'You want me to row you all *that* way?' he asked. 'I think you should hire a bigger boat and one with a sail. Mantes is too far for me.'

'You won't go anywhere near it,' Daniel assured him. 'You'll lose your passengers well before then.'

Mantes was over thirty miles away and he had no intention of visiting the pretty riverside town. It was a destination that he invented on purpose. If Daniel did manage to get Janssen out of prison and convey four fugitives out of Paris, pursuit would be inevitable. Guards at every gate would be questioned as would those who kept watch on the river. Boatmen were bound to be asked about passengers who'd recently hired them. Alphonse Cornudet would say that the people he'd rowed out of the city were on their way to Mantes. It would send the chasing pack in the wrong direction.

The old man was grumpy but Ronan Flynn had insisted that he was trustworthy. Once engaged, Cornudet was very dependable. He simply liked to be paid well for his services.

'Take this, Monsieur,' said Daniel, fishing in the purse for some coins. 'It will show you how keen we are to retain your services.'

'I'm the best boatman on the river.'

'Then you deserve to be well paid.'

'Thank you,' said Cornudet with something approaching a smile as Daniel pressed coins into his hand. 'You are very kind.'

'There'll be more when we get there.'

'I'll be interested to see where it is, Monsieur Daron.'

'I'll have made up my mind by tomorrow,' promised Daniel, 'though it may be the next day when we actually leave. Whatever happens, I'll be here to see you in the morning.'

Cornudet pocketed the money. 'I'll be waiting.'

* * *

Even a river veteran like the old man could not be expected to row five people downstream, especially as they would have luggage with them. In any case, Daniel reasoned, it would be foolish of them to try to escape from the city together. The party needed to split into two groups and leave by different means. To that end, he mounted his horse and rode towards the western gate. He was now dressed as Marcel Daron again. Challenged by the guards, he produced his forged documents and answered a volley of questions about how he'd spent his time while in the city and why he was leaving. There were far more guards than he'd encountered on his way into Paris and they were obviously on the alert. At length, he was given his papers and waved through. He cantered out the gates and went in the direction of the Seine.

After a couple of miles, he found a quiet spot on the river that seemed to fit all his requirements. Shielded by some trees, it was on a bend where it would be easy to unload passengers from a skiff. Travel by water was slow. To have a chance of outrunning any pursuit, they had to move fast by land. Having made his decision, Daniel rode back to Paris and took care to enter by a different gate so that he wouldn't be recognised by the guards who'd seen him earlier. There was far less trouble getting into the city. It was only those wanting to leave who were being questioned and, in some cases, searched. The hunt for Jacques Serval's killer was clearly still going on. When a guard stood back to let Marcel Daron go into the capital, he didn't realise that he had just let the wanted man slip through his fingers.

Daniel was familiar with the geography of Paris now. He was able to take a short cut that took him through a maze of streets to Ronan Flynn's bakery. As he arrived at the shop, he saw that the Irishman had finished work for the day and was about to return home in his cart.

'Wait!' he called.

'Holy Mary!' cried Flynn, seeing him approach. 'What the devil are you doing here?' Daniel's horse trotted up to the cart. 'I thought you'd be well clear of us by now.'

'I was missing the pleasure of your company.'

'You lying hound, Dan Rawson! No red-blooded man on earth would spend time with an old rascal like me when he's got someone like Amalia dancing attendance on him. In your place, I know exactly what I'd be doing right now and it's not simply holding hands with her.' He whistled in admiration. 'I'd no idea a Dutch woman could be so gorgeous.'

'I need to ask you another favour, Ronan.'

Flynn closed an eye. 'It's not another boat you're after, is it?'

'No, I've hired Monsieur Cornudet on your recommendation. I'm sure that he won't let us down.'

'If he does,' vowed Flynn, raising a fist, 'he'll have to answer to me. Alphonse knows that you're a friend of mine.'

'I'm an extremely grateful friend, Ronan.'

'You're not as grateful as I was when you saved me from being shot as target practice by my captors. Until you suddenly came along, I thought my time on this earth was up. A whole heap of gratitude was piled up that day, Dan.'

'That's why I felt able to come to you.'

'So what's this new favour you want from me?' asked Flynn, rubbing his hands together. 'I suppose there's no chance that you want me to take care of Amalia for you, is there?'

'None at all,' said Daniel with a laugh. 'I'd offer you Beatrix but she may not have the same appeal.' Flynn groaned in disapproval. 'All that I have for you this time is a very simple request.'

'What is it?'

'Where can I find a small coach?'

Emanuel Janssen was beginning to wonder if it had all been a dream. Awakened in the night by one of the turnkeys, he'd been told that his daughter, assistant and servant were all safe and well. Equally reassuring was the news that the tapestry on which he'd laboured so long had been rescued from the house. Brief details of what had happened had been contained in the letter delivered to him by means of a stone tossed through the bars. Because it was unsigned, he didn't know who his benefactor might be or if it was all some cruel joke being played on him by the gaolers. The most extraordinary thing about the letter was that it held out the possibility of escape. How it might actually take place was not specified but it had given Janssen the first surge of hope since he'd been imprisoned.

As he sat on the chair in his cell and pretended to read one of the books he was allowed to have, Janssen brooded on the strange event in the night. One way to verify that it had occurred was to read the letter again but he had already obeyed the sender's order to destroy it. After reading it several times and savouring each line, the pattern-maker had swallowed the missive. Nobody else would ever see it now. Had it been a dream? Was he being taunted by the men who kept him there? Or, worst of all, was his mind finally crumbling in the sustained horror of confinement, leaving him prone to wild fantasies? Janssen was confused.

What helped him to cling tightly to hope was the character of the man who'd visited him. He'd been friendly, sincere and spoke in Dutch. His letter had reinforced the impression of someone who could be trusted. Any attempt at escape would involve great danger and considerable daring yet Janssen was not frightened at the prospect. During his fleeting appearance, the nocturnal stranger had imparted confidence. It gave the Dutchman an inner strength. There was no chance of his having weird dreams in the coming night. Responding to the advice in the letter, he'd remain wide awake.

Amalia Janssen had also done Daniel's bidding. In an effort to change her appearance, she'd darkened her hair with dye, taken the colour out of her cheeks with a white powder and put on some old clothing. She'd even bought a pair of spectacles to complete her disguise. What she could never do completely was to hide the beauty of her features and Daniel relished the opportunity to look at them again. Amalia was eager for his approval.

'Do I look different?' she asked.

'Yes, Amalia,' he said with a fond smile. 'You're different and yet essentially the same.'

'Will it help?'

'I'm sure that it will.'

He met all three of them at the tavern where they were staying and spent the first few minutes trying to calm Beatrix's frayed nerves. She could not understand why it was taking so long to put his plan into operation. Dopff, too, was plainly unsettled but his faith in Daniel remained steadfast. He considered the soldier to be their saviour. Without Daniel's intervention, they would still be living in fear in the same house, watched over night and day. They now had a degree of freedom and a promise of escape from the city. Most important of all was the hope that they'd be joined in their flight by his master. How that feat could be achieved, he didn't know but he was won over by Daniel's iron resolve. Beatrix didn't share Dopff's belief in their ultimate success but, after listening to Daniel, she at least began to fret in silence instead of expressing her anxiety aloud.

Wanting to speak alone with her, Daniel took Amalia for a walk. He was delighted when she took his arm so that they could stroll as if husband and wife. Pedestrians and carriages went up and down the boulevard but nobody accorded them more than a cursory glance. They fitted comfortably into the scene. When they reached the river, they went along the bank together until they got within sight of the wharf where Cornudet's boat was usually to be found. In fact, the skiff was now out on the water as the old man rowed some passengers upstream. Daniel indicated the wharf and told Amalia what he had in mind. She was thrown into a mild panic.

'I can't leave without Father,' she protested.

'He'll be with me, Amalia.'

'Why can't we be together?'

'It's safer if you go separately,' Daniel explained. 'The police are still hunting for you, Kees and Beatrix. Your descriptions will have been passed to everyone on guard at one of the exits. If all three of you try to leave together, you might be stopped. Even that disguise of yours may not save you.'

'Let me go in the boat with Father,' she urged.

'No, Amalia. He must come with me. If and when I do manage to get him out of the Bastille, it will only be a matter of time before his escape is discovered. A hue and cry will be set up. The city gates will be closed. We have to be through them before that happens. If your father leaves by boat,' Daniel pointed out, 'then you can easily be overhauled by a faster vessel because a search will certainly be made of the river. There's something else,' he added. 'When you're reunited after all this time, you'll simply want to hug each other. Anyone will see at once that you're father and daughter. Nothing can hide that fact, Amalia.'

'What about Beatrix?'

'She'll come with me.'

'Does that mean I'll be alone in the boat with Kees?'

'It's the best way to escape detection. The two of you will look like close friends, enjoying a trip on the river. You're far less likely to attract attention that way.'

'I suppose that's true,' she said, reluctantly accepting his logic. 'But I'd still rather be with Father.' She squeezed his arm on impulse. 'And I'd much prefer to be with you, Daniel.'

'Thank you, Amalia.'

'Instead of that, our servant will have the privilege.'

'Beatrix is our weak spot,' said Daniel, 'and the one person who could ruin everything. Were she in the boat when you were questioned by the river guards, her nerve might fail her. All three of you would be captured then.'

'If she travels in the coach,' Amalia argued, 'she could endanger Father for the same reason.'

'I don't think that will happen.'

'It could do, Daniel.'

'It's imperative that Beatrix leaves the city in the coach. I need both her and her luggage with me.' He rubbed her arm gently and ventured a kiss on her forehead. 'In due course, you'll realise why.'

In his fine house in Amsterdam, Emanuel Janssen had glass in his windows and a fire in every room to take off the autumnal chill. There were no such refinements at the Bastille. The wind howled all evening and blew the rain into his cell through the slits carved in the thick stone walls. He did, however, have other concessions. He had a comfortable mattress on which to sleep, a small table and a chair, some books and a wooden bucket in which he could relieve himself. From time to time, the bucket was emptied, a luxury that was denied those below ground or those in open cages under the roof. In a storm like the one now pelting the Bastille, prisoners in the *calottes* would be whipped by the wind and soaked to the skin. As his gaolers kept telling him, Janssen was comparatively lucky.

It was only since his nameless visitor had appeared during the previous night that the Dutchman dared to believe in luck. Until then, he had rued his ill fortune. With frightening speed, he'd gone from talking with the French king at Versailles to inhabiting a lonely cell in a prison. Instead of being treated with exaggerated respect, he was met by sneers and jeers. Instead of sharing a home with his beloved daughter, he was cut off from all contact with her. Speculating on what might have happened to her had caused him intense grief. For the first time, he'd now heard word of her.

The gaoler on duty that evening was a stocky man with bandy legs and a malicious sense of humour. To make the prisoner suffer, he taunted him with the prospect of execution, going into gory details about what would be done to him. He'd also told Janssen that his daughter had been arrested, deflowered and put to work in a brothel. Other falsehoods were used to torture the Dutchman.

'Do you see how lucky you are?' said the turnkey, waddling over to the bars. 'Listen to that rain outside. You're snug and warm and in the best possible place. You should be thankful for that.'

'I'd be more thankful if you'd empty my bucket,' said Janssen.

'Ask someone else.'

'It's almost overflowing.'

'Then you shouldn't shit so much,' said the man with a harsh guffaw. 'Or maybe we shouldn't give you so much food.'

Janssen said nothing. He knew enough French to issue a sharp retort but it would only be to his detriment. When he'd made even the slightest complaint in the past, he'd been denied the next meal or threatened with violence. To a man as fastidious as him, living in such dreadful conditions was a daily trial. Yet he'd learnt to hold his tongue for fear of reprisals. The men outside the cell held more than a set of keys. They controlled him completely. To upset them was to increase the severity of his deprivation. The sensible course of action was to be obedient and undemanding. Whatever the provocation, Janssen had to rein in his temper.

'Oh,' said the man, goading him, 'I've got some more news about that daughter of yours. Sergeant Bermutier has met her.'

'Has he?'

'Yes, I spoke to him when he was going off duty this evening. He told me he'd spent a whole night fucking her in every way known to man and woman. I thought you'd like to know that.'

'Thank you,' said Janssen, turning away in disgust.

'I know you think the French are all monsters but we have very soft hearts really. That's why we're going to let your daughter watch when you're executed next week.'

His grating laughter reverberated around the tower.

Rain made the decision for him. It lashed down so hard that Daniel had to seize the advantages it gave him. Scouring the streets, it kept people in their homes or shepherded them into taverns and other places where they could escape the downpour.

It made visibility much more difficult. Though he was only yards away from some of the other turnkeys who scurried towards the Bastille, he recognised none of the faces through the deluge. Everyone was keeping his head down. By the time he went into the prison, Daniel was drenched. His shoes splashed through the puddles that had formed in the undulations and water dripped off his cap on to his face. Having their own problems with the storm, the others ignored him.

From the shelter of the gatehouse, the duty sergeant checked the names of incoming gaolers, barking them out above the noise of the wind and the relentless patter of the rain. For once in his career as a turnkey, Daniel was glad to plunge into the dark safety of the *cachots*. Water was seeping in there from a broken drain but at least he was out of the storm. Some of the others took off their uniforms to wring them out or removed their sodden shoes to dry them before a brazier. Daniel was forced to keep his coat on. Hidden beneath it was the loaded pistol he'd acquired on his journey to Paris. A dagger was concealed in his breeches as were some short lengths of rope.

Everyone else was complaining about the rain but Daniel was hoping that the storm would last. It was an ideal accomplice.

Janssen, by contrast, was cursing the storm. He'd got used to the rain that was blown in on him. What troubled him was the swirling wind that invaded his cell, blowing out his candle time and again. Eventually, he gave up even trying to read and adjourned to his bed. Light from a lantern illuminated the area outside, enabling him to watch every move made by his turnkey. In addition to Janssen, the man looked after other prisoners in the tower and he moved slowly between them, feeding them, giving them fresh water and making sure that everything was as it should be in their respective cells. Two of his charges were French aristocrats and they merited politeness from him. All that the Dutchman received was derision. When the turnkey had finished ministering to the prisoners, he drank from a flagon of beer before settling down on the long bench. As was customary, he was soon fast asleep.

The prisoner watched, waited and prayed. Hour followed tedious hour and nothing happened. The storm raged on outside. The turnkey began to snore and occasionally broke wind in his sleep. Janssen grew more and more weary. When another hour crept slowly by, his eyelids began to droop and he had to stifle a yawn. The man was not coming. It was the only conclusion to draw. Janssen had either had his hopes deliberately raised so that they could be dashed again or his earlier visitor had been unable to reach him again. All that he could do was to give up the struggle and surrender to sleep. Within minutes of closing his eyes, he was slumbering peacefully.

What brought him awake was a sharp nudge in the ribs. He tried to protest but there was a hand cupped over his mouth. When he squinted in the dawn light, he saw that there were two people in his cell. One of them lay full-length on the floor. The other one removed his hand from the prisoner's mouth.

'We have to be quick,' he said. 'Help me to take off his uniform so that you can put it on.'

Recognising the voice, Janssen did as he was told, buoyed up by the fact that his mysterious friend had somehow overpowered the turnkey, unlocked the cell and dragged the unconscious man into it. Between them, they stripped the turnkey. While Janssen clambered into the uniform, his rescuer tied the man up then lifted him on to the mattress. The last thing he did was to put a gag in place.

'We don't want him to call for help, do we?' he said.

'What's your name?' asked Janssen.

'Marcel Daron.'

'Why are you doing this?'

'Let's save explanations for later.'

He pulled the sheet over the turnkey so that it looked as if the prisoner was still asleep. Then he led Janssen out of the cell and locked it behind them, hanging the keys on a hook on the wall. Giving Janssen his cap, he told him to keep his head down. They descended the stairs at speed and stepped out into the courtyard that was still being swept by rain. The turnkeys who'd arrived to replace them did not even look up to see their face. They were too intent on reaching the shelter of the tower. Doing as he was told, Janssen stayed close to his rescuer and joined the men gathered at the gate. There was safety in the crowd. Nobody spoke to them. When the massive door swung open, they went out as part of a sodden exodus.

Janssen was overcome with gratitude but he dare not speak until the crowd began to disperse. Having been penned up in a cell for so long, he didn't mind the wind or the rain. The relief of getting out of the Bastille at last made him impervious to the elements. Only when the two of them were alone did he break the silence.

'What did you say your name was?' he said.

'Rawson,' replied the other. 'Captain Daniel Rawson.'

The rain was easing when they arrived at the wharf but that did nothing to lessen the intensity of Cornudet's grumbling. He had simply not expected them in such weather. Since the storm had been so fierce, he'd hauled his skiff out of the river and turned it over so that it would not get waterlogged. As he and Daniel lowered it back on to the Seine, the boatman was aggrieved.

'Why couldn't you pick a day when the sun was shining?'

'We have no choice, Monsieur,' said Daniel.

'I ought to be in bed, resting my old bones. My wife thinks I'm a fool to go on the river today?'

'Did you tell her how much you'll earn?'

'That's beside the point, Monsieur,' said Cornudet.

'Is it? I've only paid you half the fare. When you drop the passengers off, you'll get the remainder.'

'Where am I supposed to be taking them?'

'It's the best part of two miles downstream,' said Daniel. 'You'll know the place because I'll wave to you from the bank. We'll get there some time ahead of you.'

'I thought you'd be coming in the boat.'

'I've lightened your load for you.'

'Why did you do that?'

'I think they deserve to be alone,' said Daniel, indicating Amalia and Dopff, who stood side by side and gazed at each other as they'd been instructed to do. 'You may as well know the truth, Monsieur Cornudet. They're young lovers, running away to get married in Mantes. Take pity on them.'

The boatman's tone changed. 'Oh,' he said, amused, 'I am to help a romance to flower, am I? Why didn't you say so? That makes all the difference, Monsieur Daron. I'm not so old that I can't remember what it's like to be young and in love. You leave them to me,' he went on. 'I'll look after them.'

'Thank you,' said Daniel. 'I knew that you would.'

Now that the boat was bobbing on the water, the passengers could climb aboard. Dopff went first, carrying a bag but without the tapestry this time. Amalia paused at the top of the stone stairs for a whispered farewell to Daniel.

'When can I see him?' she begged.

'When we are well clear of the city,' he told her.

'I can't wait!'

'Forget about him for the moment. Remember that you're eloping with the man you love. Fasten all your attention on him.'

'Kees is more embarrassed than I am.'

'It's only for a short while.'

Amalia was concerned. 'What if you don't get out of the city?'

'Then you have no alternative,' said Daniel, kissing his fingers before touching her lips with them. 'You'll *have* to marry Kees then.'

The coach was a fairly ramshackle affair. It was no more than a wooden box on a cart but it served their purpose. Rolling over the cobblestones, it gave its occupants an uncomfortable ride. They were happy to endure it. Emanuel Janssen was overjoyed that he was travelling with his latest tapestry, neatly folded up at his feet. Seated beside him was Beatrix, ordinarily his servant but elevated to a new station on this occasion. Janssen did not object. After repeated humiliation in the Bastille, he was not one to stand on his dignity. He willingly acquiesced in everything that was asked of him. Beatrix had been less ready to comply but the promise of escape was enough to persuade her. They were finally leaving a place she'd come to hate and fear in equal proportions.

The rain was still persistent enough to make the guards huddle against the walls at the city gate. Only one of them stepped forward to challenge the coach driver. Daniel's hat was pulled down over his forehead so that nobody would identify him as the man who'd ridden out of Paris the previous day. To complete the disguise, he'd even changed his name. Instead of masquerading as Marcel Daron, he handed over the papers he'd taken from

Jacques Serval after their fight. Satisfied that the driver was a French citizen, the guard thrust the document back at him.

'What about your passengers?' he said.

'Don't disturb them, Monsieur,' warned Daniel. 'They're fast asleep. I'm taking them to Mantes for a wedding.' He pulled some more papers from inside his coat and gave them to the guard. 'Neither of *them* is getting married, as you'll see.'

Shielding the papers from the rain with one hand, the guard read the names. One was the genuine passport that had allowed Beatrix Udderzook, a Dutch servant, into the city. The other was a clever forgery and would have got her out again as Emma Lantin, a Frenchwoman. In fact, it was being used to get Janssen out of Paris instead. The guard took a long time inspecting the papers and Daniel began to fear that Beatrix's name would arouse suspicion. After their flight from the house, the name of Amalia Janssen would certainly have been given to the guards at every exit. Daniel had hoped that the servant's name would not be known.

The man looked in the back of the coach and saw two stout women, leaning against each other and apparently asleep. Janssen was wearing a dress borrowed from his servant. The hood of his cape obscured his head and face. At Daniel's suggestion, he'd readily shaved off his beard.

The guard sniggered and handed the papers back to Daniel.

'You're right, my friend,' he said. 'They're an ugly pair.'

The turnkey who'd been knocked out by the butt of a pistol took a long time to recover consciousness. When he did so, he found himself bound hand and foot. A gag prevented him from doing anything but make a muffled noise. Realising that he was under a sheet, he began to thresh around until he rolled off the mattress and on to the floor. As the sheet was peeled away, he lay there half-naked, twitching violently like a large fish hauled on to the deck of a ship. The guard who'd been resting on the bench leapt up in alarm at the sight.

'Where's Janssen?' he demanded.

News of the escape spread around the prison like wildfire, causing anger and amazement. Emanuel Janssen was being held at the Bastille at the express command of King Louis. Nobody looked forward to conveying news of the escape at Versailles. There would be dire repercussions. The fugitive had to be recaptured as soon as possible. When the police were informed, riders were dispatched to every exit of the city with orders that nobody was to leave unless they were wholly above suspicion. Guards on duty were questioned about those whom they'd already allowed out that morning. Information was gathered from all sources and taken back at a gallop to the Lieutenant-General of Police. He scrutinised it for a long time before he pronounced his verdict.

'Janssen is still in the city,' he declared. 'Find him!'

Five miles away, dressed in a more manly fashion now, the tapestry-maker sat in the coach with an arm around his daughter. Beatrix was opposite them while Dopff was perched beside the driver. Since there were five of them, Daniel did not push the horse too fast. Nursing him along, he left the main road and plunged off into some woods where they could rest and eat some of the food stored in the coach. The rain had now stopped and the sun was peeping through the clouds. It was a portent of something but Daniel had no idea what it might be.

CHAPTER TWELVE

The Confederate Army was on the move. Now that the campaign season had drawn to an end with an impasse in the Low Countries, it was possible for a large-scale withdrawal of troops to winter quarters. Dutch regiments maintained a presence on the western borders but most British soldiers were pulled back. The long marches taxed the patience and energy of Hugh Dobbs. As soon as they stopped for a rest on their latest journey, he sat down beneath a tree with his back to the trunk. Tom Hillier was with him.

'I hate marching,' said Dobbs. 'I've got delicate feet.'

'You should've joined the cavalry,' advised Hillier.

'I can't ride a horse.'

'It only takes a little practice. I learnt to ride when I was a boy. We had a couple of ponies at the farm.'

Dobbs became reflective. 'I grew up in a small town with nothing to do except fight with the other boys. I was bored, Tom. That's why I was tricked into joining the army. The recruiting sergeant made it sound such an exciting life. When they marched into town with the drums beating, I was the first in the queue to sign up.'

'When did you start to regret it?'

'When I realised I'd have somebody yelling at me all day long.'

'You get used to that.'

'Well, I haven't. Sergeants are all bloody slave-drivers and corporals are not much better.'

Hillier smiled. 'I'll remind you of that when *you* get promoted.'

'Not me,' said Dobbs. 'I'm not nasty enough and I'd never want the responsibility. What about you?'

'I've only been here five minutes,' Hillier reminded him. 'It's far too early to think about promotion of any kind. That's years away. I've learnt to take one day at a time.'

'When we're on the march, they're all the same.'

'What about marching into battle?'

'That *is* different,' conceded Dobbs. 'The first time I did it, my hands were shaking so much I could hardly hold my drumsticks. I had no idea there'd be so much noise. It was deafening and it went on for hours. The worst part of it was afterwards.'

'Why was that?'

'It was carnage, Tom. The sight of all those dead or dying men made me puke. There were horses, too, hundreds of them scattered across the battlefield, some blown to pieces by cannon. I'd never seen so much blood.'

'It must have been hideous.'

'The stink was terrible. It took days for the burial teams to toss all our casualties into a grave. You could smell the stench from miles away. That's one thing the recruiting sergeant *didn't* warn us about,' he said, bitterly. 'He reckoned that soldiering was an adventure.'

'It is, Hugh.'

'That's not what I've found.'

'I had an adventure right at the start,' said Hillier. 'Some idiot hid my drum at the top of a tree and I had to climb up to get it.'

Dobbs grinned. 'I still don't know how you managed that. I pulled off all of the lower branches to make it more difficult.'

'I was determined to get it back.'

'You must have had help.'

'No,' said Hillier, 'everybody who walked past simply laughed at me. They thought I'd never climb up there.'

Daniel Rawson's advice had been sound. Because he made no mention of the assistance given by the captain, Hillier had earned the respect of the other drummers. It had taken a fight with Dobbs to win him over completely but they were now good friends. The problem for Hillier was that not all officers were as helpful as Captain Rawson.

'There's one benefit about this marching,' said Hillier.

'I haven't noticed it.'

'Major Cracknell has kept out of my way.'

'That man is a swine, Tom.'

'He's an officer so he'll always have the whip hand over us.'

'He picked on you again and again.'

'I know,' said Hillier, thinking of the punishments he'd endured. 'It was very unpleasant. But I think he's lost interest in me now.'

'Don't believe that for a second.'

'Oh?'

'Cruel bastards like Major Cracknell never give up. That man wants to break you, Tom, and he'll keep chasing after you until he does. I'm sorry,' said Dobbs, 'but you mustn't deceive yourself. The major will be back.'

* * *

Now that he'd escaped the cumulative indignities of imprisonment, Emanuel Janssen tried to make light of them in order not to distress his daughter. His claims to have been well treated did not convince Amalia. She could see the change in his appearance. He'd lost weight and looked older. He was pale and drawn with a distant fear in his eyes. Amalia was reminded of a time when her father had been ill and she'd nursed him back to health. She sensed that he'd need even more care to recover from his experience in the Bastille.

'They didn't hurt you in any way?' she asked.

'They took me away from you, Amalia,' he said, 'and nothing could be more painful than that. I spent each and every day worrying about you.'

They were resting in the woods and Janssen was sharing a quiet moment with his daughter. Dopff was as delighted as any of them to see his master and kept glancing across at him to make sure that he really was there. Certain that they'd be caught before they left Paris, Beatrix had been terrified throughout their flight. With the tension suddenly eased, she sobbed incessantly with relief. Lacking the words to console her, Dopff put his arms around her and patted her back. Over her shoulder, he took another look at Janssen and smiled in awe, as if beholding a miracle.

Daniel had left them beside the coach while he walked back to the edge of the woods. Through his telescope, he'd been watching the main road for signs of pursuit. Since the escape would definitely have been discovered by now, he'd expected search parties to be sent out but none appeared on the main road. Daniel concluded that they must have reason to believe the fugitives were still within the city walls. It was a boon to them. Their journey through France would be much easier without a posse on their heels but he was very conscious that other dangers would lie ahead. After a few more minutes, Daniel went back to rejoin the others. Janssen immediately came across to him and shook his hand warmly.

'Amalia has been telling me what you did for them, Captain Rawson,' he said, effusively. 'We're forever in your debt.'

'I did what was expected of me, that's all,' said Daniel.

'You're far too modest. What you achieved beggars belief. The Duke of Marlborough will hear of this.'

'My task is to make sure that you reach him safely.'

'According to my daughter, you can do *anything*.'

'That's very flattering but quite untrue.'

'Amalia rarely exaggerates, Captain Rawson.'

'I think it wiser if you don't call me that,' said Daniel. 'We're still on French soil. Until we leave it, my name is Marcel Daron.'

'I'll remember that, Monsieur Daron.'

'And, in the event of our being stopped, the rest of you must answer to the names on your forged papers.'

'Does that mean I'm to travel as Mademoiselle Lantin?' asked Janssen with a wry smile. 'Posing as a woman was a new experience for me. I'm glad I didn't have to speak as Emma Lantin.'

'That will be Beatrix's name from now on. We must be on our way,' he continued, raising his voice to address the others. 'We need to put distance between ourselves and Paris.'

Amalia and Beatrix returned to the coach and climbed in. Dopff clambered up on to the driving seat. Before he got into the vehicle, Janssen had a question for Daniel.

'How good is your memory?' he asked.

'It's fairly reliable, I think.'

'I'm sure it's better than mine. We need to have a long talk. The last time I was at Versailles, I overheard discussions about the war that would be of great interest to the Duke. I want to tell someone about them before I forget.'

'You could always put them on paper,' said Daniel.

'I was about to do that when I was arrested so I was unable to pass on the information to a British agent in the city. I think I'd prefer to confide in you,' said Janssen. 'As a soldier, you'll be able to decide if the intelligence has any real value.'

'I will.'

'Was it explained to you how I worked in Paris?'

'Yes,' said Daniel. 'Whenever you had anything that might be useful, you passed it on to a man named Pierre Lefeaux.'

'He was such a delightful fellow,' recalled Janssen. 'He and his wife became good friends of mine. Pierre was so courageous. He made what I was doing feel very ordinary by comparison. He was the one who took the risks. I don't suppose that you had any dealings with them, by any chance?'

It was not the time to tell him the truth about the fate of his two friends. Janssen was still elated by his escape. Daniel felt that it would be wrong to deprive him of his joy or to upset the others by describing what he'd seen when he visited the Lefeaux household.

'No,' he said, shaking his head. 'I never had that pleasure.'

Ronan Flynn was a dutiful son-in-law. Twice a week, he drove Charlotte and their baby to the village where her parents had their cottage, making sure that he had a supply of the day's bread with them. It was only three miles away from Paris so he could get there and back in an afternoon. When his wife was dressed for the outing, he helped her up on to the cart then passed up

Louise. Wrapped in a shawl, the baby was fast asleep and even the joggling of the cart and the tumult in the streets didn't wake her up. The little family was off on what they believed would be an enjoyable excursion. As they approached one of the city gates, however, they encountered a problem. The gates were locked and armed guards stood in front of them, turning people back. Charlotte was worried.

'What's wrong?' she said.

'I'll go and find out, my darling.'

'Mother and Father are expecting us, Ronan.'

'We'll get to them somehow,' he promised.

Handing her the reins, he hopped down from the cart and walked past a line of others wanting to leave the capital. There was a coach, two carts and a number of horsemen. Flynn strode to the head of the queue where a man was arguing vociferously with one of the guards. It reached the point where the guard lifted his musket to threaten him. Raising both hands in a gesture of surrender, the man backed away and swore under his breath. Flynn spoke to the guard.

'We have to visit my wife's parents,' he said.

'Nobody is leaving today,' warned the guard.

'What's the reason?'

'All the city gates have been shut. Visitors can come in but we've been ordered to let nobody out unless they have authority.'

'Well, *we* have authority,' said Flynn. 'We're good citizens and we pay our taxes regularly. That surely entitles us to come and go as we wish.' He turned to point down the queue. 'That's my wife, sitting on the cart with our baby in her arms. Surely, you can let us out?'

'No, Monsieur.'

'But we're completely harmless.'

'That makes no difference. We have our orders.'

'Who issued these bleeding orders?' asked Flynn, temper rising.

'It was the Lieutenant-General of Police.'

'Did he have the grace to say why?'

'He did, Monsieur,' replied the guard. 'An important prisoner has escaped from the Bastille. We must make sure that he doesn't leave Paris.'

'He must be very important if you're taking measures like this. Who is the fellow?'

'That's none of your business.'

'It *is* my business if it spoils a family visit. Who did they have locked away in the Bastille? To cause all this upheaval, he must have been a foreign prince at least.'

'He was a Dutchman,' said the guard. 'That's all I know. Now please turn back.'

Seeing that the guard was adamant, Flynn gave up. It was annoying to him and would be a grave disappointment to his wife's parents. They'd be very anxious when Flynn and Charlotte failed to turn up and their free bread would be sorely missed. The Irishman had almost reached the cart when he realised what the guard had just told him. A Dutchman had somehow escaped from the Bastille and was on the run. Into Flynn's mind came the image of three guests who'd stayed at his house recently. He thought about a boat that had been hired and a coach that was sought. He remembered a number of isolated clues that now fitted neatly together to make a perfect whole. Forgetting his anger at the disruption to their visit, he opened his mouth wide and roared with laughter.

'Dan Rawson!' he said to himself. 'You're a clever old devil!'

* * *

The coach kept up steady speed. Daniel was careful to pace the horse, stopping occasionally to let it rest or drink from a stream. When they set off after one such break, Amalia volunteered to sit beside Daniel, allowing Dopff to travel inside the coach for once. Warmed by the afternoon sun, she surveyed the rolling countryside ahead.

'How far will we go today?' she wondered.

'As far as we can before the light disappears,' he said. 'We'll look for a wayside inn. We'll have been driving for several hours by then. The horse will deserve a good feed and a long rest.'

'What happened to your own horse?'

'I had to trade it in to buy this coach.'

'We must pay something of the cost,' said Amalia, seriously. 'It's wrong that you should pay for everything. I have plenty of money as well as my jewellery.'

'Hold on to it in case we need it.'

'Are you sure?'

'I still have some reserves left.'

'Very well, Daniel.'

'And remember that when we're with strangers, I'm not Daniel anymore. I'm Marcel Daron. The others have been warned.'

'I won't forget.'

Sitting close together, neither of them noticed the discomfort of the bare wooden seat or the loud creaking of the vehicle as it swayed to and fro. They were wholly preoccupied with each other. When one wheel hit a deep pothole, however, they were very much aware of it. The coach lurched violently sideways for a second before righting itself with a bump. Amalia was thrown against Daniel and he put an arm around her, pulling her close in a moment of intimacy that caused a frisson in both of them. It was minutes before he released her.

'When we find a suitable inn,' said Daniel at length, 'I suggest that you and Beatrix share one room while your father occupies another with Kees.'

'What about you?'

'I'll sleep in the coach.'

'You can't sleep in this,' she protested.

'One of us has to,' he explained, 'and I'm the only person with any weapons. I want everything of real value to be hidden in the coach in case we're stopped and searched. The tapestry will remain here as well. Someone has to stand guard during the night.'

'But it's so unfair on you.'

'Then you can act as a sentry instead,' he teased.

'We could guard the coach together,' she said, blurting out the suggestion without considering what it would entail.

'I don't think your father would approve of that, appealing as the idea is. In any case, you'll be busy elsewhere, keeping Beatrix under control. If anyone is likely to give us away, it's your servant. You have to watch her carefully.'

'Beatrix is much better since we left Paris.'

'She still needs a close eye kept on her,' he said. 'At the first sign of trouble, I'm afraid that she may let us all down.'

'Then I'll do as you say.'

They rode on in companionable silence for a while, scanning the horizon and feeling a slight chill as the sun was obscured by clouds. Every so often the wheels would squelch through a puddle left by the heavy rain and throw moisture into the air. Though animals grazed in some of the fields, they didn't see anybody else for miles. Daniel was already planning ahead, thinking about the next stage of their journey and trying to work out when and where to cross the French border. Amalia's mind was fixed on something beyond that.

'What will happen when we reach Holland?' she said.

'I'm to take you to The Hague.'

'Why?'

'Because people there wish to hear about your father's stay in France,' said Daniel. 'Nobody else has ever got so close to King Louis. What he can tell us may affect the progress of the war next year.'

'What then?'

'You'll be allowed to return home to Amsterdam and resume your normal life. Once everyone realises that your father didn't betray his country, he'll be seen as something of a hero.'

'I don't think he feels like a hero. He's still very shaken by what happened to him in the Bastille. It will always haunt him.'

'The ugly memories will fade in time, I'm sure.'

'What about you?' she asked. 'If and when you take us back to The Hague, what will you do afterwards?'

'I'll return to my regiment to give a full report.'

'And then?'

'I'll await the return of our commander-in-chief before I can rejoin his staff. Oh,' he added, looking deep into her eyes, 'there is something else I intend to do.'

'And what's that?'

'I'll find time to visit Amsterdam and call on a very special friend.' She laughed in delight. 'Can I have an address, please?'

After a testing march, they set up camp early that evening. The first thing that Hugh Dobbs did was to go to the nearby stream so that he could dangle his bare feet in the water. Tom Hillier sat beside him, letting his own feet get washed by the current.

'We'll have a decent rest at long last,' said Dobbs. 'We'll be here for a few days at least.'

'How do you know that?'

'I overheard Lieutenant Ainsley say so.'

Hillier chuckled. 'One of these days, the lieutenant will catch you listening and box your ears.'

'That's why I always loiter near him. He's never really strict. If I was caught eavesdropping by Major Cracknell,' said Dobbs, 'he wouldn't just box my ears, he'd cut the pair of them off.'

'We haven't seen the major all day,' noted Hillier.

'I daresay he's seen us, Tom.'

'Why is he keeping his distance?'

'He's just biding his time.' Dobbs picked up a stone and tossed it idly into the water. 'Have you heard from Sergeant Welbeck?'

'Not a single word, Hugh.'

'He's a poor bloody uncle.'

'I told you before,' said Hillier. 'He denies there's any family tie between us. I was hurt at first but I've come to see that he's doing me a favour. If I kept turning to him all the time for support, I'd never be my own man.'

'I still think he's letting you down badly, Tom. Ah, well,' he said with an arm around his friend, 'since nobody else will teach you, I'll have to take you under my wing. We'll wait until tomorrow night.'

'What for, Hugh?'

'Didn't you see that town we passed a couple of miles back?'

'Yes, it was very pretty.'

'It's more than pretty,' said Dobbs with a cackle. 'We camped near there two years ago and some of us sneaked into the town for some sport. It was amazing, Tom. It cost me a week's wages but it was worth every bit of it. She was the best I've ever had.'

'What are you talking about?'

'With a brisk walk, we could get there in under half an hour, though it might take us a lot longer to get back to camp.'

'Why?'

'We'll be exhausted, you buffoon.'

Hillier was perplexed. 'I'm not sure that I follow you.'

'Manhood,' said Dobbs. 'I'm talking about satisfying our urges between the warm thighs of a woman. You can't hold on to your virginity for ever, Tom. It's high time you learnt to fuck.'

To reinforce the message, he pushed his friend into the stream with a big splash. The cold water helped to cool Hillier's blushes.

The inn was on the edge of a village and it served their needs well. While the others slept inside the building, Daniel stayed in the courtyard, curled up inside the coach with a pistol at his side. He shared an early breakfast with his friends, leaving an ostler to harness the horse. Before they left, Daniel took Kees Dopff aside.

'I'd like you to sit beside me today,' he said. 'Have you ever driven a cart or a coach?' Dopff shook his head. 'Then I'll have to teach you,' Daniel went on. 'In case something happens to me, you must be able to take over. There's nobody else I can ask.'

Dopff was pleased to be offered the chance of taking the reins but worried by the suggestion that Daniel might not be with them indefinitely. He could not imagine how the four of them would possibly survive without him. The others climbed into the coach and the little Dutchman took his place beside Daniel. It gave him a sense of being useful again. Having lost his roles as cook and keeper of the tapestry, he was ready to embrace a new challenge. When Daniel flicked the reins to set the horse off, Dopff watched the driver's every move.

It was a dull day with low cloud and the promise of more rain. Daniel hoped that they were not caught in another downpour. He pushed the horse a little harder than before without taxing it too much. When the animal was trotting over level ground, Daniel handed the reins over for the first time. Dopff took them nervously as if expecting the horse to react mutinously to the change of driver. Instead it continued to trot at the same unvarying pace. Dopff turned to Daniel and nodded happily. He was clearly going to enjoy being in charge. Controlling the coach seemed remarkably easy.

His confidence steadily grew. It was soon dented. They came to a series of deep ruts that made the whole vehicle sway crazily from side to side then Dopff mistakenly took the horse off the track altogether. When they crested a low hill, he saw another problem looming. At the bottom of the slope was a ford, the fast-flowing water creating white foam. Fearing that they'd be trapped in the stream, he thrust the reins at Daniel but they were immediately put back into his hands. Dopff was even more nervous when Daniel jumped to the ground from the moving vehicle and took the bridle to lead the horse through the water. It was very shallow and hardly reached his shins. Safe on the other bank, Dopff felt a sense of pride. He'd been alone on the driving seat when they'd negotiated the hazard. He grinned for a whole mile.

They paused at midday to have a light meal. Since Dopff was eager to renew his education as a coach driver, Daniel let him take the reins again. The Dutchman's main concern was to keep the horse on the winding track. Daniel, on the other hand, was more worried about the weather. A storm was brewing. The clouds were darker and more menacing. Though the windows were mere open rectangles, those in the coach did have a measure of protection. The two drivers had none. Seeing a copse ahead, Daniel wondered if it was better to seek shelter there until the storm had blown over.

In the event, he was given no choice between stopping and driving on. Shortly after they entered the copse, they had unwelcome company. Three horsemen appeared out of nowhere. One blocked their passage, forcing Dopff to pull on the reins and bring the coach to a halt, while the other two came up behind. All three of them held pistols. The leader of the highwaymen was a handsome man in his thirties with a well-groomed black beard.

'Well, now,' he said, smirking, 'what do we have here?'

'We're in a hurry, friend,' replied Daniel. 'We don't wish to be caught in the rain. Pray stand aside, if you will.'

'I will not. I want to see who your passengers are.'

There was nothing that Daniel could do. While the leader flicked his pistol to make Daniel and Dopff hold their hands in the air, the other men ordered the passengers to get out. Beatrix alighted first, petrified by the sight of loaded weapons. Janssen came next, helping his daughter after him. As soon as the men saw Amalia, they licked their lips. One of them, a squat individual with a patch over one eye, dismounted in order to search them. Choosing Amalia first, he took the opportunity to grope her. She stepped back in disgust and her father tried to push the man away. Janssen was punched in the face and fell back against the coach. He had no more strength to resist being searched. Beatrix screamed when the man ran his hands over her. It was a disappointing haul. He held up the few valuables he'd managed to find on them.

'Search these two,' said the leader, indicating Daniel and

Dopff. 'Maybe they'll have something worth stealing.'

They were made to climb down from the driving seat. The man found a small purse on Dopff and an even smaller one on Daniel. Of more interest to him was the pistol that Daniel was carrying. It was tossed up to the leader.

'This is an army pistol,' he observed, studying it. 'Did you serve in the army?'

'Yes,' replied Daniel, 'and I was proud to do so.'

'How many years did you follow the drum?'

'Twelve.'

'That may save your life,' said the other, weighing him up. 'I was a soldier myself. I like a man who fights for his country.'

'What shall we do with the others?' asked the searcher.

'I haven't decided yet.'

'I say we shoot the two men and let the women live so that we can take it in turns at night.'

'Oh, the ladies will survive, have no fear of that.'

'Shall I kill this one?' said the squat man, holding a pistol to Janssen's temple. 'He's no use to us at all.'

'Yes, he is,' cried Daniel. 'Shoot him and you throw away the chance to make a lot of money.' He turned to the leader. 'Tell him to lower the pistol.'

'Do as he suggests,' said the leader and the man obeyed. 'Now what's this about a lot of money?'

'Is the name of Emanuel Janssen familiar to you?' asked Daniel, looking around the three men. When he received blank stares from the trio, he pressed on. 'This gentleman is the finest tapestry-maker in Europe. His work hangs in the capital cities of almost every nation. He and his daughter have been living in Paris where he's been weaving his latest tapestry. This,' he went on, touching Dopff, 'is his assistant.' Dopff smiled uneasily.

'We're on our way to deliver a tapestry commissioned by the Bishop of Beauvais. If you don't believe me, we can show it to you.'

'Do that,' said the leader, interest aroused. 'But let's have no tricks, soldier. Make one false move and I'll shoot you between the eyes.'

Daniel reached into the coach to bring out the tapestry then he and Dopff carefully unfolded it on the grass. The highwaymen were astonished at the size and quality of it.

'Nothing but the finest materials have been used,' said Daniel.

'Yes,' said Janssen, taking his cue. 'What you are looking at is Picardy wool, Italian silk and gold and silver thread from Cyprus.'

Daniel took over again. 'Imagine the cost,' he said. 'The bishop is very wealthy. He wishes to have another tapestry made by Emanuel Janssen. Can you hear what I'm saying to you? Hold the tapestry and its creator to ransom, and you'd all be rich men.'

'That makes sense,' urged the squat man.

'Be quiet, Gustave!' snapped the leader.

'Bishops always have far too much money.'

'True enough. I'd be delighted to make one of them part with it. First, I wish to know something,' he went on, turning a suspicious eye on Daniel. 'If that tapestry is destined for the Bishop of Beauvais, why does it depict a battle? Surely a prelate would choose something more spiritual to hang on his wall?'

'You're clearly unaware of his links with the army,' said Daniel, inventing the tale as he went along. 'In his younger days, he served as an army chaplain. His brother holds the rank of general and actually fought in the battle you see laid out before you. It will not hang in the bishop's palace. It's a gift for his brother. The second tapestry,' he explained, 'will show a religious scene.' He felt a first spot of rain. 'You can see how delicate this is,' he went on. 'With your permission, we'll fold it up again.'

'Do that, soldier.'

As Daniel tried to bend down, Janssen stepped forward to stop him. He insisted on folding the tapestry himself. Aided by Dopff, he handled it with a care and reverence that showed he must have woven it. They lifted it gently back into the coach. Any lingering doubts the leader might have about Emanuel Janssen were swept away. The rain now began to fall in earnest.

'What do we do?' asked Gustave.

'Get them in the coach and take them to the house,' said the leader. 'We need to write a letter to the Bishop of Beauvais.'

The house was less than a mile away. It turned out to be a derelict cottage on an abandoned farm. With a loaded pistol levelled at him by one of the men, Daniel drove the coach into a dilapidated barn and brought it to a halt. In defiance of the countless holes in the roof, the horse managed to find a dry spot. The passengers were ordered out and tied up in turn. Daniel, Janssen and Dopff were bound hand and foot. The two women simply had their hands tied behind their back. Gustave bent over to steal a kiss from Amalia. The leader grabbed him by the collar and pulled him back.

'Show more respect,' he warned. 'If I learn that either of these women has been molested, you'll get nothing of the ransom.'

'That's unfair!' wailed Gustave.

'Waiting heightens the appetite.'

'I'm ready for her *now*.'

'You'll get your turn in due course. Stay and guard them.'

'Where will you be?'

'Armand and I are going to the house to compose the letter. You can have the pleasure of delivering it to the Bishop of Beauvais.'

'I want another kind of pleasure first.'

'Later.'

'Yes,' said Armand, shooting a lascivious glance at Amalia, 'while you're riding to Beauvais, we'll be playing cards.'

The leader smiled. 'The winner has the pretty one and,' he went on, pointing to Beatrix, 'the loser gets the ugly one.'

'I want them both,' said Gustave.

'For the moment, you can simply look at them.'

After issuing another warning to Gustave, the leader ran across to the cottage with Armand, leaving the captives seated on the ground in a semicircle. Gustave walked around them to make sure that they were securely bound. When he reached Amalia, he leered at her.

'Don't you dare touch my daughter!' yelled Janssen.

'I'll do what I like when the time comes.'

'When you get your ransom,' Daniel told him, 'you'll have enough money to buy any woman you choose.'

Gustave leered again. 'I'll have this one free!'

Sitting down a few yards away, he rested his pistol on his thigh and ogled Amalia. She lowered her head in despair. Beatrix had already resorted to prayer, closing her eyes and sending urgent pleas up to heaven. Dopff was utterly distraught, fearing for the safety of the tapestry as much as for his own life. Janssen was grateful to Daniel, knowing that his intervention had saved two of them from being shot dead. All that Daniel had done, however, was to buy some time. When it was discovered that the Bishop of Beauvais had no knowledge of any tapestry woven by

Emanuel Janssen, the highwaymen would wreak their revenge. Amalia and Beatrix would be raped. In all likelihood, the men would be brutally killed. The beautiful tapestry woven at royal command would be in the hands of ruthless bandits. Turning a woeful face to Daniel, Janssen spoke to him in Dutch.

'Is there *nothing* we can do?'

CHAPTER THIRTEEN

Daniel Rawson was concentrating hard. All that he had gained so far was a temporary respite. Had he not distracted the highwaymen with the promise of ransom money, he, Dopff and Janssen would almost certainly be dead now, leaving the women at the mercy of their captors. As it was, there was only limited time before the other two men returned to the barn to take their pleasure with Amalia and Beatrix. That thought burnt inside his brain. The others were looking to him for salvation. Powerless themselves, their only hope was that Daniel could somehow come to their rescue. He could feel the intensity of their desperation. It spurred him on.

There was one small but significant advantage. Gustave had no interest in him. Through his single, glinting eye, the only person that their guard wished to look at was Amalia. Grinning inanely, he let his imagination roam, undressing, fondling, biting, abusing her at will, sucking all the sweetness out of her lips. Daniel had already been working to loosen the rope around his wrists. He and Dopff were farthest away from Gustave, sitting side by side. Daniel wriggled even closer so that he could reach behind Dopff's back. With his own bonds slackened, he had enough freedom of movement to untie the other man's rope, instructing him to return the favour. Dopff's hands were trembling as he plucked at the rope holding Daniel's arms together but he managed to release the knot eventually. Unseen by their captor, the two men shook hands behind their backs. It was a start.

Daniel's ankles were still tightly bound and it would be more difficult to untie them. Gustave was sure to see him out of the corner of his eye. Somehow he had to be distracted. The man's impatience came to Daniel's aid. Throbbing with lust and dazzled by the beauty of the defenceless young woman sitting only yards away, he hauled himself up to take a first kiss from Amalia. When she turned her head away in horror, he grabbed her hair and forced her to face him.

'Leave her alone!' yelled Janssen.

'Why?' taunted Gustave, hitting him across the cheek. 'What are you going to do to stop me?'

'I'll tell the others.'

Gustave laughed derisively and went back to Amalia.

'Wait!' shouted Daniel.

'Be quiet!' snarled Gustave, annoyed to be deprived of his kiss yet again. 'I'll deal with you in a minute.'

'But I've got some good news for you.'

The highwayman glowered at him. 'What do you mean?'

'I can tell you why these people didn't have much money with them,' said Daniel. 'They've hidden their valuables in the coach.'

Janssen was outraged. 'Why tell him that?'

'One of the seats lifts up,' Daniel continued. 'There's money and jewellery there along with some saddlebags.'

'Is this true?' demanded Gustave.

'See for yourself if you don't believe me.'

Spitting on the floor, Gustave wiped the back of his hand across his mouth and went to investigate. Janssen was appalled at what he saw as a betrayal and Amalia stared at Daniel in disbelief. He ignored both of them. As soon as Gustave opened the door of the coach to search inside, Daniel swiftly undid the rope around his ankles then kept it in his hands as he leapt to his feet. Gustave, meanwhile, had lifted the seat to discover the valuables. He held one of the purses in his hand and felt its weight. His cry of triumph became an instant gurgle of pain as Daniel slipped the rope over the man's head to use as a garrotte. Taken completely by surprise, the Frenchman was slow to react. Daniel was merciless. Using all of his considerable strength, he tightened the rope by degrees and gradually squeezed the last vestiges of life out of the highwayman. Gustave struggled, flailed his arms and even tried to kick his attacker's legs from under him but Daniel was far too powerful. With a final twist of the rope, he pulled Gustave's head backwards then released him. The dead body slumped to the floor.

Amalia was shocked, Beatrix horrified and Janssen ashamed that he'd misjudged Daniel. Thrilled to have helped in the escape, Dopff held up his hands to show that they were free then undid the rope around his ankles. The first person Daniel released was Amalia, lifting her up to hug her. When the others were untied, he retrieved Gustave's pistol from the floor and tucked it into his belt.

'We must go,' he said, ushering them into the coach. 'The Bishop of Beauvais will be waiting for his tapestry.'

Though the cottage was largely derelict, the highwaymen had taken the trouble to make part of it habitable so that it could be used from time to time as a place to spend the night.

Upstairs rooms had been allowed to decay but the parlour and kitchen had not. They'd repaired doors, made new shutters and supported the main beam with a stout timber upright. When the place had been swept clean and mattresses brought in, it was a useful hiding place. The two men sat either side of a table in the kitchen, drinking some of the wine they stored there. It had been a profitable day and they had much to celebrate. After a long discussion about its contents, Armand had penned a ransom demand in spidery handwriting.

The leader of the little gang had then produced a pack of cards so that they could decide who'd first have the privilege of an hour naked on one of the mattresses with their lovely female captive. It added spice and incentive to the game. As the cards were dealt, they were in high spirits. Their capture of the travellers had been a stroke of good fortune. Money and pleasure had been dropped into their laps and there was promise of a huge ransom. Armand picked up his cards and smiled inwardly. With such a hand, he felt that he was bound to win. It was the other man who heard the noise.

'What was that?' said the leader, straining his ears.

'I heard nothing.'

'It sounded like hoof beats.'

'You must be mistaken,' said Armand, drooling over the cards he held. 'All I can hear is the sound of the wind.'

'Let's go and see,' said the other, getting to his feet.

'Play the game first. I want to win.'

'That can wait, Armand. There was a definite noise.'

Opening the rear door of the cottage, he went out into the rain and looked towards the open door of the barn. The coach was no longer there and their own horses had also disappeared.

'Armand!' he cried. 'Come quickly!'

He ran across to the barn and saw Gustave stretched out on the floor, his neck bruised and his head twisted at an unnatural angle. Armand soon arrived to stand over the dead body. The highwaymen were mystified. During their time in the cottage, they'd lost everything.

'How could they possibly have done it?' wondered Armand.

The leader pondered. 'It was the coachman,' he decided.

They rode for miles before they felt it was safe to stop. Dopff had driven the coach, pulling along the horse tethered to it. Daniel had taken charge of the other horses stolen from the highwaymen, riding one and leading the other by the reins. Having spent all of his life in the army, he'd often been in situations where he'd had to kill or be killed. He never harboured regrets. The moment that Gustave had been strangled, Daniel had forgotten him but the death could not be so easily dismissed by the others. Beatrix was still sickened by what she'd witnessed, Dopff was dismayed and Janssen, though grateful to be rescued by Daniel for the second time, was aghast at the cold efficiency with which he'd taken a man's life.

Amalia was caught up in a tangle of emotions. She felt relief, disgust, hope, fear and remorse. Daniel had saved her from being raped and intense gratitude was thus uppermost in her mind. But he'd done so by strangling someone to death in front of her and it had been nauseating to watch. It made her look at Daniel in a slightly different way. Loving him for his bravery, she was also wary of him now. His strength was frightening. She'd only seen his kindness and tenderness before. Watching him as a soldier, trained to kill, had been a chastening experience. While accepting that it had been a necessary death, she was still very disturbed by it.

The storm had spent its force now and no longer battered them. As the others tried to get their breath back, Daniel inspected the saddlebags on the three horses. They were full of weapons and of plunder from previous ambushes. He gathered all the money up and put it under the seat in the coach. Then he selected a dagger and a pistol, glad that there was plenty of ammunition to go with it. There was still enough light for him to study the map he'd kept hidden in his coat. Amalia and her father came over to interrupt him.

'Where are we going?' asked Janssen.

'Well, it won't be to Beauvais,' replied Daniel, 'I can tell you that much. We need to strike north-east. Since I'll ride one of the horses, the load will be lightened somewhat. We can press on harder.'

'I can ride as well, if need be, and Amalia is a very competent horsewoman. Riding is one of the few things we did together.'

'I enjoy it,' she confirmed. 'It was something I missed in Paris because Father was too busy. I'll be glad to take one of the horses.'

'That will speed us up considerably,' said Daniel. 'Kees will be our coachman and Beatrix his only passenger. The coach will be much easier to pull.' He indicated the three animals. 'Choose any horse you wish.'

Janssen went off to do so but Amalia lingered beside Daniel.

'I haven't been able to thank you properly,' she said. 'You saved me from that awful man. I hated what you did but I admired your courage in doing it.'

'I'm sorry you had to be there when it happened.'

'None of us had any choice in the matter.'

'We'll take care not to be caught like that again,' he said.

She looked over her shoulder. 'What about those men?'

'They'll never catch up with us on foot, Amalia.'

'They might find other horses somehow,' she said, 'then they'd be certain to come after us.'

'They'd be very foolish to do so,' said Daniel. 'We have their weapons and ammunition. In any case,' he added, folding up his map, 'they'll be riding in the wrong direction altogether. They think we're going to Beauvais.'

Tom Hillier was looking forward to the experience with an uneasy mixture of timidity, excitement and trepidation. At first he tried to get out of it, providing endless feeble excuses. Hugh Dobbs refused to accept any of them, insisting that he joined the three of them who intended to visit the town that night. Hillier was committed. He liked girls but had had very little to do with them when working on the family farm. It was only at dances and harvest festival celebrations that he spent any real time in female company and he'd always felt awkward in doing so. It was one thing to share ribald jokes with his new friends but quite another to go to bed with a woman. The possible fear of failure tormented him.

Some armies allowed prostitutes to travel with the troops or gave them ready access wherever they pitched camp. The Duke of Marlborough had done his best to stamp out such practices, believing that soldiers fought best when not distracted by pleasures of the flesh. Women did accompany his army with the baggage wagons but they were the actual or common-law wives of particular individuals and, as such, were not seen as posing any threat. Marlborough had fought in armies where venereal diseases had disabled some of the men and he didn't want his own soldiers to be affected in that way. Lust, however, could never be wholly controlled, especially in virile young men. Those eager for sexual passion would always find it somewhere.

As the hour for departure drew near, Hillier lay on his back in the tent with his hands behind his head, wishing for a thunderstorm or some other obstacle to prevent them from leaving. Dobbs rolled over and shook him by the arm.

'It won't be long now, Tom,' he said.

'You'd better go without me, Hugh. I don't feel well.'

'I was as sick as a dog before my first time but she made it so easy for me. My head was in the clouds for days.'

'What if we're caught leaving the camp?' asked Hillier.

'We won't be.'

'I still think it's too risky.'

'The only risk you take is of catching something nasty between the sheets and that won't happen here. The women are as clean as can be. What you'll be getting is healthy recreation.'

'I'm not sure that I'm old enough, Hugh.'

'Of course, you are,' said Dobbs. 'I was only fifteen.'

There was no escape. Resigning himself to the inevitable, Hillier brooded on what lay ahead. Two of the other drummers were joining the escapade. As he listened to them trading memoirs about previous visits to brothels, Hillier felt even more unready for the challenge. The time eventually came for them to set out. The camp was in darkness. Dobbs took the lead because he'd already reconnoitred the position of the picquets. They followed him in single file with Hillier at the rear. Dodging between the bushes, they reached the stream and paddled across it. Hillier caught up with his friend.

'My breeches are soaked, Hugh,' he complained.

'They'll have plenty of time to dry when you take them off,' said Dobbs. 'Now stay close and keep your voice down.'

Only when they were well clear of the camp could the four

of them relax and talk freely. Hillier still worried about the consequences of leaving camp without permission but the others were obsessed with what lay ahead. Their language became cruder, their expectations more colourful. Hillier was made to feel like a callow outsider. Dobbs poked him with a friendly elbow.

'Don't worry, Tom,' he said. 'If you lived on a farm, you probably fucked a sheep or two in your time,' he added jokingly.

'We kept dairy cows.'

'Then you must have seen them mounted by a bull. What they did was only natural. It's the same with a woman. You're the lusty young bull mounting a warm, welcoming cow with lovely udders to play with and suck. I'll wager that you love every second.'

Hillier did not share his confidence. When the town was at last conjured out of the gloom, his mouth went dry and sweat broke out on his face. Dobbs clearly had an excellent memory. He picked his way through the streets as if he'd been raised there. Candles flickered in some windows but most houses were dark. Dobbs stopped outside one where a finger of light could be seen between the shutters.

'This is it,' he announced, rubbing his hands.

Hillier looked up at it with apprehension. The house was large. Built of local stone, it had a thatched roof with prominent eaves. From inside they could hear the sound of muffled voices. As if in proof of its credentials as a brothel, the door suddenly opened and two soldiers tumbled out, laughing happily as they did up their uniforms. They rolled off down the street on their way back to camp.

'There you are,' said Dobbs, 'I told you they always give you what you want. Knock the door, Tom.'

Hillier quailed. 'Me?'

'You must be first.'

'I'd rather wait, Hugh.'

'Stop arguing and knock the door.'

'Yes,' said one of the others, 'we want our money's worth.'

Hillier stepped forward and tapped on the door, scared of what he might find on the other side of it. The door was opened by a woman holding a candle. He could see that she was fat, middle-aged and raddled. She wore a silk dress with a low décolletage and bared her snaggly teeth in a welcoming grin.

'Don't just stand there, Tom,' said Dobbs, pushing him over the threshold. 'Manhood awaits you.'

For the second time in a row, Daniel chose to spend the night sleeping upright in the coach. It stood beside the stables in which their horses had been stalled. The inn was fairly remote but he took no chances. Two loaded pistols were at hand in case of nocturnal intruders. The brush with the highwaymen had been unpleasant but it had yielded rewards. They now had three horses at their disposal and had found a substantial amount of money in the saddlebags. Daniel was sitting on top of it.

He came awake periodically to check that all was well then returned to his slumbers. It was when he opened his eyes for the third time that he thought he glimpsed movement in the darkness. He reached for one of the pistols and stared through a window. Nothing was there yet he was convinced he'd seen something. Deciding that it must have been a dog or even a fox, he put the pistol aside. Almost immediately he snatched it up again as he heard footsteps.

'Daniel,' called a voice softly. 'Are you there?'

It was Amalia, wrapped up in a cloak. When she reached the

coach, she smiled in through the window. He opened the door and helped her in.

'What are *you* doing here at this time of night?' he said.

'I wanted to speak to you.'

'There are more convenient moments to do that, Amalia.'

'We're never really alone during the day.'

'Sit down,' he invited, moving over so that she could perch beside him. 'Beatrix will raise the whole inn when she realises that you're not there in the bed.'

'She's a heavy sleeper,' said Amalia. 'You'd have to fire a pistol to wake her up once she dozes off.'

'What did you want to say to me?'

'I owe you an apology, Daniel.'

'That's not true at all.'

'It is,' she insisted. 'After all you'd done for us, I didn't trust you. When you told that man where we'd hidden our valuables, I thought you were only trying to save your own skin. Instead, you merely wanted to distract him.' She gave a shrug. 'I'm ashamed that I thought so badly of you at the time.'

'Not at all,' he said, stroking her arm. 'Your father and the others must have felt exactly the same. Kees had managed to undo the rope around my wrists. I needed Gustave's attention elsewhere so that I could untie my feet. You know the rest.'

'That's the other apology I must make.'

'What is?'

'I was shocked at what you did to that man. There was a moment when I actually felt sorry for him even though he was so repulsive. I'd never seen anything like that before.'

'I hope you never have to do so again, Amalia.'

'It's been in my mind ever since,' she said. 'I was lying in bed thinking about it. Looking back, it was so unjust of me. It was almost as if I was blaming you for what happened whereas you *had* to do what you did. That man deserved it. We both know what he had in mind for me and Beatrix. The horror was unimaginable.'

'No apology is necessary,' he told her.

'I believe that it is. I thought ill of you.'

'To save lives, you often have to take one, Amalia. It's a rule of military life. I wasn't going to let that oaf molest you. He'll get no sympathy from me.'

'Nor from me,' she said.

'Are the others still sickened by what I did?'

'Beatrix will never get over it. She talked of nothing else until she fell asleep. She began to wonder what you did to that man who was watching our house in Paris.'

'It's just as well she wasn't there at the time.'

'Father was upset,' Amalia went on, 'but more for my sake than his own. He was hurt that I should've been forced to watch but I'm not as delicate as he seems to think. What happened to us in Paris has made me a lot stronger.'

'Adversity can often bring out the best in people.'

'As for Kees, I fancy that he was as revolted as the rest of us.'

'I hope they'll all forgive me in time.'

'They *admire* you, Daniel, but you did upset them.'

'Everyone likes pork on their plate but nobody wants to see the pig being killed.' She recoiled in surprise. 'I'm sorry,' he said, 'that was a rather vulgar way of putting it.'

'Nevertheless, it was probably accurate.'

'You must go back to bed, Amalia.'

'Are we still friends?' she asked, quietly.

'We're very good friends,' he told her. 'Nothing will change that. Do you feel any better for speaking to me?'

'Yes, I do.'

'Then go back to your room. I'll walk you to the door.'

'There's no hurry, is there?'

'We both need our sleep.'

'I'm enjoying it here, Daniel.'

'You should be resting in a proper bed.'

'Can I stay just a little longer?'

'It's late, Amalia.'

'I'll go in a few minutes,' she said, snuggling up against him. 'You won't send me away, will you?'

He put an arm around her. 'It would never cross my mind.'

'Thank you, Daniel.'

They fell asleep together.

It was a revelation. The woman was young, shapely, compliant and experienced. She made Hillier feel wanted and unthreatened. Her skin was smooth, her hair silken and her lips sweeter than anything he'd ever tasted before. His only regret was that it was over so quickly. What pleased him most was that it was very different from the way his friends had described it. Instead of the wild rutting they'd all talked about, Hillier had enjoyed a gentle encounter, full of soft caresses and tenderness. During the short time it had taken, he'd been madly in love with the woman, wanting to make her his own. It was only when he left the room and Dobbs went straight into it that he realised he was merely sharing her with others.

The walk back to camp gave them a chance for comparison. Hillier's friends were loud-mouthed and boastful. He didn't join in the banter. They seemed to be talking about something that had never happened to him. Dobbs tried to prompt him.

'Did you enjoy it?' he asked.

'Yes, Hugh.'

'Do you feel any different now?'

'I do,' admitted Hillier.

'We picked the right girl. Have you ever felt such a body? I rode her for ages. Why didn't you stay longer?'

'I had what I wanted.'

Dobbs giggled. 'Did she take you in her mouth?'

'I had what I wanted,' repeated Hillier, refusing to be drawn.

While the others went into details of their respective couplings, Hillier held his peace. He was still uncertain whether to feel ashamed or exhilarated. Visiting a brothel was something he'd looked on as anathema before. In losing his virginity, he'd also sacrificed his respectability. But he was a drummer now, able to grab the passing pleasures of a soldier's life. The pleasure in this case had been indescribable. He could still feel the blood bubbling in his veins and taste her luscious kisses. A sense of remorse intruded. He wondered what his parents would think of him if they knew what he'd done. It would be seen as sordid, immoral and unbecoming. They would be badly wounded. His pleasure was tempered by repentance.

Another question suddenly loomed and it had a frightening immediacy. What would his uncle, Henry Welbeck, say?

'Shall we go again tomorrow night?' Dobbs asked him.

'I don't know, Hugh.'

'But she *liked* you, Tom. She told me.'

'I haven't any money,' said Hillier.

'Borrow some. That's what I'll do.'

'I'll see how I feel in the morning.'

'How do you feel now, that's the main thing? Are you glad that you came with us? Didn't I say it'd be the making of you?'

'It was good,' said Hillier, warmed by the memory. 'Thank you for taking me. It was very good.'

They ambled along in the darkness until they saw the campfires ahead. Dobbs hushed them all into silence and took over the lead, trying to find the route by which they'd left earlier. They went in single file with Hillier at the rear. Reaching the stream, Dobbs went along the bank in search of a place to cross. The youth directly behind Dobbs suddenly tripped, bumped into him and burst out laughing.

'Be quiet!' hissed Dobbs.

'I'm sorry, Hugh.'

The damage had already been done. Hearing the noise, two of the sentries came to see what had caused it. In response to their challenge, Dobbs took to his heels.

'Run!' he called.

The other three raced after him, running along the bank until they reached a point where it dipped down low. Following their leader, they plunged into the water and splashed their way across. Hillier kept up with them until he'd almost gained the other bank. His foot then caught in some weeds and he fell headlong into the stream. By the time he'd disentangled his foot and got back up again, it was too late. The sentries were waiting for him. He found himself looking at the barrels of their muskets.

Fine weather and an early start allowed them to make good speed on the following day. Janssen rode well and Amalia proved herself a capable horsewoman, handling a spirited mount without undue difficulty. Dopff, too, was developing into an able coachman though he still had trouble controlling the horse's speed. Daniel kept leaving the others so that he could ride ahead and act as a scout. There was nothing to delay them this time. Hours passed by without incident. During a period of rest, Janssen took him aside.

'I still haven't told you what I found out,' he said.

'Then do so now.'

'It's become a little confused in my mind, I fear. During those weeks in the Bastille, I rather lost my bearings.'

'I can understand why,' said Daniel.

'Where shall I start?'

'Go back to the time when you were last in touch with Pierre Lefeaux. All the intelligence you sent him would have reached us. What else is there to add?'

'I overheard a conversation between the king and one of his advisers. They were talking about next year's campaigns.'

'That sounds promising. What exactly was said?'

Janssen's account was rambling but full of interesting detail. It led on to other intelligence that he'd gleaned. Daniel was patient, drawing the information slowly out of him and sifting it as he did so. Until his arrest, the tapestry-maker had been an assiduous spy. His weakness was an inability to distinguish fact from anecdote. Much of what he said was of no military value to the Allies but it was offset by some significant intelligence. At the end of their conversation, Janssen sought information of another kind.

'Tell me what happened to Pierre Lefeaux,' he requested. 'When I mentioned his name before, I sensed that you were not telling me the whole truth.'

'Monsieur Lefeaux is no longer able to help us,' said Daniel, his face impassive. 'That's all you need to know.'

'Has he been arrested as well?'

'It amounts to that.'

'You're holding something back from me,' said Janssen. 'Pierre and his wife were dear friends of mine. I'm entitled to be told what became of them. Is Pierre still alive?'

'No,' confessed Daniel.

'What happened to him?'

'He was executed.'

'What about his wife?'

'She met the same fate.'

Janssen reeled as if from a blow. 'This is my fault,' he said, eyes filled with contrition. 'I must have blundered in some way and caused their deaths. I'll never forgive myself for that.'

'I suspect that it may have been the other way round,' said Daniel, sadly. 'Monsieur Lefeaux was probably caught first and your name was beaten out of him. There was clear evidence he'd been tortured. The French police are searching for our agents all the time. You've no need to feel any guilt.'

'I'm bound to, Daniel,' said Janssen. 'All I ever wanted to do with my life was to weave tapestries and bring up my daughter. It was madness for me to go to Paris in the first place.'

'I disagree. The rewards have been considerable.'

'Forgive me if I fail to see any of them. As a result of what I did, two good people were put to death, I was imprisoned and Amalia and the others were locked in a nightmare. I know how close you are to the Duke,' he went on, taking Daniel by the shoulders. 'Can you please ask him when this damnable war will end?'

Major Simon Cracknell kept him waiting. Ordinarily, he would have no dealings with anyone caught absent without leave but, when the name of Tom Hillier passed before him, he took a keen interest. The young drummer was kept under guard all morning. It was only after he'd washed his luncheon down with a glass of wine that the major chose to send for the miscreant. With a guard at his side, Hillier came into the major's tent looking exhausted and fearful. The major made him stand there in silence for a few minutes while he pretended to read the report on the table in front of him.

'Well?' he said at length, looking up. 'What do you have to say for yourself?'

'I would like to make an unreserved apology, sir.'

'To whom?'

'To you, Major.'

'Any apology needs to be directed at the British army for breaking its regulations. You're well aware of them by now.'

'I am, sir,' admitted Hillier.

'So why did you flout them?'

'It was a mistake.'

'It was a very bad mistake,' said Cracknell, 'but I want to know what lies behind it. What possessed you to go absent without leave?'

'It was only for a short time.'

'One minute is too long. Regulations are there to be obeyed. You seem unable to grasp that fact.' He flicked a glance at the report. 'What were the names of the others?'

'I was on my own, sir.'

'Don't lie to me.'

'I went for a walk in the night and strayed outside the boundary. That's all that happened, Major.'

'Then perhaps you'll explain why this report differs from your account. According to this, you were part of a group. Instead of going for a walk, you were actually caught running as hard as you could.'

'I was eager to return to camp, sir.'

'You should never have left it in the first place.'

'I accept that, Major.'

'Give me the names of your companions.'

'I had none,' said Hillier, determined not to give his friends away. 'I was alone.'

'And where had you been during the night?'

'I told you, Major. I went for a stroll.'

'And did that stroll, by any chance, take you towards the town?'

'No, sir.'

'Are you telling me that you didn't leave camp in order to roister in a tavern or dip your prick in some greasy whore?'

Hillier blushed. 'I went nowhere near the town, sir.'

'What about your friends?'

'There *were* no friends, Major.'

'In some respects,' said Cracknell, 'I suppose that's correct. When you fell over in the stream, none of your so-called friends stopped to help you up. They thought only of themselves. That being the case, you've no need to be misled by false loyalty. They left you to face the punishment they should all share.'

'There was nobody else involved, Major,' insisted Hillier.

The officer sat back in his chair. 'What view do you think your uncle would take of all this?'

'That's not for me to say, sir.'

'Sergeant Welbeck will be very disappointed to hear that a nephew of his sneaked off to wallow in some filthy brothel. He'll be even more upset to hear that you don't have the courage to name the others who took part in the sorry escapade. You'd never have done this on your own, would you? I think you were led astray by them.'

'I went of my own accord, Major.'

'Are you willing to suffer while the other culprits go free?'

Hillier made no reply. Getting to his feet, Cracknell walked across to stand in front of him and fix him with a cold stare. Wanting to blink and swallow hard, the drummer steeled himself to do neither. Whatever else he did, he resolved not to show weakness. The major was intent on humbling him. Self-respect made Hillier stand there without flinching.

'This is your last chance,' said Cracknell, making each word feel like a pinprick. 'Name your companions or I'll be forced to increase the severity of the punishment.' Hillier said nothing. Losing his patience, the major waved a hand. 'Take him away and stand guard over him. He's to be allowed neither food nor water.'

Welbeck was giving instructions to a corporal when he saw his visitor. Hugh Dobbs was hurrying towards him between the parallel lines of tents. His manner was furtive and his expression doleful. Welbeck dismissed the corporal with a peremptory nod then folded his arms, breathing in deeply through his nose.

'Go straight back where you came from,' he said when the drummer reached him. 'I want to hear no more tittle-tattle.'

'But this is important, Sergeant.'

'Behaving like a soldier is the only thing of importance in the army. I suggest that you grow up and start doing it.'

'Don't you want to hear what Major Cracknell has done?'

'No, lad, I do not.'

'But you'll be there when it happens.'

'I told you to stop bothering me,' said Welbeck. 'If you come within ten yards of me again, I'll have you put under armed guard.'

'That's where Tom is at the moment.'

The sergeant narrowed his lids. 'What did you say?'

'Tom Hillier was absent without leave last night. He was taken before Major Cracknell. But,' he went on, turning away, 'since you don't want to know anything about your own nephew, I won't tell you the news. You'll find it out soon enough anyway.'

Welbeck grabbed his shoulder and spun him round so that Dobbs was looking up into the sergeant's unforgiving face. Though his tone was brusque, he could not hide the flicker of interest.

'What news?' he demanded.

'On the major's orders, Tom is going to be flogged.'

Chapter Fourteen

Fortune could not favour them indefinitely. After the shock of being ambushed and held captive, they'd enjoyed a relatively clear run along the French roads. Three of them were on horseback and, though Amalia was accustomed to riding side-saddle, she was coping well in a less ladylike sitting position. Dopff provided the real surprise. His initial reluctance to act as coachman had given way to a positive relish for the task. He improved steadily and, with only two people on board, the vehicle was no strain for the powerful animal between the shafts. Dopff had overcome his natural fear of horses to develop a close relationship with this one. Whenever they rested, it was the little Dutchman who fed his horse or led it to water and he spent a lot of time simply standing beside the animal and patting it.

They encountered their first setback that afternoon. Riding ahead of them, Daniel spotted a detachment of soldiers marching towards him along the main road. He immediately galloped back to the others and diverted them on to a meandering track through a forest, hoping that it would take them in the right direction. Dopff's inexperience soon told. On a proper road, he could handle the coach with assurance but a bumpy track that constantly twisted and turned was another matter. He began to lose confidence. What broke his nerve completely was the appearance of a wild boar that darted suddenly out of some thickets and sped across their path. The coach horse neighed in alarm and bolted. Dopff tried manfully to keep hold of the reins until the overhanging branch of a tree swept him off his seat altogether.

The other horses had also been scared by the boar. Amalia and her father were struggling to control their mounts but it was Beatrix who was in most danger. As the coach careered on madly without a driver, brushing past thick bushes and bouncing off trees, she was thrown helplessly from side to side. Daniel responded at once. With a sharp dig of his heels, he galloped after the vehicle, praying that he could reach it before it overturned or was badly damaged. Beatrix's life was at stake. She was screaming hysterically. The track was narrow but there was just enough room for Daniel to pass. As he drew level, however, the coach lurched sideways and buffeted his horse, forcing him to pull back and wait until a better chance presented itself. Beatrix's howls grew more desperate by the second.

Bushes and trees then vanished magically as the coach entered a large clearing. Daniel didn't waste his opportunity. Kicking more speed out of his mount, he overtook the coach, came up alongside the horse and reached out to grab its bridle, pulling hard as he did so. The coach described a wide semicircle in the grass before finally coming to a halt. Daniel dismounted and made sure that the coach horse was sufficiently calmed before he ran to the vehicle itself. The moment he opened the door, Beatrix fell out gratefully into his arms, blubbering like a child. She was heavily bruised and frightened out of her wits but no bones had been broken.

Dopff had been less fortunate. Knocked from the driving seat, he'd tumbled to the ground and banged his head against the solid trunk of a tree. He was unconscious for several minutes and blood oozed from the gash in his skull. Amalia quickly tore off part of her petticoat to use as a bandage. She and her father crouched over Dopff until his eyelids at last flickered. They praised him for his bravery and assured him that he was not responsible for what had happened. He was still far too dazed to understand them.

Having sat Beatrix on the grass and given her a sip of water from a flagon they'd providentially filled, Daniel was able to inspect the damage to the coach. It consisted largely of scratches and dents though something had smashed a hole in one door. Daniel was more concerned about the coach horse, going over it carefully for signs of injury. Apart from several grazes, some of them spattered with blood, the animal had come through unscathed. It was now nibbling at some grass. Daniel was relieved. He'd learnt his lesson. From now on, he wouldn't foist the job of driving the coach on to Dopff. The risk was too great.

When the others eventually joined them, he reached a decision.

'I think it might be wise to break our journey for a while,' he said, 'don't you?'

Alone in the tent, still wearing the uniform soiled from his antics on the previous night, Tom Hillier had ample time for reflection. He was musing on the unfortunate turn of events that had landed him in his predicament when the tent flap was drawn back and Welbeck came in. Hillier was startled to see him.

'What are *you* doing here, Sergeant?' he asked.

'I might ask the same of you, lad.'

'I was absent without leave,' admitted the drummer.

'Why?'

'I was very foolish.'

'That's patently obvious. The question is *why?* You must be aware of the regulations by now. Why deliberately break them?'

'It was an accident, Sergeant.'

'Oh, I see,' said Welbeck with heavy sarcasm. 'You were strolling round the edge of the camp and you accidentally stepped outside its limits. The fact that it was in the middle of the night was also purely accidental, I'm sure.'

'I accept that I did wrong,' said Hillier, shamefaced.

'What use is that? You knew that you were doing wrong before you even set out. That should've deterred you.'

'I hoped that I wouldn't be caught.'

Welbeck grimaced. 'I've lost count of the number of times I've heard that pathetic bloody excuse. It's the reason that thieves steal or men commit murder. They hope they won't be caught. It's a hope that can justify any crime and – make no mistake about this, Tom – being absent without leave is a serious crime. If you disappear from camp while we're engaged in a campaign, you could be seen as a deserter.' He shook Hillier hard with both hands. 'Do you know what the army does to deserters?'

'I do, Sergeant.'

'Are you quite sure?'

'Deserters are shot.'

'Only the lucky ones,' said Welbeck. 'I can remember seeing a deserter given five hundred lashes. He was flayed to death. Is that how you want to end your time in the army?'

'No,' said Hillier in distress. 'I can't tell you how sorry I am for what I did. It won't ever happen again.'

'It shouldn't have happened this time. The only saving grace is that it wasn't your own idea. You were talked into it by others.'

'Nobody else was to blame.'

'Do you expect me to believe that?'

'I got myself into this mess alone,' affirmed Hillier.

'Where did you go? Come on, lad,' he went on as his nephew hesitated. 'I've been in the army a very long time and I know there are only a few reasons why soldiers are absent without leave. So please don't tell me you went fishing at night or collecting birds' eggs. You sneaked off to the town, didn't you?'

'I left camp without permission, Sergeant. That's all I can say.'

'And what am I to say to your mother about this incident? Am I to tell her that it took you less than six weeks in the army to catch the pox and earn yourself a flogging?'

'Please don't mention any of this to her,' begged Hillier.

'She'll want to know how you're getting on.'

'I know I'm in disgrace. Give me a chance to make amends for it.'

'And how are you going to do that, lad?' asked Welbeck with a mirthless laugh. 'You're about to be flogged. If you caught something nasty between the legs of some doxy last night, you'll spend the next couple of weeks wondering which itches most – your back or your balls.' Hillier blanched. 'Who went to the town with you?'

'I left here on my own, Sergeant.'

'Was it Dobbs, for instance?'

'Hugh Dobbs is nothing to do with this.'

'What about the other lads?'

'They were not involved,' said Hillier, firm under pressure. 'I was very stupid and I'm ready to pay the penalty for my stupidity.'

Welbeck appraised him. 'That's fair enough,' he concluded with the first whisper of sympathy. 'How are they treating you, Tom?'

'I've been under armed guard since I was caught.'

'Have they given you food and water?'

'No, Sergeant.'

'Have they allowed you to use a latrine?'

'No, Sergeant.'

'That's not right.'

'I've no complaints,' said Hillier, bravely. 'I brought this on myself. If my parents got to hear about this, it would be far worse than any punishment the army can inflict.'

'They'll hear nothing from me, Tom,' said Welbeck.

Before his nephew could thank him, the tent flap lifted and Major Cracknell stepped in. Hillier and Welbeck stood to attention.

'If you've come to plead on your nephew's behalf,' said the major, curtly, 'you're wasting your breath.'

'That isn't why I'm here, sir,' said Welbeck.

'Were he your own son, I wouldn't change my decision.'

'Nor would I expect you to, Major Cracknell.'

'He's let your family down badly.'

'He knows that only too well.'

'What he did was indefensible,' said Cracknell. 'Private Hillier was absent without leave and compounded the offence by refusing to name his companions.'

'I went out of the camp alone, Major,' said Hillier.

'Others were heard running away.'

'That may well be so but I wasn't with them. They must have been returning to camp at the same time.'

Cracknell turned to Welbeck. 'You have an accomplished liar

in your family, Sergeant. Do you condone his misconduct?'

'No, sir,' replied Welbeck. 'He's broken army regulations and must be disciplined. At the same time, however, he's entitled to privileges such as food, water and access to the latrines. I feel it my duty to report this mistreatment of him to your superior officers.'

'Damn you, man!' yelled Cracknell. 'Hillier is the offender here, not me. He doesn't deserve any privileges. He should count himself lucky that he's not been shackled. As for you, Sergeant, I'm ordering you to stay away from him.'

'Yes, Major.'

'And if there are any other members of your family who wish to join the army, keep them away from this regiment. We have certain standards to maintain. Hillier has fallen well below them.' He regarded the drummer with contempt. 'You're a disgrace to everyone,' he added. 'Even the sergeant must admit that.'

'Tom Hillier is my nephew,' said Welbeck, stoutly, 'and I'm proud to acknowledge that fact.'

They needed a long rest before they pressed on. When they did so, Daniel drove the coach with Beatrix and Dopff as his passengers. Both were still shaken by their experience. They came at length to a river, enabling Daniel to have a more accurate idea of where they actually were. He called them to a halt.

'We need to cross it,' he told them.

'Is there a bridge?' asked Janssen.

'It's three or four miles away, I fancy. You can all wait here while I ride ahead to see if it's safe to use it.'

'Shall I come with you?' offered Amalia.

'That's a kind offer but I'll be quicker on my own.'

'Take care, Daniel.'

Mounting his horse, he rode off at a canter with the river on his right. He soon vanished around the bend. The others sat on the bank and ate some of the food they'd brought with them. Dopff was too jaded to touch anything but Beatrix had a voracious appetite. Of the two of them, she was the more resilient. Dopff was detached and pensive, still blaming himself for losing control of the coach. It was a long time before Daniel returned and his news was not encouraging.

'There are guards on the bridge,' he said. 'That suggests to me that the police have decided that we managed to escape from Paris and are throwing their net wider.'

'We have false passports,' argued Janssen. 'Won't they see us safely past any patrol?'

'Not when everyone along the north-east frontier has been warned to look out for four Dutch fugitives. Even dressed as a woman, you won't deceive guards a second time.'

'Is there any other way to cross?'

'Yes,' said Daniel. 'I found a shallower spot further upstream. The water came up to my feet when I rode into it. Had it been much higher, the horse would have had to swim.'

'What about the coach?' asked Amalia.

'That could pose a problem.'

With Daniel as coachman once more, they rode along the bank until they reached the place he'd seen earlier. The river was wide but the current was not strong. A gentle gradient would allow the coach to enter the water when it was fairly horizontal but the vehicle wasn't tall enough to clear the surface. Water was bound to seep in through the doors. Realising that, an anguished Dopff waved his arms frantically. Daniel understood his concern.

'Yes, we know,' he said. 'There's a chance that the tapestry will be soaked and we can't have that. I suggest we take out everything of value. Apart from anything else, we need to lighten the coach as much as possible.'

All five of them set about emptying the coach, removing their baggage as well as the booty stowed under the seat. Daniel put some of the items in his saddlebags and took hold of the tapestry. Watched by a nervous Janssen and a trembling Dopff, he rode into the river and let the water climb inexorably up the horse's legs. At the deepest point, he was still able to remain in the saddle and kept on until he reached the other bank. Janssen and Dopff clapped their hands with glee. Heartened by what she'd seen, Amalia went next, riding more slowly but contriving to get to the other side without even wetting her shoes. She gave the others a wave of triumph. It was Janssen's turn to cross but he had more enthusiasm for the venture than his horse. The animal refused to enter the water at first and, even when it did, twice tried to turn back, threshing about as it did so. When Janssen finally emerged on the other side, his legs were soaking wet.

Riding his own horse, Daniel borrowed Amalia's mount and tugged it behind him as he headed back towards the coach. Beatrix was helped into the saddle so that Daniel could tow her across the river, taking the rest of the baggage at the same time. The exercise was repeated with Dopff in the saddle of the other horse. Pulling on the rein and urging both horses on, Daniel got them safely to the bank. There was no baggage left now. Only the coach remained.

'Are you certain that it's safe?' said Amalia, worriedly.

'There's only one way to find out,' replied Daniel. 'The trick is to have a good run at it so that we hit the water at speed. If the coach is allowed to stop at any point, then I could be in difficulty.'

'Can I help in any way?'

'Yes, please. Ride with me then lead my horse back here again. When I'm driving that coach, I don't want to worry about having to pull another horse behind us.'

'Let me come instead,' volunteered Janssen.

'I'll go, Father,' insisted Amalia.

'Well, *I* certainly wouldn't,' said Beatrix to herself.

Dopff put both hands over his eyes to show his unwillingness. As it was, Amalia accompanied Daniel, riding beside him and getting splashed this time. Once on the other bank, he dismounted and handed the reins to her, waiting until she'd gone all the way to the other bank before he even climbed up on to the coach. As he viewed his task, he began to have misgivings. Water would certainly flood into the vehicle, making it much heavier to pull. On the other hand, the horse was strong and, if kept on the move, should reach the opposite bank without undue stress. Whip at the ready, Daniel judged the line he'd take down the slope.

Biting their lips in consternation, his friends watched. While they didn't doubt his courage, they began to question his wisdom. From where they stood, it looked like a perilous undertaking. So it proved. Daniel cracked his whip to sting the horse's rump and off it went. Plunging into the water, it pulled valiantly and the coach made good progress until it reached the middle of the river. One of its wheels then struck a submerged rock with enough force to snap it away from the axle. The whole coach tipped sideways, hurling Daniel into the water. When he surfaced again, he saw the broken wheel floating off down the river. Of more immediate importance was the fact that the coach horse was trapped between the shafts, kicking madly and neighing loudly as it tried to regain its feet and keep its head above the water.

Daniel swam swiftly to its rescue. Trying to keep clear of the flashing hooves, he undid the harness to release the animal from the shafts then held on tight to the reins as he was literally hauled along by the frantic beast. While Beatrix and Dopff jumped out of the way in fright, Amalia and her father stood firm. They knew that the horse had to be stopped before it could get up any speed. The two of them therefore waded into the water and, as the horse reached them, took hold of either side of the bridle. Scrambling to his feet, Daniel added his own strength on the reins. The animal reached dry land and, though still tossing its head and neighing in protest, it slowed down. Dopff came forward to pat it on the neck and help to calm it.

'Are you all right, Daniel?' cried Amalia.

'I'm a little wetter than I intended to be.'

'You're not hurt in any way?'

'No,' he said, winding the harness up. 'If truth be told, it was rather bracing. When I've dried off a little, I can address my mind to the thorny problem of how we carry on without our coach.'

The delay was deliberate. Hillier soon realised that. If he'd been punished on the morning he'd been caught, he would now be nursing his wounds but at least the worst would be over. By postponing the event until the following day, Major Cracknell guaranteed a sleepless night for the drummer. The longer he waited, the more fearful loomed his sentence. He could almost feel the skin being stripped from his back.

There had been some relief. Thanks to Sergeant Welbeck's

intervention, he had now been given a meal and allowed to visit the latrines. Even more encouraging was the fact that his uncle had finally recognised his existence. In front of a vindictive officer, the sergeant had defended his nephew. That meant a lot to Hillier.

He was a scapegoat, receiving the punishment that Dobbs and the others should be sharing. Yet he refused to yield up their names. It was not simply out of fear of repercussions. They were his friends. If one of them had been caught in his place, Hillier felt certain that his own name wouldn't have been volunteered. Those in the lower ranks looked after each other. When he thought of what lay ahead for him, he shuddered. Flogging was a barbaric punishment and he'd seen its effects. One of the other drummers, flogged for drunkenness, still had livid marks across his back months after he'd received his lashes. Hillier had seen them. He wondered how long he'd bear his own gruesome souvenirs.

The most troubling aspect for him was not the physical agony but the sheer humiliation. Hillier would be flogged in front of the whole regiment. Since it was a first offence committed by a new recruit who'd obviously been misled, some officers would have been inclined to leniency. Major Cracknell wasn't one of them. He wanted Hillier to suffer and Sergeant Welbeck to suffer with him. Under the guise of imposing discipline, the major was also able to work off his grudge against Daniel Rawson, the sergeant's close friend. Cracknell would doubtless go out of his way to inform his enemy of Hillier's fate when the captain returned to his regiment.

He was pacing the tent anxiously when he heard a low whistle. At first he had no idea where it came from then he saw something protruding under the canvas at the rear of the tent.

It was a small bottle of brandy held by someone.

'Tom?' whispered a voice. 'Are you there?'

Hillier crouched down. 'Hugh – is that you?'

'Yes. Take a swig of this. It might help.'

Taking the bottle, he uncorked it and took a long sip. It burnt his throat and coursed through his body but it gave him new strength to face his ordeal. He corked the bottle and slipped it back into Dobbs' hand.

'Thank you,' he said.

'Don't thank me, Tom. It belongs to Sergeant Welbeck.'

Hillier had another reason to be grateful to his uncle. The brandy was starting to take full effect now. His head began to swim. Minutes later the guard came in. The prisoner was taken under escort to a patch of land behind the camp where the regiment was drawn up in a hollow square. It was a spectacle that the rank and file hated but they were forced to watch. The flogging of one soldier was also a dire warning to others. Writhing with shame, Hillier kept his eyes down. He stopped beside a wooden triangle and was ordered to remove his coat and shirt. When his wrists were tied to the triangle, he was quite defenceless. His naked back looked pale and stringy.

Major Cracknell issued the command for the punishment to begin. A burly drummer took a cat-o'-nine-tails from out of a bag and had a couple of practice swings through the air. Hillier tensed, hoping that the brandy would dull the pain in some way. If nothing else, he'd discovered that his uncle could be considerate. When the first stroke came, it made his whole body convulse, biting into his flesh like so many vicious teeth. Hillier recovered quickly, promising himself that, however searing the pain, he'd hold back any cries. Another set of hungry teeth sank into his back to be followed by a third and a fourth. Eyes closed and body already covered with blood, he tried to count the strokes but he drifted off into unconsciousness long before the tally had been completed.

They were no longer able to stay overnight at an inn. If, as Daniel suspected, the search for them had spread outside the capital, it would be too dangerous to stop. Roads were patrolled, bridges were guarded and sentries were on duty at key points on the frontier. Evading them all was paramount. What slowed the fugitives down was that they no longer had the coach at their disposal. Five of them now shared four horses. Since he was the only person able to ride bareback, Daniel sat astride the coach horse with much of their baggage. Janssen reserved the right to carry the tapestry. He and Amalia retained a horse each while Dopff led the third horse by its reins so that Beatrix could sit on it. While progress was tardy, they were able to hide more swiftly whenever someone approached.

It was a fine night with stars twinkling in the sky like distant candles. Instead of stumbling along in complete darkness, they had a modicum of light. As ever, Daniel led the way, relying on an inner compass to take him in the right direction. They stopped by a brook to refresh themselves. Janssen had grown weary.

'I think we should snatch a few hours' sleep,' he said.

'We must press on,' argued Daniel.

'But we're all dog-tired.'

'It's better to move at night than in the day when we're more likely to be seen. We're being hunted like animals. Do you want to be caught and sent back to the Bastille?'

'Perish the thought!'

'I don't think you'd be offered a comfortable cell next time.'

'I'm certain of it,' agreed Janssen. 'I'm just worried about Amalia. She almost fell off the horse at one point and Kees must be exhausted, going on foot all the time.'

'It's tiring for all of us, I know,' said Daniel, 'but we simply must persevere. It would be folly to stop now.'

'What happens when dawn breaks?'

'We'll simply have to be more circumspect.'

'How far away is the border?'

'I'm not sure.'

'Have you *any* idea where we actually are?'

Daniel was honest. 'No, I'm afraid not.'

Growing increasingly fatigued, they forced themselves to move on, keeping to a track that took them on a winding route through open countryside. Whenever they reached a village or a hamlet, they went around it. At one point, they went through a stand of trees and heard rustling noises in the undergrowth. An owl hooted above them and startled the horses. Nocturnal creatures were all round them. Daniel was used to marching through the night and going without sleep. For the others, however, it was a wholly new and debilitating experience. Every time he glanced at them, Daniel could see them flagging badly.

They were at the bottom of a hill when he caught sight of some riders silhouetted against the sky as they came over the crest. Daniel waved to the others to pull off the track. They dismounted and led their horses behind some bushes. Not daring to move or speak, they crouched behind the foliage until they heard the sound of hooves and the jingling of harness. The riders were getting ever closer. Eyes now accustomed to the darkness, Daniel peered through a gap in the bush and saw that there were six of them. Certain that they were soldiers on patrol, he hoped that they would ride past and go on their way without being aware of the presence of the fugitives. His fear was that one of their own horses would whinny or shift its feet in the long grass and make a noise. Daniel and the others were on tenterhooks. To have come so far and to be caught when they were so close to safety would be devastating. They could look for no mercy whatsoever.

Ironically, it was Dopff who gave them away. The man with no voice had been sneezing and coughing for the last couple of miles. Hand clapped over his mouth, he was doubled up as he tried to suppress the urge to sneeze again. When the impulse passed, he thought it was safe to remove the restraining palm. Before he could stop it, he was overcome by a secondary urge and sneezed aloud. Dopff put both hands penitently across his mouth but the damage had already been done. Hearing the noise, the soldiers came around the angle of the bushes to see what had caused it. Six loaded muskets were pointed at the cowering group. They'd been caught. Daniel's heart was a drum. Amalia shivered, Janssen's legs threatened to give way and Beatrix burst into tears. Dopff was reciting his prayers and begging the Almighty for forgiveness.

'Who *are* you?' demanded one of the soldiers.

It was a miracle. The man had spoken in Dutch. Fearing that they'd been captured by French soldiers, the fugitives had never considered the possibility that they'd already crossed the border. Overwhelmed with relief, they started laughing and hugging each other. Daniel held Amalia in a warm embrace.

'What's the jest?' asked the soldier.

'We'll be happy to explain it to you,' said Daniel, beaming. 'My name is Captain Rawson, attached to the staff of His Grace, the Duke of Marlborough, and I admit that I've been critical of the Dutch army in the past. Let me say before witnesses that I've never been so grateful to see some members of it as I am at this moment in time.'

The meeting was held at the home of Johannes Mytens. The visitors arrived punctually and were shown into the parlour. After greeting his friend, Willem Ketel introduced him to Gaston Loti. The Frenchman was tall, lean and well-dressed. His full-bottomed wig framed a face that was pitted with age but softened by a ready smile. Loti was intelligent, watchful and devious. As a merchant, Ketel had learnt to speak French fluently and Mytens had a sound knowledge of the language. They were therefore able to converse in French. Loti began by making some flattering remarks about The Hague, hinting that it would be a tragedy if such a fine city were ever to be under direct attack. Mytens bridled slightly.

'It would be equally unfortunate if Paris were to be under siege,' he said. 'The destruction of the magnificent French capital would be a sad sight to behold.'

'It's one that will never be seen,' said Loti with easy confidence. 'No enemy would ever get within striking distance of Paris.'

'Don't be so complacent, Monsieur Loti.'

'It's not complacency, sir, but common sense.'

'Even the best armies can be beaten,' asserted Mytens, 'and yours has been humbled on the battlefield more than once.'

'Gentlemen,' said Ketel, diving in quickly before the argument became more heated. 'Paris and The Hague are both wonderful cities. We are here to discuss how we can ensure their mutual well-being in every conceivable way.'

'I agree, Willem,' said Loti, 'and I apologise to my host if I appeared a trifle arrogant. It's a fault of my nation, alas, and none of us is entirely free from it.' His smile broadened. 'I'm sorry, sir.'

Mytens nodded. 'I accept your apology,' he said, 'and tender my own in return. This is an opportunity to bargain rather than bicker.'

'Bargain!' echoed Ketel, sucking his teeth. 'That word is music in my ears. You two are politicians and talk of compromise. I'm a merchant and therefore seasoned in haggling.'

'There's no need for haggling here, Willem,' said Loti. 'We have common needs and a common aim. All we have to discuss is how best to achieve that aim.'

'Johannes and I have already done that.'

'I and my fellow-politicians have been debating the issue since this war first started. It's not one that we sought, let's be clear about that. All that King Louis did was to confirm the right of his grandson, the Duc d'Anjou, to inherit the Spanish throne.'

'It was viewed elsewhere, not unreasonably, with great alarm,' said Mytens, jowls wobbling. 'If France is allowed to annexe Spain, it would create an empire that would hold us all in thrall. Does King Louis never tire of conquest?'

'It's not his intention to conquer Spain,' replied Loti, calmly, 'but merely to supervise the rightful succession. Your fears of a vast and aggressive French empire are much exaggerated, Monsieur Mytens. What you seem to forget is that Louis XIV is an old man. In a few years' time, he'll be seventy. At his age, he has no appetite for a long and damaging war. He'd much rather live in peace and enjoy the splendours of Versailles.'

'In his position, I'd probably wish to do the same.'

'I'm sure that we all would,' said Ketel, worried that his two friends were not getting on as well as he'd imagined. 'What better life is there for a man than to inhabit paradise and be able to select his mistresses from among the greatest beauties of France?'

'We have *our* share of beauties, Willem,' said Mytens with a touch of patriotic lechery. 'Paris has nothing to compare with some of the ladies you'll find in The Hague and Amsterdam.'

'Dutch women are a little dour for my taste,' said Loti.

'That's because you judge them by their appearance, my friend. They cannot match their French counterparts in flamboyance, I grant you, but in passion they are far superior.'

Ketel was exasperated. 'Why are we talking about women when we should be discussing the war?' he asked, adjusting his wig. 'If we can find our way to a peaceful settlement, we'll *all* have time for the pleasures of the flesh.'

'Well said, Willem,' agreed Loti.

'Yes,' added Mytens, 'we're rightly chastised. Once again I apologise, Monsieur Loti. It's a poor host who argues with a visitor.'

'Then let's proceed to a friendly debate,' said Ketel. 'Gaston knows the very nerves of state in France. He knows what the King and his advisors intend before they even put their thoughts into words. Why don't we let him enlighten us?'

Mytens turned to Loti. 'You have a rapt audience, sir.'

'Then I'll try to give a performance worthy of merit,' said the Frenchman. 'Not that this is a theatre in which all the lines have been rehearsed, mind you. I'll be speaking from the heart.'

'We'll be doing the same,' promised Ketel.

'Good.'

'What news do you have for us, Gaston?'

'The best news possible,' answered Loti, 'though it must remain between the three of us for the time being. France is weary of this pointless and inconclusive war. It serves no purpose other than to be a constant drain on the national coffers of everyone involved. We are all stupidly fighting our way into poverty.'

'That's been my contention throughout,' said Ketel.

'When winter comes and we all have time to sit back and view the situation dispassionately, we'll see the lunacy of resuming the war next spring. If wisdom prevails,' he went on, 'and if the Dutch are as ready to come to terms as the French, then there can be a formal end to the hostilities between us.'

'There'll be a definite offer of peace?' said Mytens, hopefully.

'Yes, my friend. I'll be part of a deputation that makes it.'

'What are its details?'

'They've yet to be finalised,' said Loti, 'but I assure you that they'll have considerable appeal. France will recognise your objectives and you, by the same token, must acknowledge ours.' He looked from one man to the other. 'How strong is the desire for peace here?'

'Very strong,' said Ketel. 'Johannes has been working hard to convince his friends in the States-General that the war should be abandoned. His support grows every day.'

'That's very gratifying.'

'One must not overstate it,' warned Mytens. 'Many of us long for peace but it must be on terms that we can accept. And no matter how tempting those terms may be,' he went on, 'we must be braced for a measure of resistance.'

'From whom would it come?'

'Grand Pensionary Heinsius would lead the opposition.'

'Could he not be won over?'

'Not as long as we're allied to England.'

'Aye,' said Ketel, sucking his teeth, 'there's the rub. We have to dance to England's tune. They've provided soldiers, supplies, money and our redoubtable commander-in-chief.'

'How close are he and Heinsius?' asked Loti.

'Too close, Gaston.'

'Could their friendship be blighted in some way?'

'It's difficult to see how.'

'The situation is this, Monsieur Loti,' explained Mytens. 'What we most covet is the security of our boundaries. If that could be guaranteed by France, then peace negotiations would be welcomed.'

'They'd be conducted in the utmost secrecy,' said Loti, tapping the side of his nose. 'Diplomacy is best done in the dark, gentlemen.'

'Like certain other pleasures,' noted Ketel, smirking.

'France would be prepared to make serious concessions.'

'We'd be minded to make a positive response, Gaston.'

'The eternal problem,' said Mytens, 'is the intransigence of the Duke of Marlborough. Until France renounces interest in the Spanish throne, the Duke will not hear of peace.' He tossed a shrewd glance at the Frenchman. 'Is there any possibility that that will be among the terms you offer?' he continued. 'Could the name of the Duc d'Anjou be withdrawn?'

'You're referring to King Philip V of Spain,' said Loti with a disarming grin, 'but, yes, anything is possible. Whether it's desirable from our point of view, of course, is another matter. To answer your question, Monsieur Mytens, the terms of any peace treaty will be negotiable. And let me remind you that I'm only talking about a parley between France and Holland.'

'Our allies must be taken into account.'

'Even if the Dutch army withdraws from the contest,' said Ketel, 'the Duke is likely to fight on. He's the enemy here.'

'Then we must join forces to remove him,' declared Loti.

'Let's wait until formal negotiations have taken place this winter. If they falter because of the obduracy of one man, the solution stares us in the face.' He tilted his head to one side. 'We must assassinate the Duke of Marlborough.'

CHAPTER FIFTEEN

It was almost a fortnight before Daniel Rawson was able to rejoin his regiment. In the interim, he'd been in The Hague with Amalia and her father, then had escorted them back home to Amsterdam. Daniel had been their guest for a couple of days. After his visit to Paris, he found it a treat to be in a city so clean and free from noisome smells. Not only were the streets washed regularly, they were also sprinkled with sand on occasion. What he did miss were the wide boulevards at the heart of the French capital. Amsterdam had narrow thoroughfares infested with fast-moving carriages and carts that could maim or even kill. It was a place where pedestrians had to be on constant guard.

The other advantage of the visit was that he was able to go back to the house where he and his mother had lived after their enforced flight from England twenty years earlier. In the wake of the battle of Sedgemoor, his life had suddenly been transformed. Daniel moved from a small farm to a large city, from rural tranquillity to a thriving port. Instead of speaking English, he grew up talking his mother's native language. Instead of envisaging his future as a farmer in Somerset, he nursed an ambition to join the Dutch army. It was only by a quirk of fate that, by doing so, he found himself back in the very country he'd deserted.

It was a wrench to take his leave of Amalia Janssen. Events had drawn them ineluctably together into a friendship that balanced the excitement of novelty against a feeling of permanence. Sad to part from her, he promised Amalia that he'd write whenever he could. The presence of Emanuel Janssen made it a less touching farewell than Daniel could have wished but the older man clearly approved of the friendship between the captain and his daughter. There was an unspoken commitment between Daniel and Amalia. It was sealed by a simple exchange of glances. Riding away from Amsterdam, his abiding memory of her was the night they'd shared in the privacy of the coach.

When he finally joined his regiment in winter quarters, he first reported to Marlborough's brother, General Churchill. Letters from The Hague had already informed Churchill of the captain's heroics in France but he insisted on a first-hand account. Daniel obliged readily though his version of events said nothing about an incipient romance with Amalia. Since the general was in regular correspondence with his brother, Daniel was given the latest news about the commander-in-chief, still courting allies in foreign capitals. The minute he was free to leave, he went off to find Henry Welbeck. The sergeant was in his tent. Daniel was shocked to hear what had happened.

'When was this?' he asked.

'Weeks ago, Dan.'

'How many lashes did the lad receive?'

'Eighty,' replied Welbeck.

'That was cruel.'

'It was typical of the major.'

'Did nobody intervene on his behalf?'

'Nobody had a loud enough voice.'

Daniel was deeply upset. 'If only I'd been here,' he said with compassion, 'I could have challenged Major Cracknell. At the very least, I might've got the number of lashes reduced.'

'I doubt it.'

'Why do you say that, Henry?'

'You and I are two of the reasons why the lad was punished so severely. The major is green with envy at your promotion, Dan. He'd do anything to strike back at you.'

Daniel had already discerned the connection to him. In having the hapless drummer flogged, the major would be hurting Welbeck and, by extension, the sergeant's best friend. Indirectly, Cracknell was trying to put salt on the tail of a bird whose fine plumage was now on display in Marlborough's personal staff. It grieved Daniel that Hillier had suffered additional pain because of him.

'How did he bear up?' he said.

'Very well, considering,' replied Welbeck. 'He didn't cry out or beg for mercy. Every inch of skin was stripped from his back but he didn't make a sound.' He gave a half-smile. 'I like to think that the brandy helped.'

'Did you give him that?'

'I slipped a bottle to his friend.'

'That was thoughtful.'

'He *is* my nephew, Dan.'

'You've remembered that at last, have you?'

Welbeck told him about all the other things that had occurred during his absence but they were eclipsed, in Daniel's mind, by what he'd heard about Hillier. He kept wondering if the flogging would break the drummer's spirit or simply deprive him of any interest in remaining in the army. Harsh discipline had turned many zealous soldiers into potential deserters. Daniel resolved to speak to him.

'What about you, Dan?' asked Welbeck. 'Where have you been all this time – or is it still a secret?'

'I've been to Paris,' said Daniel.

'To take tea with King Louis, I daresay.'

'No, Henry. In point of fact, the King hates the city and prefers to live well away from it in Versailles. He did invite me to dinner, as it happens, but I felt that I had to decline.'

Welbeck laughed. 'Tell the truth, you bugger.'

'The truth is that I was sent to rescue someone.'

Daniel gave him an abbreviated account of his time in France, concentrating on the escapes from the Bastille and from the three highwaymen. There was no mention of Amalia and Beatrix. It was an omission on which Welbeck soon pounced.

'What was her name?'

'Whose name?'

'*Her* name,' said the sergeant. 'I refuse to believe that Dan Rawson spent a week or so in France without meeting a woman.'

'I met two as it happened – Janssen's daughter and his servant.'

'Which one did you seduce first?'

'You're getting very coarse in your old age, Henry.'

'All right,' said Welbeck, searching for another way of asking his question, 'which one of them first studied the bedroom ceiling over your shoulder?'

'Neither of them,' said Daniel, firmly.

'You made them lie face down, did you?'

'I was too busy trying to save their lives to think about anything else. Besides, I had Emanuel Janssen and his assistant with me all the time. It was like being part of the family.'

'I still think there was a naked woman in the story.'

'You can think what you like, Henry. If you want a naked woman, I'll put in half a dozen for you. A dozen, if you prefer.'

'I've no need for them,' said Welbeck, tartly. 'They spell danger. Look what happened to Tom. He was so keen to see a pair of naked tits that he forgot he wasn't supposed to leave camp.'

'I'd like to speak to the lad.'

'Be warned, Dan. He's changed.'

'It takes a long time to recover from a flogging.'

'I'm not talking about the pain he's in. The change is inside his head. He seems to have gone off into a world of his own. If you want to know the truth,' Welbeck admitted, 'I'm worried about him.'

It was a paradox. In taking punishment on behalf of his friends, Tom Hillier had become their hero. At the very time when they wanted to show their gratitude by spending time with him, he preferred to be on his own. The flogging had isolated him in every sense. He was pleasant to Dobbs and the others but he avoided their company when he could. Being alone was his only solace. It gave him time and space to revalue what he'd suffered. The physical pain was constant. The regimental surgeon had offered him a salve for his wounds but the application of it was so agonising that he only endured it once. Various other remedies were suggested to him. None of them worked and even though the fire on his back gradually burnt less persistently, the inferno inside his head roared on with undiminished rage.

He was strolling beside the stream where he'd met his nemesis when Daniel came upon him. Hillier was astounded to see him.

'Good morning, Captain Rawson,' he said.

'How are you feeling, Tom?'

'It's getting better, sir.'

'I was shocked when your uncle told me what happened.'

'It was my own fault,' said Hillier, too embarrassed to meet his eye, 'and I've no quarrel with that. On this side of the stream, I'm abiding by army regulations. On the other bank – and that's where I was on the night – I was deemed to be absent without leave.' He pursed his lips. 'What a difference five yards of water can make to your life!'

'You went farther afield than five yards, I suspect,' said Daniel.

'I did, Captain.'

'I'm sorry that I wasn't here to help.'

'What could you have possibly done?'

'I could've remonstrated with Major Cracknell. I could've made sure that you were treated fairly from the moment of arrest.'

Hillier was moved. 'Why should you bother about me?'

'It's because you're a rarity, Tom. You're a willing recruit and we get few of them. Well, you've seen the character of the men we have. Some of them only agreed to join the army because it was a way out of prison. According to Sergeant Welbeck, the vast majority of our soldiers begin as rogues, vagabonds or drunkards. You don't fit into any of those categories. You *wanted* a career in the army.'

'That was a long time ago,' said Hillier, dreamily.

'You took your flogging like a man, I hear.'

'That's no consolation, sir.'

'It is to your uncle. Sergeant Welbeck was impressed.'

'He'd have been more impressed if I'd obeyed regulations.

But I let him down and I let myself down. My parents will be disgusted.'

'There's no reason for them to hear about it.'

'There is, Captain Rawson. My first thought was to keep it from them and I begged Uncle Henry to do likewise. It's just not possible,' said Hillier, quietly. 'I was brought up to tell my parents the truth and my conscience won't allow me to hide this. I can't lie to them.'

'Concealing the truth is not the same as telling a lie.'

'It is to me, sir.'

'In saying nothing of this,' observed Daniel, 'you'd be sparing them untold pain. More to the point, you'd be sparing yourself the ordeal of writing the letter. The army is the army, Tom. It's a hard existence. I'm sure that your parents realise that.'

'They did, Captain. They kept warning me against it.'

Daniel sighed. 'My mother warned *me* against it. She implored me to stay at home with her. My father died fighting in an army and she feared the same would happen to me.'

'Why didn't you listen to her?'

'For the same reason you didn't pay any attention to your parents,' said Daniel. 'I had an urge inside me. I wanted adventure.'

Hillier made no comment. He seemed to have drifted off into a reverie. There was a faraway look in his eye. It was almost as if Daniel was not even there.

Major Cracknell was playing cards in his tent with Lieutenant Ainley and winning handsomely. He was not pleased to be interrupted by a visitor. The lieutenant, however, seized the opportunity to cut his losses. Seeing that Daniel was intent on speaking to the major, he made an excuse and left. Cracknell tossed his cards on the table.

'You've just cost me a lot of money,' he complained.

'The lieutenant can ill afford to lose it.'

'Since when have you been concerned about Ainley's finances?'

'I don't like to see anyone being exploited, Major.'

Cracknell stood up. 'Are you accusing me of cheating?'

'No, sir, I'm not.'

'Then please refrain from making any further comment on the subject. That, after all,' he said, hands on hips, 'is not what brought you here, is it? You've come to talk about a squealing drummer with a back as red as a lobster.'

'I'm reliably informed that Private Hillier didn't squeal.'

'Perhaps not but he certainly *squirmed*.'

'You obviously took pleasure from that.'

'The pleasure I had was derived from the chance to administer a warning to the others. A good flogging keeps the rest of the men in check for a month. If I'd been lenient with Hillier, it would have encouraged others to emulate him. Dozens of them would have been sneaking off at night to the nearest brothel. I had to make an example of him. Eighty lashes were justified.'

'It was a vindictive punishment.'

'What would you have done, Captain?' asked Cracknell with a sneer. 'Would you have docked his wages or simply given him a slap on the wrist?'

'I'd have taken the circumstances into account. He was a young man, new to the army, obviously cajoled by others into leaving camp without permission. It was his first offence. If he'd been treated firmly but fairly,' argued Daniel, 'he'd have learnt his lesson. But that wasn't enough for you, Major. You wanted blood. You've been persecuting Hillier ever since you discovered that he was Sergeant Welbeck's nephew.'

'I deny that.'

'Your conduct has been malicious and unwarranted.'

'I need no lectures on conduct from you, Captain Rawson,' shouted Cracknell, exploding with anger. 'While you've been cavorting off somewhere, it's been left to me and others to maintain a high standard of discipline in this regiment. It's the duty of officers to keep the lower ranks in order. Unlike you, I don't try to befriend them. It's a sign of weakness and they need a show of strength.'

'What they need is to be able to respect an officer.'

'It's the principle on which I operate.'

'No, Major, you confuse cold fear with respect. They're very different. How can anyone respect you for what you did to Hillier? You took a harmless lad and had him beaten to a pulp to gratify your own desires. Had anyone else been caught that night,' stressed Daniel, 'you wouldn't even have been involved in the punishment.'

'I won't be criticised!' yelled Cracknell.

'You deserve more than criticism.'

'Is that a threat, Captain Rawson?'

'Take it as you wish, sir.'

'You're talking to a superior officer.'

'No, I'm not,' retorted Daniel. 'I'm talking to a cruel, jealous, twisted, malevolent, self-important bastard who's a disgrace to the uniform he wears.'

Losing his temper, Cracknell lashed out wildly with a fist but Daniel dodged the punch with ease and pushed him away. He squared up to the major, hands bunched in readiness. He looked lithe, fit and determined. He was fired by the opportunity to take revenge on behalf of Hillier and to assuage his own hatred of the man. It was a moment for which he'd always yearned. But it never came. Cracknell's anger was replaced by a sulky wariness. Aware of Daniel's reputation as a fighter, he had second thoughts about taking him on. The major was forced to back down, glowering at him but making no move. They stood there for several minutes. The tension was eventually broken by the appearance of a messenger.

'Excuse me,' said the man, entering the tent. 'Lieutenant Ainley told me that you were here, Captain Rawson. You're to report to General Churchill at once, sir. He has orders for you.'

Daniel was reluctant to leave the camp on the very day that he'd returned to it. Orders from Marlborough, however, could not be ignored. A dispatch had arrived from Vienna, instructing him to join the commander-in-chief as swiftly as possible because he was needed as an interpreter. Evidently, Marlborough knew about the success in France. Letters sent from The Hague had only given him outline details and he was anxious to hear the full story from the captain's own mouth. After a series of farewells, Daniel set out with a small escort on the road to the Austrian capital. In the company of fellow-soldiers, he was able to move much faster than he'd done during the flight from Paris. By staying in the saddle longer, they covered much more distance each day.

When they finally reached their destination, he expected Marlborough to be staying in one of the Emperor's palaces. Daniel found him ensconced instead at the home of the English ambassador in Vienna. Marlborough had been careful to avoid the formality that would have been imposed upon him if he'd been the Emperor's guest. In a private house, he was not dogged by ceremony. Daniel was given an effusive welcome and, as soon as he'd had some refreshment, pressed to give a detailed account of his trip to Paris. Both Marlborough and Adam Cardonnel were avid listeners. Distressed to hear of Pierre Lefeaux' fate, they were agog when Daniel explained how the escape from the Bastille had been engineered. He also passed on the intelligence that Janssen had taken the trouble to confide in him. As on previous occasions when he'd talked about the escapade, the names of Amalia and Beatrix did not feature.

'We owe you thanks and congratulations,' said Marlborough. 'When we heard that Janssen had been imprisoned, we abandoned all hope of ever seeing him again.'

'We wondered if we'd ever see *you* again,' added Cardonnel. 'It sounds to me as if you had some narrow escapes.'

'We did, sir,' said Daniel.

'Rather more of them than you told us about, in fact.'

'I don't follow.'

'We have another report of what took place in France. It's a shade more fulsome than your own.'

'Yes,' said Marlborough, reaching for a sealed letter on the table, 'we had a missive from Emanuel Janssen. He's put much more flesh on the story than you. You've been too self-effacing, Daniel. You said nothing about your capture by highwaymen or the crisis you met when you tried to drive a coach across a river.'

'They seemed irrelevant details, Your Grace,' said Daniel. 'My orders were to get someone out of Paris and that's what took up most of my energy. It's not something to boast about. I simply did what I felt was necessary.'

Marlborough laughed. 'Do you hear that, Adam?'

'Yes, Your Grace,' replied Cardonnel. 'I've never known a soldier less willing to take credit for his achievements.'

'It can't all be put down to modesty, I think. Daniel's loss of memory is another factor to consider.'

Daniel frowned. 'I had no loss of memory, Your Grace.'

'Then why did we not hear about Janssen's daughter, not to mention his assistant and servant? You rescued *four* people. One of them in particular has been singing your praises.'

'Oh?'

'I refer to Amalia Janssen. According to her father, she reveres you in every way. Well,' he went on, holding out the letter, 'you can read what she has to say. This was written in her own fair hand and enclosed with the missive from Janssen.'

'Thank you, Your Grace,' said Daniel, taking the letter.

'Read it in private,' suggested Marlborough. 'Later on, I trust, when your memory has been sufficiently jogged, you can tell us what *really* happened during your escape from France.'

Notwithstanding his regrets at having to leave his regiment, Daniel was delighted with his new duties. In taking part in diplomacy as an interpreter, he was helping to further the war effort. He was intrigued by the way that Marlborough persuaded Emperor Joseph to commit soldiers to the next campaign even though he gave no details of how he would deploy them. It was only at his lodging that Marlborough talked openly about the strategy for the coming year. Daniel felt honoured to be present at the discussion, a sign that his opinion was valued and his discretion taken for granted.

'Italy is the key to the whole enterprise,' said Marlborough, pointing at the map that lay open on the table. 'We must transfer all our regiments there so that we can unite with Prince Eugene and save Savoy from being overrun.'

'What of the Dutch army, Your Grace?' asked Daniel.

'It can stay in the Low Countries and do what it always does.

Namely, avoid anything resembling a full-scale battle. They and the French are kindred spirits. Instead of going on the attack, they'd rather adopt defensive positions and stare at each other over the intervening territory without firing a shot.'

'Moving our entire force to northern Italy is taking a huge risk.'

'That's precisely why the enemy will never expect it.'

'Think what happened last year,' said Cardonnel. 'Our march to the Danube was a triumph because it took the French by surprise. They never imagined we'd take so many men so far south.'

'In doing so,' resumed Marlborough, 'we were able to save the Empire from widespread destruction if not total extinction. It's the reason we're able to sit here in Vienna. By deceiving Marshal Tallard with regard to our objective, we secured the most resounding victory of the war. I look for a similar triumph in Savoy.'

'There'll be an immediate advantage,' said Daniel. 'You'll be fighting alongside a brilliant soldier. Prince Eugene has something of your own daring, Your Grace.'

'I hold him in the highest esteem.'

'You'll find him more amenable than General Slangenberg.'

'A wild elephant would be more amenable than Slangenberg,' said Marlborough, chuckling. 'At least it would charge without having to reconnoitre the battlefield three times before doing so. No,' he went on, tapping the map, 'Savoy must be the point of attack. It straddles the mountain passes between Italy and France. When we reinforce Savoy, we open up a gateway into enemy territory. It may even be possible to use the English navy to secure ports like Nice and Toulon, allowing a secondary invasion.'

'That would flutter the dovecotes in Versailles,' said Cardonnel.

'We must strike hard and strike early, Adam.'

'Thanks to the intelligence that Daniel passed on from our tapestry-maker with the sharp ears, we know that the French will concentrate their activities in the Low Countries.'

'They'll be ill-prepared for a decisive thrust into northern Italy.' Marlborough saw the doubt in Daniel's eyes. 'You have reservations, I fancy.'

'None at all about the boldness of the plan, Your Grace,' said Daniel. 'I admire it. However, three things worry me.'

'What are they?'

'First, there's the problem of getting our army there. It will involve a march through the length of Germany, across Austria, over the Alpine passes and down into the Lombardy plains.' His finger described the route on the map. 'At a rough guess, that must be twice the distance we travelled on our way to the Danube.'

'Another reason why the French will never imagine we'd attempt such a march. I know what your second objection is,' Marlborough went on, anticipating him, 'and it's been voiced before. On such a long journey, how will we keep the army in bread and forage?'

'It will place a massive burden on our quartermasters.'

'We shall have to plan ahead with the utmost care, Daniel.'

'That brings me to my third worry, Your Grace. The campaign will entail the support of our allies. Without a concerted attack,' said Daniel, 'we'd not be able to repel the French. How can we be sure that all contingents will arrive at the rendezvous together?'

'They managed it on the march to the Danube last year.'

'Yet they failed abysmally on the Moselle.'

'They did,' Marlborough conceded, 'and steps will be taken to prevent a repetition of that farce. You raise legitimate objections, Daniel, and we've looked at all three of them. With commitment and organisation, they can all be overcome. Put it another way,' he said, folding up the map. 'Where would you rather fight? Would you prefer to be bogged down in the Low Countries with the Dutch or riding into battle with Prince Eugene of Savoy?'

'I'd choose Prince Eugene every time,' said Cardonnel.

'So would I,' added Daniel, brightly. 'Italian wine tastes so much better than Dutch beer.'

Weeks rolled by with surprising speed. Daniel's command of German was put to good use in an endless round of ceremonies, meetings, dinners and balls held in celebration of Marlborough's visit. From Vienna, they went on to Berlin and thence to Hanover where the Electress Sophia, struck again by his graciousness, fawned over him. In diplomatic terms, the tour had been an unqualified success but it had been exhausting. The year was coming to an end before Daniel returned to The Hague with the embassy. His first task there was to act as an interpreter between Marlborough and Anthonie Heinsius, Grand Pensionary of Holland. A fine statesman, Heinsius still exerted great influence in his country though his power had declined a little after the death of William III. He and the commander-in-chief shared an implacable hatred of France's expansionist policies. There was a deep mutual respect between the two men.

Daniel had responded to Amalia's letter and couched his reply in the same affectionate terms that she'd used. Since they were constantly on the move, it was difficult to maintain a correspondence with her and he hoped for a chance to see Amalia when they got back to Holland. All that he contrived was a flying visit to Amsterdam but it was enough to show him that her feelings for him had not changed. On his part, he thought she looked more beautiful than ever. Being with her father in the safety of their own home had removed all her anxiety. She was happy, relaxed and enchanting.

'What time do you sail for England?' she asked.

'We leave on the morning tide, Amalia.'

'When will you be back?'

'Not until the spring,' he said.

'That's months away,' she protested.

'It will soon pass.'

'What will you do in England?'

'Oh, I think His Grace will have plenty of work for me.'

'Will you promise to write?'

'Only if you promise to reply,' he insisted.

'Please hurry back, Daniel. I'll miss you.'

'You could always visit me in England.'

'Father needs me here,' she said, resignedly.

Daniel put a hand under her chin to lift it up. 'I, too, have my needs,' he said, stealing a kiss. 'Think of me often.'

'Will you be staying in London?'

'That depends on His Grace,' he explained. 'But the first place I'll visit is Somerset.'

'Why?'

'I have to pay my respects, Amalia.'

Though the return voyage to England was uncomfortable, it had none of the horrors they'd encountered on their earlier crossing to Holland. Daniel was glad to step back on to British soil again. As soon as he could, he rode off in the direction of the West Country. Long hours in the saddle were taken up with contemplation. He missed Amalia, he thought about Henry Welbeck and he wondered how Tom Hillier was now faring. Not for the first time, he speculated on what would have happened if he and Major Cracknell had not been interrupted when they came close to exchanging blows. His worry was that, in trying to defend Hillier, he'd only made it more likely that the drummer would be singled out again for punishment. There was nothing he could do about that now.

Somerset was sprinkled with snow and spangled with frost. Its wintry prettiness was belied by a gusting wind that made his hat flap about and an icy track that caused his horse's hooves to slide from time to time. By adopting a cautious pace, he eventually reached the village and went straight to its church. The graveyard was dusted with white and the ground as hard as iron. Daniel was only a boy when he buried his father there. Captain Nathan Rawson had been one of the many rebels taken captive and hanged after the battle of Sedgemoor. Sneaking up to the gallows at night, Daniel and some friends had cut down the body and given it a hasty burial in consecrated ground. As he'd done most of the digging, Daniel remembered how soft the earth had been in July.

Since it was an unauthorised burial, they had hidden Nathan Rawson's last remains in a grave tucked away in a corner. It was several years before his son was able to return and, after explaining the situation to the priest, secure a proper Christian burial in the place where Nathan had once been baptised. Every time he came to England, Daniel made a pilgrimage to the site. The same bitter memories were resurrected. His father had been a valiant soldier who'd made the mistake of fighting for the wrong side. When the rebel army was routed, his fate was sealed and so was that of his farm. Under the threat of eviction, Daniel and his mother had loaded some belongings on to a cart and driven to the coast to take ship to Amsterdam.

Daniel reached out to brush the snowflakes from the headstone. His father's name had been chiselled in the stone along with the date of his death. Few people now remembered the blatant savagery of his execution and the public mortification attending it. His had been one of countless bodies that swung in the wind that summer. Nathan had met his end fearlessly. Daniel had been inspired by that. In his eyes, his father was no mere rebel but a hero prepared to fight for what he truly believed in. There was dignity in that.

He knelt beside the grave for a long time, pulling out weeds that had sprouted up since his last visit and clearing away the twigs that had been blown on to it. Before he rose to leave, he offered up his usual prayer for the salvation of his father's soul. A bond had been renewed. His visit to the past was over. Daniel rode slowly away from the village, his sorrow fringed with a strange feeling of pride. It stayed with him all the way back to London.

The Duke of Marlborough spent the winter months in the company of his beloved wife, Sarah, bemoaning his long absences and assuring her that the end of the war might be in sight if his calculations were proved to be correct. Details of his strategy were discussed at length with his inner circle, Daniel Rawson among them. Plans were put in place to guarantee that there would be adequate provisions for a large army on a longer march than had ever before been attempted during the war. Marlborough was brimming with confidence. He had the support of Queen Anne and of his close friend, Sidney Godolphin, Lord Treasurer and skilful manipulator of Parliament. Everything boded well for the new offensive.

Unfortunately, it was the French army that seized the initiative.

While the commander-in-chief of the Confederate armies was refining his strategy in England in April, 1706, a strong French force under Marshal Vendôme defeated a Hapsburg army at Calcinato in northern Italy. Instead of deploying his armies in defensive positions as he was wont to do, Louis XIV elected to engage the enemy. Marlborough and his staff crossed to The Hague almost a week later to be met by delay, disappointment and confusion. The Dutch had welcomed the idea of reinforcing Italy from the north. Once they realised that Marlborough intended to go there in person, they feared that he'd weaken their defences in doing so and render them vulnerable to attack.

Dutch vacillation was followed by a blank refusal to cooperate from other quarters. The Danish, Hessian, Hanoverian and Prussian commanders reneged on their earlier undertakings and withheld their support. The prospect of taking the war to Italy frightened them. It was a crushing setback for Marlborough, made worse by the fact that the careful preparations needed for a sustained march were well short of completion. There had been a woeful lack of urgency in setting up depots. It was as bad as in the previous year. Marlborough was furious and dismayed. It was almost as if his allies were deliberately holding him back. Though he tried to rectify the situation with commendable energy, it was an impossible task. The strategy he'd nurtured for so many months was now in danger of falling apart.

The final crippling blow came early in May. With great secrecy, Marshal Villars and Marshal Marsin had prepared an offensive against the position held in Alsace by the Margrave of Baden. They took the Imperialist troops by surprise and captured Haguenau, forcing Baden's men to retreat in disarray across the Rhine. The fortress of Landau, which had changed hands many times, was under siege once more. The dramatic change in French tactics had been rewarded. In Alsace, as in northern Italy, signal victories had been secured. It was an ideal start to the new campaign. At the same time, it was a declaration of intention. France was on the attack.

Daniel was at his side when Marlborough received a dispatch, telling him of the Allied defeat in Alsace. All hope of marching to Italy vanished. His bold plan would never be put into operation. They were back where they had been the previous year, losing ground to the enemy and compelled to restrict their activities to the Low Countries. Overcoming his frustration, Marlborough adapted swiftly to the change of perspective. He even found cause for optimism.

'Our intelligence from Versailles was inaccurate,' he said. 'The King has realised that you can only win a battle if you engage with the enemy. If he's ready to sanction an attack, we don't have to provoke the French any longer. They'll come at us of their own volition.'

'That will make a change, Your Grace,' said Daniel.

'It's a very welcome change.'

'What's brought it about, do you think?'

'King Louis wished to remind the Dutch of his power,' said Cardonnel. 'We know from our spies that he secretly offered peace to the States-General during the winter. Naturally, he wishes it to be negotiated on his terms. By securing these early triumphs in Italy and Alsace, he's sending a message to The Hague.'

'Unfortunately,' said Daniel, 'many people will heed it. The closer the French encroach on us, the louder are the calls in Holland for a peace settlement.'

Marlborough was adamant. 'The only way to achieve peace is to defeat the French,' he said. 'I firmly believe that we have the money, men and spirit to do it.'

'We're somewhat short of men, Your Grace,' Cardonnel told him. 'The Hanoverians and Hessians have not yet arrived and the Danish cavalry will not be here for a week or more.'

'What about the Prussians?' asked Daniel.

'King Frederick is having another tantrum, alas. He's refusing to send his contingents until we've listened to his grievances.'

'I thought they'd all been remedied, sir.'

'Since our visit, he's invented some new ones.'

'His support is more trouble than it's worth.'

'Forget about the Prussians,' said Marlborough, shaking off his depression at the prospect of action. 'Forget about the Hanoverians and the Hessians. The time for talking is over at last. Everything points to the possibility of a battle against Marshal Villeroi. By the time it takes place, we'll have sufficient forces. We may have lost our chance of a telling attack in northern Italy but we've gained something in return. We now have an opportunity for a decisive engagement on our own doorstep, so to speak. I feel exhilarated, gentlemen,' he went on, raising a fist. 'For the first time since Blenheim, I feel that destiny is at hand. Nothing will content me more than to offer battle to the French. I have every confidence that we'll achieve a complete victory.'

Chapter Sixteen

'Greetings to you, stranger!' said Welbeck, sardonically. 'This regiment is the 24ᵗʰ Foot. It's always a privilege to welcome a new officer.'

'There's no need for sarcasm, Henry.'

'How do you come to know my name, sir?'

'It was a lucky guess,' said Daniel.

'Wonders never cease.'

'Stop this horseplay, will you?'

'Why?' said the sergeant, pretending to recognise him for the first time. 'I do believe it might be our long-lost Captain Rawson.'

'You know bloody well it is.'

'We thought we'd never see you again, sir.'

'I haven't been away *that* long,' said Daniel. 'In fact, it seems like no time at all since I saw that hideous visage of yours. What's been happening in my absence?'

'There's been nothing of consequence, Dan.'

'*Something* must have occurred.'

'You know what winter quarters are like. We get up, visit the latrines, eat, drill, eat again, go back to the latrines, drill again then moan about the fools who're supposed to lead us. Whenever I look at our officers,' said Welbeck, mordantly, 'I think that a lot of villages back in England must be missing their idiots.'

'It's good to know that you have such faith in us, Henry.'

'Present company excepted, of course.'

Daniel laughed. 'Thank you.'

It was months since he'd seen his friend. For most of them, he'd not even been in the same country as Welbeck. While it was rewarding to be one of Marlborough's aides-de-camp, it did distance him from so many friends in the regiment. Simultaneously, it also set him apart from his few enemies. One of them popped into his mind.

'How has Major Cracknell been treating you?' he asked.

'He's been the soul of kindness, Dan.'

'I refuse to believe that.'

'I was joking,' said Welbeck. The major is a conceited, spiteful, self-serving cunt but you already know that.'

'I've said as much to his face,' recalled Daniel, 'though not in those precise words. He tried to hit me.'

'Really – when was this?'

'The day I left here. I offered to fight but he thought better of it. To be honest, I expected him to challenge me to a duel.'

'He's not that stupid, Dan. The major has seen you practising with a sabre. He knows you'd cut him to shreds.'

'It's no more than he deserves, Henry. Is he still harassing your nephew?' Welbeck nodded. 'What's he been up to now?'

'He's still looking for another excuse to have the lad flogged again. Since he can't find one, he keeps reprimanding Tom for trivial bloody offences that were never committed in the first place. It's upsetting to watch,' said Welbeck. 'Can't the army find the major something more useful to do than hounding a harmless drummer?'

'It's going to find him something very soon.'

'What's that?'

'Fighting a battle,' replied Daniel. 'That's the one thing Major Cracknell can do with any distinction. When he's fulfilling his duties against the Frenchies, he won't have time to bother Tom Hillier.'

Welbeck was cynical. 'There's no earthly hope of a battle with those cowardly bastards,' he said. 'They'd much rather just look over the ramparts and wave at us.'

'That's where you're wrong, Henry. His Grace has every reason to believe that Marshal Villeroi is prepared to engage us this time.'

'It will never happen.'

'It will,' said Daniel. 'The marshal is as eager to bring this war to an end as we are. According to our latest reports, he has an army of 74 battalions and 128 squadrons. I don't think he'll keep a force of that size sitting on its hands. Marshal Villeroi has two very strong incentives,' he continued. 'The first is that he wishes – like everyone else in France – to avenge the defeat at Blenheim. That still rankles at Versailles.'

'So it should, Dan. We kicked their arses hard that day.'

'The second thing that drives him on is that conviction that he's a better commander than His Grace. He thinks he proved that last year at the River Yssche.'

'We were betrayed once again by the fucking Dutch!' said Welbeck, angrily. 'Villeroi was lucky. If we'd been allowed to attack, we'd have smashed his army to smithereens.'

'We may have a second chance to do that, Henry.'

'I won't believe it till I see it.'

'You've every right to be sceptical,' said Daniel. 'We've been in this position before and nothing happened. This time, however, I'm certain that it will. Prepare for battle, Henry. Marshal Villeroi simply wants to avenge Blenheim – we have a chance to repeat it!'

Corswaren was a little village that lay in a hollow beneath the whirring sails of its windmill. The Allied armies camped nearby. It was country they knew well from previous campaigns. At their back, less than twenty miles away, was the River Meuse, curving its way south. Ahead of them were the French lines. At 1 a.m. on 23 May, Marlborough sent off Brigadier-General Cadogan, one of his most trusted men, with an advance guard. Their orders were to reconnoitre the high ground between two rivers, the Mehaigne and the Little Gheete. Conditions were poor. After three days of pelting rain, there was a thick fog that night. Two hours after dispatching Cadogan, his quartermaster, Marlborough led the main body out of camp. Captain Daniel Rawson was with him.

The advance guard had ridden beyond the village of Merdorp when they encountered a French patrol. As soon as they heard distant firing, the patrol withdrew. Though there was full daylight now, mist was still swirling unpredictably around. Cadogan could see very little at first then something uncannily reminiscent of their experience at Blenheim occurred. The mist began to thin and lift. What he saw through his telescope was a wide sweep of open country with hardly any trees and hedges to impede movement. On a high ground some four miles off, he picked up clear signs of movement. Guessing that it was Villeroi's advance guard, Cadogan promptly sent a galloper to alert Marlborough. It was not until 10 a.m that the brigadier-general and the commander-in-chief were able to survey the scene together. Marlborough was astonished at what he saw.

'It's just like Blenheim,' he said. 'It's a natural battlefield.'

He scrutinised it through his telescope. The vast expanse of land would allow huge numbers of soldiers to be aligned in rigid mass formation. It was a perfect arena for war. The rolling acres bore such a resemblance to the plain near Blenheim that Marlborough's spirits soared. As in all battles, his strategy was dictated by the nature of the terrain. Little discussion was required. It was obvious to him, his staff and the accompanying Allied officers that the engagement had to take place on the undulating plain between Taviers and Ramillies. All that remained was to deploy his cavalry and his troops. Three hours later, they were all in position. The battle of Ramillies was imminent.

'What are we waiting for?' asked Tom Hillier, holding his drum.

'Reinforcements,' said Hugh Dobbs. 'Some of our allies are late.'

'Where are they?'

'Shitting with fright behind a hedge, I expect. You can never trust foreigners, Tom. They always let you down.'

'Will there really be a battle this time?'

'That's what it looks like.'

'Who's going to win?'

'We are,' said Dobbs with a strained laugh.

He expected a comment from Hillier but his friend's attention had already wandered in a way that was wearisomely familiar. Since his flogging, Hillier had been withdrawn. Though he went through the drills with the other drummers and slept in the tent with his friends, he was no longer the fresh-faced, earnest young recruit. Eighty lashes had taken something out of him and replaced it with a brooding sadness. Instead of enjoying the company of the others, he was detached and melancholy. Nudging him in the ribs, Dobbs tried to bring him out of his dejection.

'This is what you joined the army for, Tom,' he said.

Hillier woke up. 'What's that?'

'You want to kick seven barrels of *merde* out of the Frenchies.'

'All we can do is to beat our drums.'

'Where would the rest of them be without us? We control the battle. It's the drum calls that tell the soldiers what to do.'

'It's not the same as holding a musket, Hugh.'

'Your time for doing that will come.'

'No, it won't,' said Hillier, flatly.

'I thought that was your ambition.'

'I don't have ambitions now.'

Once again Hillier's eyes glazed over as his mind drifted away. He was surrounded by thousands of men on the verge of battle yet he might have been somewhere entirely on his own. Dobbs had given up trying to understand his friend, still less hoping to talk him out of his prolonged misery. Even Hillier's uncle, Sergeant Welbeck, had failed to do that. The drummer was beyond help.

Dobbs didn't have to nudge his friend again. Someone rode up on a horse and turned the animal so that its flank knocked Hillier sideways, making him struggle to retain his balance. Looking down from the saddle was Major Cracknell.

'Watch where you're going, you numbskull,' he barked.

'I'm sorry, Major,' said Hillier, dully.

'I hope you keep your eyes open when battle commences.'

'Yes, Major.'

'You have a job to do.'

'Yes, Major.'

'Only time will tell if you've the stomach for a fight. I doubt very much if you have. It's always the same with the dregs of humanity we have to endure in our ranks. They're all cowards.'

'Begging your pardon, Major,' said Dobbs, defensively, 'but that's unfair on Tom. I know how brave he can be.'

'I don't see any bravery in dropping his breeches for a whore,' said Cracknell. 'Bravery is what a man shows in battle.'

'Yes, Major.'

'Did you hear that, Hillier?'

There was a long, considered pause. 'Yes, Major,' he said.

Daniel had never admired the Duke of Marlborough as much. He'd fought under his command in major battles before but had never been near him during the action. As part of his staff, he now had the privilege of watching him at close quarters. The person beside him was very different to the suave, urbane, congenial diplomat who was at ease in the courts of Europe. What he saw now was John Churchill, Duke of Marlborough, a soldier to his fingertips, bold, calm, decisive, vigilant, unflustered and bristling with energy, a supreme commander at the height of his powers. Despair and disappointment were behind him now. Marlborough had a golden opportunity for glory.

His army had been drawn up in standard battle formation. British battalions and squadrons were positioned in a double line near the Jeuche stream, their scarlet uniforms resplendent in the sun. The bulk of the Allied infantry – some 30,000 or more – occupied the centre ground opposite Offus and Ramillies. On their left were 69 squadrons of Dutch and Danish horse under the command of General Overkirk. Battalions of Dutch Guards were stationed on the extreme left. Daniel had noted the meticulous care with which Marlborough had sited his artillery. In all, he had 100 cannon and 20 howitzers at his disposal. A battery of 24-pounders was gathered in a cluster facing Ramillies. Other batteries overlooked the Gheete and a couple of pieces were attached to the Dutch Guards on the far left. On a battlefield as wide as this, artillery could never dictate the outcome because whole areas were beyond its reach. Marlborough had put his guns where they could do most damage and offer most protection to the cavalry and infantry.

Against this array of Allied power, Villeroi had marshalled his men along a concave line. On his extreme right were five battalions in Taviers and Franquenée. The main right wing of the Franco-Bavarian army consisted of 82 squadrons, interlined with brigades of infantry, facing the open plain. In the centre were 20 battalions and a dozen of the lethal triple-barrelled cannon were placed around Ramillies with additional foot in the rear. Overlooking the Little Gheete further north were more battalions and guns. As a final part of his deployment, Villeroi had put 50 squadrons of horse around the village of Autre-Eglise which, with Offus, was intended to anchor the left flank. There was one serious oversight. Because he deemed the marshes around the rivers impassable, the French commander had sent no troops to defend them.

Daniel was tingling with anticipatory delight as he scanned the battlefield. He felt certain that a momentous victory could be achieved. Of the two armies, neither had a marked numerical advantage but he knew that the Allied artillery was far superior. Marlborough had deployed his men in a more compact formation. While Daniel had been impressed by this, he didn't underestimate the enemy. Marshal Villeroi was an experienced and able commander, determined not to repeat the mistakes made by Marshal Tallard at Blenheim. His army was strongly posted but, as Daniel was quick to observe, in deciding to stand on the defensive, he'd surrendered the initiative. It was left to Marlborough to make the opening moves.

Early in the afternoon, the guns fired and the battle began. The extremities of the Allied line were called into play first. Attacking in the south, the Dutch Guards used their two cannon to smash a way through houses and walls. Within a couple of hours, they'd overrun both Taviers and Franquenée. Alarmed by this development, Villeroi launched a counter-attack, sending squadrons of dragoons and battalions of Swiss troops, supported by a Bavarian brigade. It was a calamitous exercise. When the dragoons dismounted among the marshes, they were at the mercy of an advancing Danish cavalry that swept quickly through them. The Swiss took to their heels in panic and most of the Bavarians joined in the retreat. There was now a serious threat to the French on their right wing.

Meanwhile, Marlborough was also probing on the other flank. Under the command of General Lord Orkney, a redoubtable Scot, the massed British battalions were dispatched in the direction of Offus, near which the enemy command post had been set up. Villeroi's judgement had failed him. Having believed the marshes on that flank to be impassable, he now watched with growing consternation as waves of British soldiers trudged through them over fascines. Every time the smoke of gunfire cleared, the lines could be seen getting ever closer, marching to the beat of the drums. With each new burst of cannon or musketry fire from the French, scores of redcoats toppled to the ground with fatal wounds or gruesome injuries. They were immediately used as stepping stones through the quagmire, dead bodies or stray limbs being gathered up indiscriminately and pressed into service as auxiliary fascines. French gunfire was unrelenting but the battalions kept surging on and the drums never faltered. Tom Hillier, Hugh Dobbs and the others kept their nerve in the hail of musket balls and maintained their line. In spite of the pounding it took, the advance continued with a sense of inevitability, climbing the slope to the ridgeline until it passed the outlying farms. It reached the very walls of Offus and Autre-Eglise, dispersing the garrisons in each village and hunting them from building to building.

Observing it all from a vantage point, Daniel was thrilled by the apparent success of the thrust on the right. He was therefore amazed when Marlborough handed him a dispatch for Orkney.

'They must withdraw immediately,' said Marlborough.

Daniel gaped. 'Withdraw?' he said. 'When they clearly have the advantage?'

'Deliver my orders, Daniel.'

'At once, Your Grace.'

'And please don't question them again.'

'No, Your Grace.'

Daniel spurred his horse into a gallop down the slope. Though he preferred to be in the thick of the fighting, he was given a taste of its ferocity as he sped across the plain. Cannon were still booming and muskets still popping. Smoke was everywhere. Wounded horses neighed in agony as they threshed about on the ground. Despairing cries of dying soldiers swelled the pandemonium. When he rode up the slope towards the main action, Daniel had to evade mounds of corpses. Lord Orkney's troops were outnumbered yet they still continued to advance, engaging in fierce hand-to-hand fighting against French and

Walloon infantry. Locating the commander amid the fray, Daniel handed him the dispatch and waited for him to read it.

Orkney was outraged. 'Pray, what's this?' he yelled. 'His Grace wishes us to retire across the Gheete? I've no mind to give ground while we're giving no quarter.'

'Those are your orders, my lord,' said Daniel.

'And damn vexatious orders they are! We're on the point of occupying Offus. We fought our way here through a blizzard of bullets and round shot. Are we to abandon what we've gained?'

'I'm sure the decision has great merit.'

Daniel left him fuming and galloped off in the opposite direction. On his way back, deafened by the noise of battle, he recognised another of Marlborough's ADCs riding towards the right flank and he wondered if the orders he'd just delivered had been countermanded. In fact, they were being reinforced. To make sure that his commands were obeyed, Marlborough sent no fewer than ten consecutive dispatches to Orkney. He even sent Cadogan, to make sure that the withdrawal was swift and orderly. The attack was called off. Angry, bewildered and feeling let down, Orkney retired with exemplary skill, sustaining losses in doing so but beating off any attempts by the French to pursue them. In obedience to Marlborough's orders, the battalions drew up on the other side of the Gheete, wholly at a loss to understand why their incisive strike had been suddenly halted.

Villeroi, meanwhile, was congratulating himself on having repulsed a dangerous attack but, as a result, he'd had to withdraw substantial forces from the centre of his line. Rather than send them back, he kept them on his left flank to counter the menace of the British battalions lined up beyond the Gheete. Marlborough's bluff had worked. Because Orkney's attack was clearly not a feint, Villeroi had unbalanced his dispositions. In strengthening the left flank, he'd seriously weakened the centre. Solid lines of infantry and cavalry had been drastically thinned down across two miles of open plain between Taviers and Ramillies.

From their position on high ground between the two villages, Marlborough had an excellent view of the entire battlefield. When Daniel realised what their commander-in-chief had done, he regretted his temerity in questioning the decision. It was a brilliant strategy.

Ramillies itself now came under attack. A dozen battalions under the command of General Schultz advanced against heavy resistance until they reached the village itself, forcing the garrison to look to its own defence rather than being able to offer support elsewhere. The grand attack on the French centre was led by General Overkirk with Allied cavalry supported by Dutch, German and Swiss infantry in the pay of the Dutch. They moved inexorably forward in four dense ranks along a line that extended from Ramillies to the Mehaigne. The real test was now coming.

Daniel was able to look down on four miles of unremitting warfare. Smoke billowed, cannon roared, cavalry charged, sabres clashed, foot soldiers traded fire, drummers beat out their calls and all the unstinting savagery of battle was released amid the tumult. Longing to be involved in it all, Daniel was forced to be an onlooker, trying to decide at which point the fighting was most intense and where the Allies were gaining the upper hand. Hurling themselves against the French centre, the Allied cavalry crashed easily through the first line of enemy horse. When they tried to penetrate even further, however, the infantry which interleaved Villeroi's cavalry responded with such a sustained volley that they were stopped in their tracks.

Of more significance was a counter-charge by the Maison du Roi, the French household cavalry, 13 squadrons in all. It was so swift, controlled and powerful that Overkirk's cavalry wilted before it. Patently, the Allied centre needed much more support. Marlborough supplied it in person.

'Are you ready for action, Daniel?' he said, taking out his sabre.

'Yes, Your Grace.'

'Then let's not miss the fun.'

'I'm with you,' shouted Daniel above the hullabaloo.

With the rest of his staff at his heels, Marlborough led the way. Having already anticipated heavy resistance in the centre, he had withdrawn some of the squadrons from the right flank to act as reinforcements to Overkirk. Because of the undulations in the terrain, the additional horse had departed from Orkney's force without being seen by Villeroi. Thinking he was still threatened by a sizeable army on his left flank, he kept several battalions away from the centre where they would have been far more use. Once again, Villeroi had been tricked by Marlborough, leaving a sector of his line vulnerable.

The arrival of their commander-in-chief at the head of fresh squadrons rallied the troops and horse in the centre. In his long scarlet coat with the sky-blue sash of the Garter, he was recognised at once by his men. Unfortunately, in making himself so visible, he also became a target for the French. Rejoicing at the chance to kill the one man who could contrive their defeat, they tried to run him down. Before Marlborough went very far, his horse stumbled at a ditch and threw its rider, leaving him defenceless on the ground. The French cavalry tried to hack their way towards him. It was a critical moment and Daniel was acutely aware of it. To lose Marlborough would be to lose the presiding genius of the

Allied army. Leaping from his horse in the middle of the melee, Daniel held its bridle and stirrup while Marlborough heaved himself up into the saddle.

There was more help at hand. Seeing their captain-general in difficulties, Major General Murray marched up rapidly with two Swiss battalions to cover his escape. Some of the pursuing French cavalry were unable to check their galloping horses and rode straight on to the gleaming bayonets of the Swiss infantry. Daniel was a grateful beneficiary. While many of the horses were impaled, it was the riders who mostly felt the thrust of cold steel and writhed in agony on the ground. Loose horses were everywhere, neighing in fear, kicking out, bumping into each other and trying to escape the burning cauldron of battle. Seizing a passing bridle, Daniel steadied the prancing stallion enough to mount it. He was now able to wield his sabre to cut a swathe through the enemy. The action was hot and he revelled in it.

Everything turned on the cavalry engagement at the heart of the battle. The elite French squadrons held the early advantage. As the battle raged on, however, and as Marlborough fed more squadrons from the right flank into the action, the balance tilted in favour of the Allies. By late afternoon, when the plain was red with blood and littered with corpses, they had built up a superiority of eight to five. There was marked progress elsewhere as well. On the extreme left of Marlborough, the Danish cavalry beyond Taviers cut through the French anchoring force on the Mehaigne and swung north to threaten Villeroi's flank.

At 4 p.m. Marlborough deemed it the moment to order his final charge. Massing his cavalry, he sent them off at a trot to gain impetus as they went along. The Maison du Roi re-gathered and formed a line to meet them. Two large, proud, urgent, tiring, bloodstained, sweat-covered bands of horsemen charged forward with murderous intent. When they met once again, there was an ear-shattering clang of sabres as they tried to cut down each other like so much human timber. Neither side gave ground. In the mounting frenzy of battle, gaping wounds were opened up, eyes gouged out, hands and arms severed, horses slashed to death and, in one case, a Dutch head cut clean from its shoulders. The French held the charge at first but the numbers told steadily against them. Bursting through the gaps in the enemy squadrons, the Allied cavalry was able to attack from the rear. The end was at last in sight.

Responding to orders, Orkney marched his men forward over the crest of a hill, deploying his forces in such a way as to give the appearance of a sizeable army. In fact, it had been seriously depleted but Villeroi was unaware of that. What preoccupied him was the threat of a second attack on his left flank. The French commander was so fearful of the phantom army beyond the marshes that he did not realise what was happening on his extreme right. The Danish cavalry had encircled the French flank from the south. At the same time, with an irresistible surge, the Allied infantry finally captured Ramillies and drove its garrison out. When the French line broke, its nerve broke with it. The panic-stricken cry of *sauve qui peut* swept through the whole army and entire brigades ran for their lives.

Marshal Villeroi had lost the battle. As a last resort, he ordered the largely unused cavalry along the Gheete to form a line in order to cover the retreat. Naked fear was the only command they obeyed. To Villeroi's disgust, all 50 squadrons deserted him and rode hell for leather through the fleeing French infantry, knocking many of them over and pummelling some to death. It was a complete rout. The whole plain was a scene of undiluted chaos as thousands of French and Bavarian troops struggled madly to get past abandoned coaches, carriages and carts, running through the mud to escape the flashing blades of the pursuing Allied cavalry. To all intents and purposes, the battle of Ramillies was over.

Behind the victory lay thousands of individual stories, none more remarkable than that of Kit Davies, a tough and spirited woman who'd disguised herself as a man in order to pursue an errant husband into the army. For twelve years she'd enjoyed the life of a roving soldier without once arousing the suspicions of her fellows. Only her husband knew her secret. Ramillies exposed the truth. Davies was injured by a shell that bounced off a church steeple and fractured her skull. When the surgeons examined her, they were dumbfounded by what they discovered. Expecting to treat a wounded man, they had incontrovertible proof that she was a woman.

Marlborough himself would have tales to tell. Apart from being rescued by Daniel Rawson when in the path of the French cavalry, he had had another lucky escape. As he mounted a horse at one point, a round shot fired from a French battery passed under his cocked leg and skimmed the saddle before decapitating Colonel Bringfield who was holding the stirrup for him. A few inches higher and the missile would have killed Marlborough. The result of the battle might then have been different.

One of the incidents that would stay locked in Daniel's mind for ever occurred when the battle was over. He found a moment to congratulate the men from his regiment on their part in the triumph. As he approached them, he saw Major Cracknell lording it over a group of junior officers, boasting about his exploits during the battle. The major was holding a glass of wine and lifting it high. He never got to drink it. A shot rang out and a musket ball burrowed deep into his brain, killing him instantly and making his fist tighten around the glass until it broke apart. The person who'd fired the shot was Tom Hillier. Daniel ran towards him but he was too slow to prevent the drummer from using the bayonet to stab his own heart. When he fell forward, the weapon hit the ground hard and went right through him, piercing the flesh and protruding from his back. Hillier had taken leave of army life altogether. Turning him over, Daniel was astonished by what he saw. It was incredible. In spite of a grotesque death, there was a contented smile on Hillier's young face.

Later on, Daniel discussed it all with Henry Welbeck.

'How did he learn to shoot like that?' asked the sergeant.

'You forget that Tom grew up on a farm like me. He'd have been taught to hunt for game. You quickly learn to shoot straight when you want to put food on the table.'

'He must have picked up a discarded musket.'

'There were thousands of those to choose from,' said Daniel.

'Tom has been biding his time, waiting for his chance.'

'Yes, Henry. I don't think he was acting on impulse. He'd taken all he could from the major and simply had to hit back. When he saw his opportunity, he couldn't resist it.'

'He's not the first soldier to shoot an officer he despised.'

'I daresay he won't be the last.'

'In one sense,' decided Welbeck, 'I suppose he did us all a favour. Everyone will be glad to see the back of Major Cracknell.'

'I'd rather have the major and Tom still alive.'

'The lad was never made for the army, Dan.'

'I disagree,' said Daniel. 'He had all the attributes. His problem was to fall into the clutches of someone like Cracknell.

From that point on, he was a marked man. The major took a delight in baiting Tom. If he'd been able to, I fancy he'd have wielded the cat-o'-nine-tails himself. Ideally, of course,' he went on, sadly, 'he'd have preferred to have *me* strung up on that triangle. Punishing Tom was a means of working off his hatred of me.'

Welbeck was distressed. 'What am I going to write to my sister?' he asked. 'She expected me to look after the lad.'

'Tell her the truth, Henry.'

'That Tom shot an officer then killed himself with a bayonet?'

'No,' said Daniel, 'I think there's a better way of putting it. Your nephew died in action at the battle of Ramillies. That's all his parents need to know. They'll think he was a hero.'

'He was, Dan,' said Welbeck. 'That's exactly what he was.'

Pursuit of the enemy continued well into the night. Stragglers were overtaken, killed or taken prisoner. Marshal Villeroi and the Elector of Bavaria narrowly missed being captured by the Allied cavalry. Their brilliant army had been reduced to a frightened rabble. Marlborough himself joined in the pursuit, determined to press home his advantage to the hilt. When darkness came, he lay on the ground under a cloak to snatch some sleep. It was not until the next day that the true scale of his triumph was known. He was at his headquarters with Cadogan and Cardonnel when Daniel Rawson brought in the details. He gave the document to Marlborough.

'Have they finished counting the numbers?' he said.

'Not quite, Your Grace,' replied Daniel, 'but I understand that you'll have a fairly accurate idea of them from that list.'

Marlborough read it out. 'Villeroi lost at least 15,000 men, killed or wounded,' he said, happily, 'and as many again have been taken prisoner. That's half their strength, gentlemen. We've crushed the French army to a pulp.'

'What of our own casualties?' wondered Cadogan.

'We lost less than 2,500 men, William.'

'God be praised!'

'Save some of that praise for our soldiers,' said Marlborough. 'They showed rare courage and endurance. The French officers lacked both. That was the essential difference between the two sides.'

'The essential difference was our commander-in-chief,' said Daniel, setting off a loud murmur of approval from the others. 'You completely outwitted Marshal Villeroi, Your Grace. In many ways, this victory was even greater than that at Blenheim.'

'There's no doubt about that, Daniel. Blenheim lasted for seven or eight hours and we lost 12,000 men. The battle of Ramillies was over in two hours and our losses were considerably smaller.' He waved the paper in his hand. 'According to this, we also acquired 50 cannon and 80 standards and colours. Huge numbers of abandoned weapons have also been recovered.'

'The victory will reverberate throughout Europe, Your Grace,' said Cardonnel. 'Our detractors will no longer be able to claim that Blenheim was merely an instance of good fortune. Ramillies has attested your superiority as a commander once and for all. And the real beauty of it is,' he added, 'that the triumph comes so early in the campaign.'

'Quite so, Adam,' agreed Marlborough, beaming. 'The summer lies before us. With God's help, we'll make the best of it.'

News of the victory was greeted with celebrations all over Europe. Not everyone, however, was pleased by the tidings. Three people were especially dismayed. Johannes Mytens, Willem Ketel and Gaston Loti found the news disconcerting. When they met at Mytens' house in The Hague, they were furious.

'There's no hope of peace now,' said Ketel.

'None at all,' said Mytens, gloomily. 'Encouraged by what he achieved at Ramillies, the Duke will want to fight on regardless. The drain on our national finances will be greater than ever.'

'Think of the loss of our soldiers, Johannes. Many more of them will be killed in battles to satisfy the Duke's craving for warfare.'

'The situation is hopeless.'

'I think not,' said Loti with smiling determination. 'Remember what we agreed, gentlemen. We have to cut the Gordian knot. Since the Duke is an insuperable barrier to peace, we have to be ruthless. He must die.'

'That's easier said than done,' remarked Ketel, scratching his head under his wig. 'I hired a man weeks ago to find out the best way to assassinate the Duke. He said it couldn't be done because it's impossible to get close enough.'

'Then we hire someone to shoot from a distance,' said Mytens.

'He's always surrounded by people.'

'In that case, we devise a way to kill him and his staff. If they can be lured into the right place, they can all be blown up in the same explosion.'

'It would never work, Johannes.'

'The Duke is only human.'

'Not if you listen to common report,' said Ketel, bitterly. 'He's being acclaimed as some kind of god. Wherever he goes, he'll be feted. That means the Duke will always have the protection of a crowd.'

'We are to hold a dinner in his honour here in The Hague,' said Mytens, 'and I'll be forced to cheer the Duke and fawn like all those obsequious fools in the States-General. If only we could use the occasion to have him shot dead.'

'He'll be far too well protected. Besides, if the bullet goes astray, it might kill someone else by mistake. Do you want Heinsius to be shot in place of the Duke?'

'No, Willem. The risk is too great. It's also difficult to see how an assassin could escape after firing a shot. Guards would be on him in a flash and our names would be tortured out of him. Our own lives would then be in danger. Well,' he continued, fingering his double chin, 'if it's not possible to shoot him, then we must find another means of killing him.'

'What we really need is the right man to do it.'

'You're chasing the wrong fox, gentleman,' said Loti, shrewdly. 'I fancy that there's a very simple way to dispose of the person who stands between us and a peaceful settlement to this ruinous war. I suggest that you leave the arrangements to me. I have the perfect assassin in mind.'

'Do you know of a man capable enough?' asked Ketel.

'I wouldn't even bother looking for one, Willem. This is not a task for any man,' he went on. 'I propose to engage a woman.'

The dinner was held in the city hall and was attended by the Grand Pensionary, members of the States-General, civic worthies and invited guests. Daniel Rawson was included in the Duke of Marlborough's party. When they arrived at the venue, they wore their dress uniforms and were given an ovation by the large crowd gathered outside to welcome them. Inside the building, they were greeted in order of seniority by Grand Pensionary Heinsius. Daniel waited patiently behind Marlborough,

Overkirk, Churchill, Cadogan, Orkney and other senior officers to shake Heinsius' hand. When he entered the hall where the long tables were in a horseshoe pattern, Daniel had a surprise that took his breath away. Amalia Janssen was there. She was wearing a gorgeous blue dress with a bell-shaped skirt, a high-necked bodice and tight sleeves, ending in a cuff above the elbow. On her head was a fontage of upright lace, pleated and in tiers. The whole effect was stunning. Daniel had never seen her looking so enchanting. He rushed across to greet her.

'I never expected to see you here, Amalia,' he said.

'Father and I were invited at the Duke's suggestion,' she told him. 'I hoped against hope that you might be here as well, Daniel.'

'His Grace wanted me beside him as an interpreter. There'll be lots of worthy but rather boring speeches that I'll have to translate from the Dutch. To be honest, I wasn't looking forward to the occasion at all. Now,' he said, gazing adoringly at her, 'I'll enjoy every second.'

'And so shall I.'

'What have you been doing since we last met?'

'Nothing of any importance,' she said. 'Nothing that could possibly compare with winning a famous victory as you did.'

Daniel grinned. 'There were one or two other people who helped to achieve that victory,' he said. 'It wasn't entirely my doing.'

'I'm sure that you played a crucial part.'

'All the plaudits should go to His Grace.'

'Have you enjoyed being part of his staff?'

'Yes and no,' he replied. 'Yes, in the sense that it's placed me at the very centre of events.'

'That must have been very exciting.'

'It was, Amalia, but it also kept me away from you for a long time and that was irksome. The months I spent in England seemed like years.'

'I'm just so pleased to see you again,' she said, touching his arm. 'When I heard about the battle, I feared that you might have been injured or even killed.'

'Nothing would keep me away from you.'

'Good evening, Captain Rawson,' said Emanuel Janssen as he joined them. 'I had a feeling you'd try to monopolise my daughter. Not that I have any objection to that, mind you.'

'I'm glad to hear it,' said Daniel.

'I've just had a brief word with your commander-in-chief. He tells me that you distinguished yourself on the battlefield yet again.'

'I was only one of thousands.'

'You're always so modest,' said Amalia.

'Would you rather I told you that I'd won the battle single-handed and that I deserved – at the very least – an earldom for my services to Queen and country?'

They shared a laugh but it was the last thing they were able to do. A gong sounded and guests were directed to their seats. Daniel was on the top table, seated beside Marlborough. He was sorry that Amalia and her father were so far away from him. It was difficult to see them properly at the far end of the table. Simply having Amalia in the same room, however, had transformed the occasion. What he'd envisaged as a dull, formal event now took on the aura of a very special day in his life. The meal was excellent, the wine plentiful and the speeches interminable. Some were in English but those in Dutch required translation.

Toasts were even more plentiful than the speeches. A number of civic dignitaries felt it incumbent upon them to rise to their feet, glass in hand, and blurt out a toast. Daniel took particular interest in a member of the States-General who proposed a toast, noting that his name was Johannes Mytens. His interest sprang not from the fulsome remarks made by the man but from his dazzling companion. Mytens sat next to a handsome, poised, full-bodied woman in her twenties. At an assembly dominated by men, she had real presence. Dressed in the French fashion, she turned many heads in the course of the evening, Marlborough's included. She looked too young to be Mytens' wife and he would hardly parade a mistress at such a function. Daniel was certain that she wasn't his daughter. In appearance and manners, she stood out from the more restrained and staid Dutch women around her. At one point, she caught his eye and gave him a quizzical smile.

When the dinner was over, guests adjourned for drinks in an adjoining chamber. Daniel was desperate to speak to Amalia but at first he couldn't see her in the crowd. Only by standing on his toes did he finally pick her out. Before he could make his way to her, a hand grasped him firmly by the wrist. He turned to face the woman whom he'd noticed during the dinner. She was even more striking at close quarters and her perfume had a bewitching aroma. She spoke in French.

'Captain Rawson?' she asked with another quizzical smile.

'Yes,' he replied.

'I couldn't help noticing that you were acting as the Duke of Marlborough's interpreter this evening. I took the liberty of asking for your name.'

'I see.'

'I'm Hélène du Vivier and I have a special reason to be grateful to the Duke. Thanks to his success against the Lines of Brabant last year, I recovered a sizeable estate commandeered by the French. Several hundreds of acres were involved as well as a fine mansion. I was able to move back into my own home again. I only wish that my dear husband – who was somewhat older than I – had still been alive to experience the joy of regaining what was ours. Until it was occupied by the French, the estate had been in his family for generations.'

'I'm glad that we were able to help you, Madame,' he said.

'Is there any way that I might be permitted to speak to the Duke?' she went on, talking now in passable English. 'As you can hear, I do have some knowledge of his language.' She squeezed his wrist. 'I would love to have the opportunity of thanking him in person. It would only take two minutes, if that. Would you be so kind as to introduce me to him, Captain Rawson?'

'I'd be happy to do so, Madame.'

'Thank you.'

Her voice was a soft purr and she momentarily stroked the back of his hand before releasing it. Daniel was stirred. Had he not met Amalia and come under her spell, he would certainly have tried to develop this new acquaintance. Hélène du Vivier was patently a woman of the world. Though her husband had died, he decided, she was no grieving widow but someone leading an independent existence. She searched his eyes. In any other woman, he would have found it almost brazen. In her, however, it seemed teasingly sophisticated. Daniel was curious.

'May I ask how you come to be here?' he wondered.

'My uncle, Johannes, brought me,' she explained. 'He was one of the many people who proposed a toast. He's a member of the States-General.'

'That would be Johannes Mytens, then.'

'You *know* him?'

'I remember him introducing himself when he gave us the toast.'

'Then you have an excellent memory, Captain.'

'Some things are impossible to forget,' he said with a smile. 'If your uncle is here, why doesn't *he* take you to meet His Grace?'

'Uncle Johannes had to leave, I'm afraid,' she said. 'My aunt is not well and he was anxious to get back to her. This was an occasion he could not miss so I took Aunt Jenifer's place at his side. Her loss was my gain.'

People were already departing and the crush had thinned out considerably. Daniel could see Marlborough in a corner, talking to his brother and a couple of Dutch officers. It seemed like a convenient moment to interrupt him. He took Hélène du Vivier across to the group and introduced her. When she began to tell Marlborough why she held him in such high esteem, Daniel slipped away. He didn't get very far. Amalia had come looking for him.

'I thought you'd sneaked off,' she said.

'I'd never do that without speaking to you first, Amalia.'

'That's what I hoped.'

'You've made a tedious event into a joyful one.'

She giggled at the compliment. 'Thank you, Daniel.' She glanced towards Hélène du Vivier. 'I saw you talking to that lady.'

'I was talking to her but thinking of you.'

'Then you were the only man in the room doing so. All the others were staring at her – even Father. In fact, he was the one who recognised her eventually. I thought there was something familiar about her but I couldn't put her name to her face.'

Daniel was interested, 'You recognised Madame du Vivier?'

'That wasn't her name when we saw her in Paris.'

'What was it?'

'I can't remember and neither could Father. What was carved

into our memory, however, was her performance. I'd never been to the theatre before,' she admitted, 'and had no idea what a wondrous place it could be. Most of their names have gone but I do recall that the playwright was a gentleman called Molière.'

'Let me understand this, Amalia,' he said, wanting the facts confirmed. 'You went to the theatre in Paris and saw Hélène du Vivier onstage?'

'Yes, Daniel – she's an actress.'

The startling news made him swing round to look at the woman. Marlborough was clearly enthralled by Hélène du Vivier. Whatever she was saying, it made him smile graciously and nod enthusiastically. His companions were equally fascinated. Daniel wondered how many other women would, on first acquaintance, have the elegance and aplomb to hold the attention of such important military figures. They hung on every word and reacted to every gesture. She was giving another well-rehearsed performance. It was abruptly interrupted. A loud scream rang out on the other side of the room and there was general commotion. Everyone looked in the direction from which the sound had come. Daniel and Amalia were among them. Word quickly spread that someone had just fainted, causing a shocked woman nearby to scream. The tension slowly faded away.

Daniel looked back at Marlborough in time to see him placing a kiss on Hélène du Vivier's hand before she withdrew. After a salvo of farewells, she flitted off into the crowd. Daniel was suspicious. His mind was racing. What was a Parisian actress doing at such a function? If she really was there with her uncle, why had she not left with him to return to a sick aunt? Or why had her Uncle Johannes not remained for the few minutes it would have taken her to meet the evening's honoured guest? The scream had been unusually piercing from someone who'd merely seen someone faint. A gasp of surprise would have been more likely and it would have been muffled by the hubbub. Daniel came swiftly to the conclusion that the scream was a way of diverting attention. He had no idea of the purpose of the distraction until he saw Marlborough raise his wine glass to his lips.

'Your Grace!' yelled Daniel, charging across to him to take him by the elbow. 'I crave a moment with you.'

'Need the request be quite so dramatic?' said Marlborough as he was led aside. 'Is there a problem?'

'I believe that there could be. May I have your glass, please?'

'You surely do not wish to drink my wine?'

'I want to make certain that nobody drinks it, Your Grace.' He took the glass and sniffed it. Daniel pulled a face at the sour smell. 'This wine has been poisoned,' he said.

'That's absurd, Daniel. Who could possibly wish to poison it?'

'It was the lady to whom you were speaking.'

'What – Madame du Vivier? She was utterly charming.'

'Her charm was very practised, Your Grace,' said Daniel, 'and her name was not Hélène du Vivier. She's an actress from Paris and I believe she was here to assassinate you.'

Johannes Mytens raised a glass of wine to offer a very different toast.

'Let's drink to the death of the Duke of Marlborough!'

The others were quick to join in the celebration. Willem Ketel sucked his teeth, Gaston Loti grinned in triumph and the woman who'd assumed the name of Hélène du Vivier congratulated herself on one of her finest performances. In her private life, she was Loti's mistress and the two Dutchmen were very envious of him. The four of them were in Mytens' house, relishing what they believed would be a critical turning point in the war. Even though the Allied army had secured a resounding victory at the battle of Ramillies, the death of their commander-in-chief would sap their determination to continue fighting against the French. Peace negotiations would be inevitable.

'Our decision was wise,' said Loti, complacently. 'Cut off the head and the body lacks any direction. Remove the Duke, as we did this evening, and his army will collapse.'

'The person we have to thank,' said Mytens, 'is my beautiful niece, Hélène du Vivier.' The men laughed and raised their glasses to her. 'You were so convincing that I really thought I *was* your uncle.'

'You were equally convincing,' she told him. 'It was rather amusing to hear you propose a toast to a long and happy life for the Duke when you were actually involved in a plot to kill him.'

'It was one of many nice touches, I feel. Inventing a sick aunt for you was another one. In fact, my wife is in rude health and staying with her sister in Utrecht.'

'I'm relieved to hear it. I was very concerned about her.'

'I know that you share our commitment to peace, my dear,' said Ketel, taking the chance to slip a sly hand around her waist, 'but what you did deserves rich reward.' He offered her a purse. 'This will show you how eternally grateful we are to you.'

'Thank you,' she said, taking the purse.

'When our countries are no longer at war, I'll make a point of visiting Paris in order to see you perform in the theatre.'

'There's been no greater stage than this,' put in Loti. 'How many other actresses have the opportunity to end a wasteful conflict and restore peace to Europe?'

'Someone should write a play about it,' said Mytens. The bell rang at the front door. 'That will be the report for which we've been waiting – certain news that the Duke of Marlborough died in agony from poison. Pray, excuse me.'

Setting his glass aside, Mytens went off to greet the messenger in person. It was too important a task to delegate to a servant. When he reached the front door, he drew back the bolts and threw open the door with a flourish, expecting to see the man appointed to bring the glad tidings. Instead he was looking at the drawn sword of Daniel Rawson. Four soldiers were at Daniel's back.

'What's the meaning of this?' demanded Mytens.

'You are under arrest,' said Daniel, pushing past him to enter the house. He went into the parlour and saw the woman. 'I have sad news for you, Madame du Vivier,' he announced. 'His Grace, the Duke of Marlborough, is alive and in good health. The poison you slipped into his wine is being examined by an apothecary. His Grace never touched it.' He looked at the others. 'You are doubtless parties to this conspiracy so I have the pleasure of placing you all under arrest.'

'You mistake us, Captain Rawson,' said the woman, producing her most charming smile. 'We have no reason to wish the Duke dead.'

'In that case,' he said with an answering smile, 'we have no reason to execute you but your execution will nevertheless take place.' He brandished his sword. 'Seize them!'

Mytens was already being held by one of the soldiers. The other three each moved to arrest one of the conspirators. Ketel gibbered wildly as he was grabbed and the woman protested by trying to smack the soldier away. Loti had no intention of being taken. From inside his coat, he pulled out a pistol and cocked it.

The soldier trying to arrest him immediately moved away. The other soldiers also took a cautious step backwards. Only Daniel had the courage to approach him.

'There's no escape,' he told Loti. 'The house is surrounded.'

Loti aimed the pistol at him. 'Put your sword aside,' he ordered. When Daniel obeyed, he found the gun jammed against his temple. 'Stand back, all of you,' Loti went on, 'or the captain will have his brains blown out.'

'Do as he says,' advised Daniel.

The soldiers released their captives at once. The woman immediately moved across to Loti's side. She was gloating.

'You don't look quite so pleased with yourself now, Captain Rawson,' she said. 'I should have poisoned *your* wine as well. Who came to suspect me?'

'I did,' replied Daniel, 'though I had significant help from a young lady named Amalia Janssen. She happened to be in Paris some months ago and saw you appearing in a play. Your performance was memorable, it seems. Because of that, the life of our commander-in-chief was indirectly saved.'

'This is no time for conversation,' said Loti, taking control. 'You are our means of getting out of here, Captain Rawson. As long as we have you at our mercy, nobody will dare to touch us.'

'What about us?' bleated Ketel. 'We can't stay here now.'

'Let us come with you,' said Mytens. 'We're in this together.'

'This gentleman is going nowhere,' said Daniel, turning to face Loti. 'I'm refusing to budge an inch.'

'Would you rather I pull this trigger?' Loti threatened, pressing the barrel against Daniel's forehead. 'Would you rather have your skull blown apart?'

Daniel was calm. 'Yes,' he replied, levelly. 'When you're a

soldier, you expect to die at some stage. If my time has come, I'd much rather be dispatched with a merciful bullet than by a more agonising means. Pull the trigger if you must, sir,' he continued, 'but remember this. You can only kill *me*. As soon as you've done that, these soldiers will hack you to death with their swords. An empty pistol will be no defence against excruciating pain.'

Loti's eyelids fluttered and the corner of his mouth twitched. His confidence was seeping away. Daniel held his gaze defiantly. He could see the doubt, fear and hesitation in the Frenchman's eyes. While Loti was unsure what to do, the woman made a positive decision.

'Shoot him, Pierre!' she cried 'If we must die, take him with us.'

The brief distraction was timely. In urging Loti to shoot Daniel, she'd inadvertently rescued him. As the Frenchman looked at her, Daniel's hand came up in a flash and knocked the weapon aside, causing it to go off with a bang and fire its bullet harmlessly through a window. Before Loti could move, Daniel felled him with a punch to the chin and stood over him. The soldiers took hold of the other three prisoners. Having heard the gunshot and the noise of shattered glass, other soldiers rushed into the house. Daniel motioned two of them over to haul Loti to his feet. He then turned to the woman.

'You're a fine actress,' he said with unfeigned sincerity, 'and it was a privilege to watch you at work. I'll be interested to see what kind of performance you manage to give on the scaffold.'

The dinner in The Hague was only a short interruption to the more serious business of conquest. Though the battle of Ramillies had draped the Allies in glory, the French army had not surrendered. They were rapidly regrouping in order to return to the fight. There were still months of campaigning ahead. Marlborough was keen to get back to action. On the day after the dinner, therefore, he gathered his party together. Daniel was allowed only a limited time to bid farewell to Amalia Janssen.

'Where will you go next?' she said.

'We'll go wherever we can be of most use, Amalia.'

'You're of most use when you're beside the Duke. Had it not been for you, Daniel, he might now be lying in a coffin.'

'We must both share the credit for that,' he said. 'It was only when you identified that lady for me that I became suspicious. If you and your father had not attended the theatre in Paris, then we'd all be grieving His Grace's death. The worst part of it would be that those responsible would have got away with it.'

'They reckoned without Captain Daniel Rawson.'

'We were lucky this time, Amalia. I've no doubt whatsoever that there'll be other attempts to assassinate His Grace. The more success we achieve on the battlefield, the more danger he'll be in. We must heed the warning we had last night and protect him carefully.'

'I hope you'll remember to protect yourself as well.'

'I will, Amalia.' The sound of horses made him glance across at Marlborough and the others. 'It's time to go, alas. Seeing you again, if only for a fleeting moment, has been an absolute delight.'

'The feeling is mutual.'

'I've no idea when we shall meet again. When the campaign is over for this year, I'll be returning to England with His Grace.'

'Then that's where we shall have to see each other.'

'How can that be? You'll be with your father in Amsterdam.'

'Not for the whole winter,' she explained. 'The Duke is a true connoisseur. He was telling Father about this wonderful palace that's being built for him.'

'Blenheim Palace will take years to complete.'

'I know, Daniel. We'll visit it when we're in England.'

'Why should you do that?'

'The Duke has kindly commissioned Father to weave a tapestry that celebrates the battle of Ramillies. It will hang in a place of honour at the palace. Father will need lots of advice, of course, from someone who actually took part in the battle.' She smiled gleefully. 'The Duke suggested that you might be the ideal person.'

Daniel was thrilled. Needing to leave with the others, he had no time to tell her how pleased he was. He simply enfolded Amalia in his arms and expressed his joy in a long, sweet, succulent kiss.